W9-DES-886

THE
BIGAMIST

BOOKS BY RONA HALSALL

Keep You Safe

Love You Gone

The Honeymoon

Her Mother's Lies

One Mistake

The Ex-Boyfriend

The Liar's Daughter

The Guest Room

The Wife Next Door

THE
BIGAMIST

RONA HALSALL

bookouture

Published by Bookouture in 2023

An imprint of Storyfire Ltd.
Carmelite House
50 Victoria Embankment
London EC4Y 0DZ

www.bookouture.com

Copyright © Rona Halsall, 2023

Rona Halsall has asserted her right to be identified as the author of this work.

All rights reserved. No part of this publication may be reproduced, stored in any retrieval system, or transmitted, in any form or by any means, electronic, mechanical, photocopying, recording or otherwise, without the prior written permission of the publishers.

ISBN: 978-1-80314-163-3
eBook ISBN: 978-1-80314-162-6

This book is a work of fiction. Names, characters, businesses, organizations, places and events other than those clearly in the public domain, are either the product of the author's imagination or are used fictitiously. Any resemblance to actual persons, living or dead, events or locales is entirely coincidental.

For my lovely husband, David, who has been dealt all the tough cards and keeps on smiling. Rest in peace, my love xxx

PROLOGUE

Emma sat in the waiting room of the antenatal clinic, one hand resting on top of her eight-month-old bump, the other turning the pages of a well-thumbed house and homes magazine. She was looking for interior design ideas for the new house her architect husband, Sam, was building for them.

It was not easy or cheap, building your own home. Especially when she had a clear idea of what she wanted. There would need to be four bedrooms, of course, to accommodate the family she envisioned, this child being the first of three. After all, she was only thirty-four, plenty of time to have three kids before she was forty-two. That was her mental cut-off point for having children. It was good to have a deadline, she'd found, otherwise things didn't tend to happen. She needed a studio space to paint in, and an office area for her day job as a virtual PA. Sam also wanted an office, as he intended to run his architectural practice from home, and there was no way on earth they'd be able to share, being chalk and cheese in their concepts of what constituted tidiness.

Heartburn gnawed at her chest and she sat up straighter, thinking it might help to ease the pain, but it didn't. She gave a frustrated huff. Nobody had warned her pregnancy would be this uncomfortable. For months and months. The pages flicked by, nothing catching her eye, but then she wasn't in the mood. It was hard to think about these things with her first baby about to arrive in the next few weeks and the reality of giving birth looming.

She tucked a strand of limp honey-coloured hair behind her ear, hoping her curls would come back once the baby had arrived. She hated how her pregnant self looked, all bedraggled and puffy and tired, her face round now, her cheekbones camouflaged by a layer of fat. She flicked over more pages, making her mind focus on houses again.

A picture at the top of the page made her do a double take, her heart suddenly racing. She blinked, not believing what she was seeing. Peered more closely at the photo. *No, it couldn't be, could it?*

The photograph showed a modern room, white and minimalist, with a stunning peacock-blue sofa, above which hung a striking abstract painting in red and gold. Two ephemeral figures entwined around one heart. She was sure it was a painting that belonged to *her*. Unique. A one-off. As far as she aware, it was carefully wrapped and stored, along with other artworks and the majority of her possessions, in a storage unit in Manchester. This was the city where she'd been living before the move north to Appleby in Cumbria.

What's my picture doing on a stranger's wall?

She knew the nurse would be calling her name to go in and see the consultant any time now; the woman before her had been in there for ages already. There was no time to look at the article properly now. No time to work out what was going on.

Furtively, she glanced around the waiting room. There were two other women. One had her headphones on and her eyes closed, listening to something on her phone. The other was trying to entertain a toddler with a box of building blocks.

Quickly, Emma tore the page from the magazine and stuffed it in her handbag to study when she had more time and felt a little calmer. Her heart was pounding, the shock of seeing the picture no doubt sending her blood pressure to heights that weren't healthy for a pregnant woman.

She was sure it was her painting, even though she'd been wrong about a lot of things recently, her brain already on maternity leave. She was about to pull the page from her bag and have another look when she heard her name being called. It would have to wait.

Half an hour later, she found her car in the car park and squeezed herself behind the steering wheel. She opened her bag and pulled out the article. It had been playing on her mind all the way through the consultation and she'd hardly heard a word the doctor had said.

There was no doubting it was her painting. *So how did it get there?*

The photo was at the top of an article about an award-winning house in Northumberland. Other pictures, scattered between the prose, showed a modern building, overlooking the sea, all wood and glass and utterly wonderful. It was the perfect place for large works of art – all the walls were white, the ceilings high, the floors wood, carefully chosen furniture kept to a minimum. Absolutely no clutter whatsoever. She scanned the words, not really reading them, until she found something that made her eyes widen. Her husband's name. Her heart felt like it had stopped for a second as she found a connection she hadn't anticipated. He'd designed the place.

She checked the date of the article and found it was three months old. He hadn't mentioned anything to her, which was odd because it was something to be proud of, a magazine like this showcasing his talents. It was exactly what he needed to promote his practice and pull in some more prestigious projects.

Anger burned in her chest. Even if he'd just lent the picture to the owner for the photo shoot, he had no business doing that. No right touching any of her pictures and especially not this one.

She rang his number, ready for a difficult conversation.

'Hello.' A woman's voice.

Emma frowned, puzzled, but she knew she'd got the right number. Sam must be busy and his client had answered his phone, which was definitely out of order. Her annoyance ratcheted up another notch, her voice strident, impatient. 'Hi, it's Emma, Sam's wife. Do you think I could speak to him, please?'

Silence for a beat. 'What are you talking about? *I'm* his wife.'

The tone of her voice told Emma this wasn't a joke, and her mouth dropped open as the meaning of the words hit home. No, she must have misheard. *His wife?*

'Hello,' the other woman snapped. 'Hello, are you still there? Sam told me about you,' she hissed. 'Said some weirdo was stalking him. You leave him alone or I'll be calling the police. Do you hear me?'

The line went dead, and Emma clutched the steering wheel as her world went spinning out of control.

PART ONE

CHAPTER ONE

FOURTEEN MONTHS AGO

Emma stood in the doorway, hands stuffed into her coat pockets, wondering if she was brave enough to go in to join the bereavement group. Whether she was ready. The event was in a local community centre and she'd imagined a circle of chairs and everyone standing up one by one and saying their names and telling their stories, the atmosphere sombre. Thankfully, she could see it wasn't like that at all.

The room was cheerful, the walls painted yellow. Opposite the door, a noticeboard was filled with children's pictures, painted by nursery-aged kids by the looks of it. Next to that, another noticeboard with a collage of coloured leaflets advertising a range of local support services. Chairs were grouped together in twos, threes and fours around low tables. There was a big table pushed against a wall, stacked with a range of snacks and drinks. Soft music played in the background. Some people were playing cards, a couple of elderly ladies were knitting, others standing, chatting like they'd known each other for years, which maybe they had.

There weren't as many people as she'd imagined there might be. A quick headcount totalled twelve, including her, if she decided to go in rather than turn tail and dash back home. That was her instinct, but she knew she needed to step inside if she was ever going to move out of this rut she'd been stuck in these last few months.

The previous week, she'd scared herself. She remembered, with a shudder, how she'd woken up with the mother of all headaches, staggering out of bed and into the bathroom, her mouth so dry her tongue was stuck to the roof of her mouth. She guzzled water from the tap and sat on the edge of the bath, her eyes squinting against the light, wondering how much she'd drunk this time. Her fingers rubbed at her temples and she squeezed her eyes shut, then blinked them open in the hope she'd be able to see properly.

That was when she noticed the packets of painkillers lined up on the vanity unit beside the sink. Five of them. Paraceta-mol. The blister packs had been taken out of the boxes and stacked neatly on top. One hundred and sixty tablets, waiting to be taken, an empty gin bottle sitting next to them. There was no doubt what her plan had been. With trembling hands, she checked the bin, relieved to find no evidence she'd actually taken a big dose of painkillers. She'd read about paracetamol, how an overdose, even an unintentional one, could cause irre-versible damage to your internal organs.

It was a turning point, a recognition she needed help. The doctor had suggested the bereavement group, not trusting her with medication. So here she was, standing in the doorway, not able to make herself step into the room.

One other person was behaving like she was, seemingly unsure what they were supposed to do. He was leaning against the wall by the food table, his hands also stuffed in his pockets, his eyes fixed on the floor. A small woman with short grey hair streaked with purple and a round, jolly face appeared from the kitchen area with a plate of samosas. She spotted Emma in the doorway, beckoned for her to come in.

'Hello! I'm Debs. I organise the group. You must be Emma. We spoke on the phone, didn't we? Or have I got that wrong?'

Emma swallowed and forced herself to move forwards, struggling to muster a smile. 'No, you're right. I'm Emma.'

'Well, it's lovely to see you.' Debs reached out and gave her shoulder a gentle rub. 'I know it's a bit daunting coming to a group like this, especially given the circumstances, but everyone's in the same boat. They've all lost someone dear to them.' She gave a reassuring smile. 'The first meeting is always the hardest, but it'll get easier. They're such a friendly bunch.'

Emma followed Debs as she went to put the samosas on the table, casting nervous glances at the other attendees. 'We start informally, while I'm getting organised,' Debs continued, wiping her hands on a tea towel slung over one shoulder. 'Then I'll introduce any new people to everyone. We have a fantastic speaker, Faith Barclay, who set the group up. She's marvellous, so supportive. Anyway, she'll do a ten-minute chat, then lead the discussion, wherever it goes, depending on what people want to share. She tends to go with the flow, nice and informal, whatever helps people cope with the grieving process.' She surveyed the loaded table, giving a satisfied nod.

Emma managed to find her voice, wondering how long it would be before she could make a getaway without appearing rude. 'What happens after Faith's talk?'

'We have something to eat and a natter.' Debs put a hand on Emma's arm. 'But don't feel obliged to stay to the end. You go whenever you want if you're not feeling comfortable. Honestly, I understand this is hard and nobody is judging. We've all been through it.' She gave her arm a final pat. 'Getting yourself here is a big step in the right direction, so you should be proud of yourself.'

Emma blushed, not feeling proud at all, but conceding Debs had a point. It was a start.

'Can I take your coat?' Debs pointed to a row of hooks by the door. 'I'll hang it over there for you if you like?'

Emma wriggled out of her coat and Debs bustled off. She pulled at the cuffs of her shirt, feeling awkward, like the new girl at school. But it was a small group, and she'd received some sympathetic smiles as she'd ventured across the room. She was surprised to see so many younger people there; she'd imagined that most bereaved people would be elderly, but maybe they dealt with it better. Maybe it was the younger generation who found grief harder to take and needed more support. It was also about equal men and women, which was another surprise.

She found a chair at an unoccupied table and waited, her hands tucked between her knees, relieved when Debs called them together a few minutes later. Now the attention was on the speaker, she felt a little less conspicuous, and found herself starting to relax.

Faith Barclay was tall for a woman, at least six foot. She had golden hair falling down her back, large blue eyes in a pale oval face, and she wore no make-up. She was striking to look at, with high cheekbones and clear skin, and Emma couldn't help but wonder if she was Scandinavian. The crow's feet at the corners of her eyes suggested she might be older than she looked at first glance, and as Emma studied her, she could see her blonde hair was streaked with white.

Her voice, when she started her talk, was low and gentle, the words spreading over Emma like a comforting blanket. She sniffed as she listened, wiping at her eyes with a bunch of tissues pulled from the box on the table. She wasn't the only one. Others were feeling emotional too and somehow, for once, it actually felt okay. No, it was better than okay. It was a relief, this permission to join in a communal recognition of the pain of loss. She sat, with tears running down her face, listening to some of the stories shared by others and taking in Faith's responses, her advice to embrace the emotions instead of fighting them.

Accepting sadness as part of the process. It wouldn't be for ever and they would get through it. Emma clung to her words, grieving for all the plans that would never come to fruition, people she would never see again, a life that would never be the same.

She sat on her own once the discussion had finished, lost in her thoughts while everyone started making their way towards the food table. Her fingers tore at the tissues scrunched in her hands as her mind wandered through the wreckage of her life.

'How are you doing?' Faith's voice made her look up. 'Can I join you for a moment?'

Emma wiped at her tear-stained face, cleared her throat. 'Yes, yes, of course.'

Faith sank into the chair next to her. 'Debs said it was your first time at the meeting and I wanted to check in with you, see if there's anything I can help you with.'

Emma blinked. There was so much she needed help with it felt wrong to burden someone else with her woes. She ventured a fleeting smile. 'Your talk was great.' She looked at Faith, saw the concern in her eyes. 'To be honest...' She sighed, looked down at her hands, her voice cracking when she spoke. 'I'm having a really difficult time.'

'I thought as much.' Faith leant towards her. 'Do you want to tell me about it?'

Emma fiddled with the tissues, not sure if she could.

'A problem shared is a problem halved, as my mum liked to say. I think it's true, though. It always feels better to articulate feelings, don't you think? And when we've been bereaved, sometimes we struggle to find someone to articulate them to. Especially if it's our significant other who has passed away.' Faith gave an encouraging smile. 'But I would genuinely like to help. So... when you're ready, let those words flow.'

Emma was silent, not sure where to begin, knowing the minute she started talking, she'd be choked up and would make

for once. 'I definitely will. You need to tell me about what happened at the Reading Festival. You've got me wondering now.'

Faith laughed. 'Oh, it'll be worth coming for the punchline to that little drama alone. I'm sorry we don't have time to do it justice tonight, but it looks like Debs is winding things up.' She reached over and patted Emma's knee again, more serious now. Their eyes met. 'You can do this. I know you can.' And for the first time, Emma thought maybe she could.

The man she'd seen leaning on the wall when she first came in walked over to join them, surprising her when he sat next to Faith. She'd spotted him during the evening, staying resolutely by himself, not mingling, and she recognised the look of sadness in his eyes. 'I hope you don't mind.' He smiled shyly at Emma. 'I'm giving Faith a lift home and it looks like everyone is going now.'

Emma had been so engrossed in her conversation with Faith she hadn't noticed the room emptying, only a couple of women left, deep in conversation at another table.

'Goodness, we lost track of time.' Faith grinned at the man. 'Emma, this is my little brother, Sam. It's his first time at one of these meetings too.' She rolled her eyes. 'It's taken me weeks to get him to come.' Emma's eyes met Sam's and she felt a jolt run through her, heat rushing to her cheeks. *Faith's brother?* At first glance he looked quite different to his sister, but now she could see the shape of the face was the same, with the high cheekbones and straight nose. She glanced away, worried he'd think she was staring. Faith stood. 'I'll just go and say goodbye to Debs. Won't be a minute.'

'Are you local?' Sam asked, when they were alone, an awkward silence sitting between them. 'I can give you a lift home, if you like.'

He was softly spoken, his hair swept back off his face, falling in dark waves to his collar, his brown eyes flecked with hints of gold round the iris. His whole demeanour was gentle, including the smile he gave her, just a slight upturn of the lips. It was like his dimmer switch had been turned down, and she understood how grief did that to a person. She felt the same about herself, her natural exuberance all but extinguished.

'Oh, I... well, I don't want to trouble you. It's not far to walk.'

He laughed. 'Have you heard the rain? You'll get soaked. Honestly, it's no trouble.'

It had been dry when she'd walked to the centre, but now she could hear the rain hammering on the roof. She looked at him again, her blush deepening, making her cheeks burn. 'Thank you. That would be great.'

They started chatting about the evening while they waited for Faith to return, slipping into conversation. He was as easy to talk to as his sister, but with a quirky sense of humour that had her giggling. He was clearly an observer of people, and they compared notes about their fellow attendees, Sam putting forward his theories about who they were and what they did for a living. Pure invention, but games like this were her favourite.

'Sorry I took so long,' Faith said when she finally reappeared, looking a little flustered, hitching her bag over her shoulder. 'Debs wanted to tie down some dates for the rest of the year and it took a bit of juggling to work out how to fit everything in.'

Sam stood, offering a hand to help Emma to her feet. She took it, enjoying the warmth of his skin, the firmness of his grip, the way his hand enveloped hers. A frisson ran through her body. It felt like the start of something.

CHAPTER TWO

The bereavement group meetings became the highlight of Emma's week. It was something to look forward to, something to aim for. Each week, Faith asked them to identify a goal for the coming days, something tangible they could hold on to as a mark of progress. It gave Emma a focus, a distraction, to stop her wallowing in misery.

She and Faith had become firm friends, an unexpected benefit, which delighted Emma. She'd missed female companionship, but her old group of friends had no idea how to talk to her now, and she couldn't face their pity. A new friendship was exactly what she needed.

They'd bumped into each other in the vegetable aisle at the supermarket, commiserated with each other about how they hated food shopping.

'Do you fancy a coffee?' Faith had asked as they queued up for the checkout. 'My treat. I need a caffeine boost to get me through the rest of my day.'

'That would be lovely,' Emma found herself saying, and actually meaning it. The conversation flowed, and before she realised, an hour had gone. They swapped numbers, promising to do it again sometime soon. She got home full of a new energy, a smile on her face as she did a bit of long-overdue housework. She even found herself humming.

A couple of days later, Faith messaged her with a link to a concert she wanted to go to, asking if she fancied coming along. It turned out to be such a fun night and Emma got home with hardly any voice left after singing along with the band for almost two hours. She slept through the night, the first time since she'd been living on her own. It turned out Faith was exactly the tonic she needed, showing her life still had a lot to offer after all.

After six weeks of going to the group, Sam had also become a friend, always seeking her out after the discussion part of the session. He seemed to prefer to be on his own for the first part of the meetings and she understood, preferring it herself as she could allow her emotions free rein without feeling embarrassed. They didn't talk about grief, or who they had lost, but focused on anything and everything else. Talking to him was fun, their conversations unexpected, always making her giggle because he had such an individual sense of humour.

'You and Sam seem to have hit it off,' Faith said after the last meeting, with a conspiratorial smile, clearly fishing for information.

Emma couldn't meet her eye, a blush warming her cheeks. 'We have a lot in common since we're both creatives.' She looked up and Faith laughed.

'I'm so happy you've found a friend in each other. It's clearly doing you both good. And look how far you've come. Restarting work. Painting again. And feeling able to share some things with the group too. You know, that's wonderful progress.' She glanced at her brother, who was perusing the food table. 'There's such a difference in Sam as well. He's throwing himself into a new project, enthusing about things like the architectural geek he is.'

Emma caught Faith's eye, glad of the chance to ask the question that had been preying on her mind. 'The only thing is... I don't know who he's grieving. He never speaks in the group discussions and I don't feel I can ask him directly.'

Faith pulled a face. 'Well, it's for him to tell you, not me. I think you're going to have to wait until he's ready. But what I will say is he's a changed man since you two met.' She put an arm round Emma and gave her a hug. 'I'm happy for you both. My advice would be to go with the flow and enjoy each other's company.'

Emma was frustrated not to get a straight answer, but reading between the lines, she had an inkling Sam was in a similar position to her. She'd take Faith's advice, though, and wait. After all, who knew him better than his own sister?

The following week, Sam invited her on a day trip to the Lake District where he was looking at a site near Windermere for a prospective job. He dropped her off in the village to have a wander around while he went to visit the clients, arranging to meet her at one of the pubs for lunch.

She pottered in and out of the little shops, then found a café by the lake where she could sit outside, soaking up the ambience. It was a long time since she'd felt so relaxed, she realised, breathing in the crisp, clean air, her eyes fixed on the view. It would be so much nicer living in a place like this than in a city, she mused. Living in the countryside would be a complete contrast to her previous life, a definite new beginning and exactly what she needed if she was going to move on from the trauma.

Sam was bouncing with enthusiasm when he joined her at the pub they'd chosen for lunch.

'I can't wait to get going on this one,' he said when he brought the drinks over to the table along with a couple of menus. 'Quite an ambitious project given the state of the place and their budget, so we'll have to see how it pans out. It sometimes takes years for people to get all their ducks in a row so we can get started.' She had never seen him so animated and loved the way he was passionate about his work. 'I see it as my job to give them something to strive for and a budget to achieve, then it's up to them when they're ready.'

Emma picked up her gin and tonic and took a sip, looking out of the bay window and up at the neighbouring fells. 'It would be lovely to live here, wouldn't it?' Waterfalls jostled down the slopes to a lightly wooded valley at the bottom. Grey stone walls bisected the hillside, sheep roaming high up on summer pasture, pale dots in the distance. So peaceful and calm, she thought, already picturing herself in a little stone studio at the bottom of the garden of a whitewashed cottage. She'd always had a vivid imagination, but this image was so three-dimensional and real, she could almost believe it existed.

Sam's demeanour changed in an instant, the joy falling from his face. He looked down at his drink, squaring the beer mat up with the edge of the table. There was an awkward pause before he spoke. 'I used to live not far from here. Coniston. It's fairly quiet as Lake District villages go, but the roads get rammed with visitors in the summer. Honestly, it's a bit of a nightmare. Takes ages to get anywhere.' He picked up his pint, took a big gulp, licking the foam from his upper lip.

Emma took another sip of her drink, processing this new information, wondering how best to probe further. She gave him a quizzical look. 'I didn't know you came from this neck of the woods.'

Sam shook his head. 'No, it's not where I grew up. But my wife's family have lived in Coniston for generations.'

His wife. Now she was getting somewhere. 'So...' she asked tentatively, 'it's your wife who died?'

He looked at his beer like it had the answer and he was wondering whether to tell her or not. He took another big gulp and she felt guilty to have asked him such a direct question.

She put a hand on his arm, knowing she was in the wrong. 'Sorry. Please, you don't have to answer. Not if it's... too raw.'

So far theirs had been a friendship that they'd navigated carefully, like two magnetic poles trying not to be attracted to each other. Hadn't they both made a point of emphasising that it wasn't romantic? But when he took her hand, something he'd never done before, it was clear there was a pull neither of them could deny.

His fingers felt warm and comforting, the physical contact a pleasure she hadn't realised she'd missed. He started speaking, his eyes on the table, his free hand fiddling with a spare beer mat, turning it round and round on the tabletop.

'I met Alice when I got a placement at the architects' practice where she worked with her uncle. It was a family firm going way back and with an excellent local reputation. They were doing all the eco designs I was interested in, and we hit it off straight away.'

Emma felt a prickle of jealousy at the back of her neck and took a sip of her gin while she forced the unwelcome emotion away. The poor woman was dead, nothing to be jealous about at all. She was the one who was here holding this gorgeous man's hand.

'Anyway, long story short, we started seeing each other and after a while we got married. We moved into a cottage in Coniston, near her family's farm.'

'Sounds idyllic,' Emma murmured, wanting this for herself. She was appalled at the way her thoughts had jumped several stages ahead and she reined herself back. He hadn't finished the story and she needed to listen. She took another sip of her drink.

He sighed, putting the beer mat down, his hand shaking slightly. 'It was wonderful, until the fire.'

She spluttered, not having expected such a blunt and shocking statement. Started coughing as her drink went down the wrong way. He didn't seem to notice, lost in his memories, his hand clasping hers a little tighter.

'Unfortunately, Alice...' He swallowed. 'She died. Our cottage stood away from the village, and by the time the fire was noticed, it was too late.' He chewed at his lip, still not looking at her. 'I was working away at the time, and now... well, I can't go back to Coniston.' He shook his head. Blinked a few times. 'Too much history.'

She squeezed his hand, gave him a sympathetic look. 'I'm so sorry about your wife. I hadn't liked to ask who you were grieving for and I apologise if you feel I backed you into a corner there. It wasn't my intention.' She sighed. 'You know, I'm just so curious about people. I suppose it comes from being a portrait painter. You have to dive into the essence of who a person is to get the best out of your image.' She squeezed his hand again, thinking she could definitely grow accustomed to this new intimacy between them. 'I'm so sorry.'

'It's fine. I'm getting used to talking about it.' His eyes met hers then and she felt a depth of connection that hadn't been there before. As though a barrier had been lifted with his revelation. A vulnerability exposed. She had to fight the urge to lean forward and kiss him. 'To be honest, I've been wanting to tell you but didn't know how.' His fingers interlaced with hers and she hoped he was feeling the same pulses of electricity that were making her heart race. 'It helps to talk about it. I've learnt that from the bereavement group. And I know I don't speak in front of everyone, but I have spoken about it to some of the people there. I'm better when it's one-to-one.'

She nodded, understanding completely. She'd been the same at first.

A companionable silence settled between them, their hands still clasped together, his thumb lightly grazing the back of her hand. Was he waiting for her to tell her own story? She swallowed, aware she hadn't shared everything with the group. Just snippets about her progress, how she was managing to pick up the threads of her life, never the cause of her grief.

She took a deep breath. 'My husband had an accident too.' Her mind filled with the voice of Zach's supervisor when she'd answered his phone call. *The scaffolding collapsed.* Terrible images of falling metal poles and planks of wood filled her mind. They were working on a ten-storey apartment block, replacing the cladding. She shuddered, a flood of emotion surging through her. 'But let's not talk about the past,' she said, quickly, sweeping the images to the back of her mind where she wanted them to stay. She had no intention of sifting through that traumatic experience in Sam's presence. 'We can save it for the group.'

She tried to gather her thoughts. She was glad he'd opened up, but there was something about the way he'd told her, the starkness of it, completely unadorned by emotion, that made her uneasy. She couldn't have spoken so calmly about what happened to Zach. But she reminded herself of Faith's words, that everyone experienced and expressed grief differently. *Better not to judge.*

CHAPTER THREE

They were lying in bed, wrapped in each other's arms, something that was happening more often these days. It was one of those conversations that started with a fantasy question. 'If you could build a new house, what would you want?' Sam asked her. 'Money no object. Anywhere you liked.'

She laughed and turned to him. 'I have been thinking about buying a house, as it happens. After my husband's accident, the company admitted liability and paid out compensation.'

He raised an eyebrow, before taking her hand and kissing her knuckles. 'Oh, you sound like the perfect client, madam. Come on then, tell me... what would your dream home look like?'

She snuggled closer, smiled to herself. She liked this sort of game.

'I can't get the Lake District out of my mind. It was so peaceful and the air was so fresh. And all that space. I'd love to be out of the city.' She opened her eyes and looked at him, saw his smile had faded. His wife had died in a fire in the Lake District, she remembered, and cursed her insensitivity. 'But I understand you wouldn't want to be there because of... you know.'

He was silent for a little while. *Damn my stupid mouth.* Why did she have to go and ruin things? They were practically living together now, their lives becoming more entwined by the week, and she was happier than she'd been for a long time. Her life had blossomed into something beautiful again. Only last week, she'd picked up a commission for a husband-and-wife portrait for their anniversary, and the virtual PA work had taken off now she'd had a blast on social media and got her name out there.

'If it's hillsides and trees and lots of space you're after,' he said, eventually, 'there are plenty of other lovely places to choose from in Cumbria outside the Lake District itself, you know. Much cheaper too.'

'You're right,' she said, a wave of relief flowing through her, happy to go along with any suggestion at this stage. It was only a game, after all. 'So, let's narrow down the location to somewhere near the Lake District, okay?' She tapped into the vision in her mind, so clear she could almost touch it. 'Now... I'd like four bedrooms, because I will be having three children.'

She glanced at him then to see how he responded to that part of the plan. It was way too early in their relationship to be talking about children, but she couldn't resist testing the water. Not wanting children would be a deal-breaker for her, however attractive a man might be. Ever since she'd hit thirty, she was desperate for a family, and after the distress of her miscarriage, and time ticking by, becoming a mother had morphed into something of an obsession. She'd believed her dream had died after Zach's accident, but now her hopes had been reborn.

'Only three?' he mused, a twinkle in his eye.

'I suppose they could share bedrooms,' she ventured, 'so four or five is not out of the question.'

He laughed then. Kissed the tip of her nose. 'And what else would this dream home need?'

By the time they'd finished, she'd created a smallholding, a bevy of children playing outside, helping to muck out the two ponies and the pygmy goats and dig up potatoes from the expansive vegetable patch and collect the eggs laid by a flock of chickens. As fantasies went, this was one she would enjoy living in, and it was a bonus that now she'd created it, she'd be able to visit it in her mind whenever she felt the need.

Three weeks later, Sam burst through the door of her apartment with a roll of paper under his arm. 'I've had such a good day, you will not believe this.'

He cleared her small dining table and unrolled the paper, revealing a number of sketches of a property. He beamed at her. 'This is it. Your dream home.'

She was astounded, couldn't believe how perfectly he'd managed to capture her fantasy on pieces of paper. This was exactly the home she wanted to live in with her imaginary family. Delighted didn't begin to explain how she felt. What she loved, though, was that he had listened. Really listened. The thoughts in her head had become the thoughts in *his* head, which he'd then made into something tangible and real. How many people were so connected? It seemed like some sort of magic. But that was love, wasn't it? The powerful draw towards someone, on a level you didn't understand, before you even knew them properly.

'Wow, it all seems possible now,' she said, poring over his designs, making suggestions for little tweaks here and there. 'I don't suppose you've thought as far as putting a figure on all this, have you?'

His arm was wrapped around her waist, holding her close, and she knew in that moment, with a certainty she'd never felt about anything else in her life, that she wanted this house and she wanted to share it with Sam.

'Well, obviously there's the small matter of finding a suitable plot. But in terms of build costs, I would imagine around the five hundred thousand mark.' He shrugged. 'Obviously if you decided you definitely wanted to go ahead, then I'd cost it out properly, but that's a ballpark figure.'

He glanced at her and she looked down at the drawings, making calculations in her mind. She was renting her apartment at the moment, but now the compensation had come through, wouldn't this be a good investment instead of throwing money away on rent? 'And how much would a plot be?'

He laughed then. 'How long's a piece of string? Location makes a heck of a difference in terms of price, but if you wanted to be in Cumbria, we could look round the edges, see what we could find. I don't know. Quarter of a million, maybe?'

We. He was talking about 'we', like they were in this together. Their project. Her excitement mounted. All her broken dreams were piecing themselves back together again. She was being given a second chance and she was going to grab it with both hands.

'Let's do it,' she said, her smile so wide her cheeks ached, joy bubbling up inside. 'If you can find a plot that will work, I'm up for it.'

It was only later, when they were lying in bed, Sam fast asleep, her eyes wide open staring at the ceiling, that she actually listened to her doubts. It was a heck of a lot of money and everything was happening quickly. Was this what was really bothering her, or was it something else?

CHAPTER FOUR

From the moment Emma had agreed to go ahead with the idea for the new house, Sam had been bouncing around like a bunny on steroids. He seemed lighter, happier, more attentive. If she'd had reservations in the beginning, now she was sure he was the man she wanted to build a life with. His enthusiasm was contagious, his laughter infectious, his ideas engrossing.

All his spare time was spent pursuing their project, tweaking the design, researching heating and lighting, roofing and window systems to make the place carbon neutral. His dedication to their future was without fault. She wasn't so fascinated by all the details, but she was suddenly committed to a project she hadn't known she wanted until he'd presented her with the plans. Building *their* dream home.

It was tricky to keep the momentum of their project going when he worked away a lot, but she had to accept it went with his job. There were a lot of site visits to do, and many projects didn't seem to get any further than putting in applications for planning permission. He'd turn up on a Sunday night every week, regular as clockwork, and leave again on a Thursday morning, travelling all over the UK. He didn't even have his own home at the moment, unsure where he wanted to settle since his wife had died. For the time being, he'd been staying with Faith between his trips away. She'd asked him about working weekends, but he said that was the only time some of his clients were at home and had time to discuss things properly. It worked and it seemed he wasn't about to change the pattern.

He moved into her flat the week after he'd shown her the house designs. He'd demonstrated a commitment to their future without even having to say anything and she realised how she'd missed being part of a couple. The cosying up on the sofa, chatting while they made a meal together, the warmth of another body in her bed, his hands on her skin, his breath in her hair.

Ten weeks after he moved in, he burst through the door on a Sunday evening, eyes shining, a big grin on his face. She'd been waiting for him to come home, excited and nervous to tell him her news, not sure what his response would be.

'You'll never guess what I've found,' he said, dumping his bags on the floor while he rooted in his briefcase, pulling out a couple of sheets of paper. He thrust them towards her and she took them, curious to know what had got him so excited.

Her heart flipped when she realised what she was looking at. 'A plot? You've found a plot for the house?' She studied the paper again. 'Where is it?'

'It's on the edge of Appleby, which used to be the county town of Westmorland until it was lumped into the bigger county of Cumbria. It's the most gorgeous little place. Red sandstone buildings, a river running through the middle, and it even has a castle. They have a horse fair there every year. You might have heard of it?'

She shook her head, but was already thinking she liked the sound of the place.

'It's a wonderful little town. I would imagine crime levels are practically zero. Which can't be said for Manchester, can it?'

He pulled his laptop out of his bag, put it on the dining table and opened a tab. 'Look, here's some drone footage I found earlier.'

She watched, flying over the scenery like a bird in the sky, taking in the market square, the lovely old church at one end, the river running round it in a semicircle. The main street heading up the hill, the shops giving way to pretty cottages, all the way to the castle gates at the top. They flew over the ancient castle, with its crenellated walls protecting a square Norman keep at one end, with the mansion part of the castle facing it across a great expanse of lawn.

'That part of the castle is a hotel,' Sam said, pointing to the mansion. 'And they do weddings there. I've been inside. It's gorgeous and the food is amazing.'

Emma's ears pricked up. Was Sam hinting at something? She studied his face, but he was engrossed in the footage, which was heading out of the town now, rolling hills opening out on either side.

'Oh, wait a minute.' He rewound the footage a few seconds, his voice excited. 'Look, this is where the site is.' She peered at the screen. 'You can see it's got a derelict farmhouse on it at the moment. Beyond saving, so I think we'll be fine to demolish and start again. And because there's a house there already, I don't imagine planning permission will be an issue.'

He showed her where the house would be positioned on the site, running through his designs, showing her the view she would wake up to each morning, bringing it all to life in her mind. She could see the children playing in the treehouse in the garden, could hear the little stream bubbling over the stones, the wind in the trees, could smell the lavender and the herbs she would plant by the kitchen door. She could already see her light-filled studio in the garden.

He grinned at her. 'How do you fancy a visit next weekend? I've booked us a room in the castle. Then you can see the place for yourself.' There was no mistaking the excitement in his voice; he was practically bursting with joy. 'I think this is it, I really do. We've looked and looked, haven't we? Literally the whole county, for weeks, and this one has just come onto the market and it's perfect. Absolutely perfect.' His eyes met hers. 'You're not going to get a better opportunity. Plots like this are like gold dust.' He grabbed her hands, held them tight. 'I can create the perfect home for you.'

'For me?' she asked, wanting him to understand what she was asking. 'I don't want it to be only for me.'

He laughed. 'You and your family. That's what I meant. It'll be everything you've dreamed of. I promise.'

She gazed at him, wanting him to say more, unsure what he was thinking, besides his obvious enthusiasm for the project. In her heart, she was disappointed. Was he thinking about this as a project, or as a future home for them to share? Was she a client or a partner? That was what she couldn't work out. Now was the time, she decided, to tell him her own news. Then she would know where she stood instead of second-guessing.

'I've got something to tell you,' she said, nerves twisting in her stomach. 'In fact, shall we sit down?' She led him to the sofa and sank into the cushions, pulling him down next to her. 'Now this might come as a bit of a surprise, but...' She glanced up at him, noting the uncertainty in his eyes, and flashed him a smile, because news like this was joyful. Properly joyful, and she couldn't help herself. 'We're expecting a baby.'

The news burst out of her as a triumphant declaration, because that was how it felt. The one thing she'd yearned for was actually going to happen and she couldn't mask her delight, however nervous she was of his reaction.

His expression changed from curious to confused. Possibly shocked. His jaw dropped, his mouth forming a silent 'o', and for a moment she wondered if it was a flash of fear or panic in his eyes.

'Oh. My. God,' he said, eventually, obviously bewildered. 'But I thought you said you were on the pill?'

It wasn't the reaction she'd been hoping for and her jaw tightened, her voice sharp. 'I *am* on the pill. But I had a stomach bug, remember, and sometimes you can get pregnant after something like that.' She shrugged. 'I'm just guessing. I don't know how it's happened. But I'm pregnant with our baby.'

'A baby. Wow.'

He didn't sound excited. She should have waited for a better moment, she realised, watching Sam's face go through several different emotions, a knot of fear in her belly as she studied his frozen smile.

His eyes squeezed shut and he pinched his nose. A moment later, a tear rolled down his cheek. 'Our baby,' he whispered, his voice thick with emotion. 'I'm going to be a dad. Bloody hell. I can't believe it.' He shook his head, and then he was laughing and crying at the same time, a huge grin on his face. 'I'm going to be a dad!' he shouted, fist-pumping the air.

She let out a relieved breath, delighted now with his response, allowing her own joy to bubble inside her. It was going to be okay. More than that, he seemed to be as delighted as she was.

He gathered her to him, smothered her with kisses, before holding her tight, his chin resting on the top of her head. 'I'll admit it's a bit of a shock, I was thinking we'd build a house, then start a family, but hey, does it matter?' Then he was laughing again and she was crying and she could honestly say she'd never been happier in her whole life.

With a final kiss, he released her from his embrace, grabbing hold of her hands. There was no mistaking the love in his eyes. 'Honestly, Emma, this is the best news. I can't wait to tell Faith. Oh my God, I can't tell you how excited I am.' He jumped up and started dancing around the room, pulling her with him, until she couldn't move for laughing.

Her whole body was weak with relief, his response so much better than she'd dared to imagine. In her mind, she was thinking he might leave and she'd never set eyes on him again. But now he was giving her all the right signals. Out of breath, she dropped onto the sofa, Sam finding a footstool so she could put her feet up while he flicked the kettle on and found some biscuits in the cupboard.

He fussed around her all night, making the evening meal and running the hoover round the apartment, putting a wash on. It wasn't what she'd expected. She'd resigned herself to the fact she'd still be looking after herself most of the time, but that clearly wasn't what Sam wanted.

The next day, he brought her breakfast in bed, something nobody had ever done before. To her it was a symbol of love, of caring, wanting to nurture his partner and their child. *His partner.* The label sent a frisson of delight through her.

Moments later, her mind took her back to Zach and his accident, snuffing out her happy mood. Life goes on, she told herself, annoyed with this unwelcome intrusion, and she had every right to live it. Enjoy it. Revel in the new adventure that was unfolding in front of her. A future with Sam by her side and his children in the house he was going to build for them all. Never had she wanted something more.

'I've registered your interest with the auctioneer and set up an account,' he said as he picked up his mug of coffee, settling himself beside her on the bed. 'The auction is two weeks away, so we can do the site visit next weekend, then we've got time to crunch the numbers, make sure it's within budget.' He turned to her, eyes shining, and she thought she'd never seen him look so happy. He was as excited as she was about their future together and that made her heart skip with joy. 'The more I think about it, the more I think we should do it. It's a fantastic location, a great investment whatever happens, and you'll get exactly the house you want.'

There was a little voice in her head asking if it was the right way to spend a big chunk of the compensation payout. It was a lot of money, more than she'd ever contemplated having in her life. In truth, having this big lump sum scared her. She'd always been a bit impulsive, never good at saving, and she'd promised herself she wouldn't do anything stupid. She'd eke the money out, make it last. She tried to do some mental calculations, wondering if she needed to keep more back for the future, to make sure her other needs were covered. Because once the money was gone, she wouldn't be getting it back.

But then... She pulled herself up. A house could be sold. It was an investment. She wasn't spending the money at all, she was putting it into a property that would make the asset grow. She smiled to herself and snuggled closer to Sam, his words rooting themselves in her mind. *A great investment.*

The following day, she met up with Faith for lunch, having taken a detour to a little shop that sold the most adorable baby clothes. She couldn't resist buying a couple of outfits, and pulled them out of the bag to show Faith while they were waiting for their food to arrive.

'Aren't these gorgeous,' she said, holding one up. 'I can't wait to show Sam.'

Faith slowly lowered her drink, her eyes on stalks, her expression one of total shock as she understood what Emma was talking about. 'A baby?' she gasped. 'You're having Sam's baby?'

Emma felt the blush travelling up her neck, burning her cheeks. Faith was the first person she'd spoken to about it and she'd imagined she would be as happy as Sam had been about the news. Now she felt wrong-footed, confused. 'I thought... well, I assumed he'd already told you.'

Faith's expression transformed into a delighted grin. 'No, he hasn't, but Emma, that's amazing news!'

Their meals arrived then and they began to eat, Faith talking between mouthfuls as she asked a stream of questions about due dates and names and how they would manage in the flat.

'Did he tell you about the building plot he's found?' Emma was not planning on still being in the flat when the baby was born, but Faith seemed to be a bit behind on their plans.

Faith nodded. 'Oh yes, he did. It sounds so exciting.' She sliced a piece of steak and put it in her mouth, frowning as she chewed. 'Awkward timing, though, isn't it? These things take so long to sort themselves out.' She leant towards Emma. 'You don't think it's too soon, do you?' As soon as she'd spoken, she appeared to back-pedal, flapping a hand as if she was trying to waft her comment away like a pesky fly. 'I'm sorry, that was a stupid thing to say. But you've only known each other two minutes and he's my baby brother and, well, I don't know... Sorry, ignore me. I'm being stupid.' She picked up her drink, as flustered as Emma had ever seen her, managing a smile as she raised her glass. 'Congratulations.'

Emma grinned, nothing able to dim her delight. She didn't care what other people thought. As long as she and Sam were happy about the baby, nothing else mattered. 'I know it might take a bit of getting used to, but you're going to be an auntie.'

Faith seemed to melt then, a smile wriggling onto her lips as she tucked into the rest of her meal, pausing to ask about birthing preferences and how Emma was feeling in herself, whether she needed any help.

'You know, Emma,' she laughed, as they were saying their goodbyes outside, 'you're just full of surprises.' Emma laughed with her, a flutter of unease in her chest, as she wondered exactly what the other surprises had been.

Later, when she was walking home, she couldn't get the conversation with Faith out of her head. *Was* it too soon? It was a question she had asked herself, but then she hadn't actually chosen to get pregnant, so it wasn't about deciding whether it was the right time to have a baby. This was about facing reality and deciding, as a couple, they were happy to go forward together to bring up their child.

The unease was back. *Why hadn't Sam told his sister the news? He'd said he couldn't wait to tell her, and he'd obviously spoken to her, because she knew about the building plot, so why not tell her about the baby at the same time?*

CHAPTER FIVE

For the last few weeks, Emma's life had been a blur of activity and she felt like she was living on a permanent adrenaline high. She'd fallen in love with Appleby after their visit, and had managed to secure the building plot at auction for a little over the budget she'd set. Now her mind was busy with plans.

It was Monday night and Sam had just got back from work, presenting her with a big bunch of flowers. 'For you, my love.' He kissed her, then held her tight, letting out a big sigh. 'I love the nights I can come back to you,' he murmured, his breath tickling her ear as he spoke. She tingled with pleasure. 'And... get this... I might have found us somewhere to rent in Appleby while the build is ongoing.'

Her body tensed. She hadn't thought about moving up there before the house was ready, but the idea blossomed in her mind into a thing of beauty. It was the perfect solution. It would solve so many of the problems that had niggled at her since she'd discovered she was pregnant. She didn't want to grow a baby in Manchester, where the air was clogged with diesel fumes and memories of Zach. She wanted space and fresh air and nothing but Sam beside her. She was more than ready, she realised, to move on physically as well as mentally.

'Oh my God! Really?' She pulled away from his embrace, excitement fizzing inside.

He nodded. 'I've got the details here.' He fished his phone out of his pocket, brought something up on the screen and passed it to her. 'It's a holiday cottage, but they'll do a winter let for us. Timing should be perfect.' He beamed at her. 'And if we're happy to pay a premium for a few months, we can have it for a full year. That should give us plenty of time for the build.'

Her eyes widened when she saw the red sandstone cottage, picture perfect with its climbing roses, nestled in a backdrop of mature trees.

'I've already rung the owner. It's ours if we want it. But we'll need to pay a deposit.' He looked awkward then, his eyes sliding away from hers. 'The thing is... I'm a bit stuck for cash at the moment.' He grimaced. 'Would you be able to pay?'

Her eyes narrowed. They hadn't discussed joint finances, but she understood it was something they needed to tackle pretty soon. Maybe now? He was basically her house guest for four nights a week, then he went to work on his other projects and stayed wherever he could, sometimes with his clients. A nomadic lifestyle, he'd said, which had suited him as a widower. He hadn't been ready to settle, unsure where he wanted to be. So he travelled, staying with Faith between projects. He'd pay for their groceries every now and again, treat Emma to meals out, but that was about it in terms of a financial contribution.

She caught his eye and he frowned. 'What? I'm totally up against it financially until the Milnrow job pays. I think I might have mentioned it.' He had. Several times. To the point where it had been getting a little tedious and her bank card had been busier than usual, paying for everything. He gave her an apologetic smile. 'More good news, though. I signed the project off today, so it won't be long till the money comes in.'

Still she didn't say anything, a bead of unease sitting in her chest.

He cocked his head, giving her a quizzical look. 'You don't mind fronting this one, do you? Then I should be fine to pay you my share going forward. If that's what we're doing.'

She nodded, relieved he'd mentioned sharing the costs. 'Okay. But if we're going to be a partnership, then it's only fair we split the living costs.'

He didn't reply, moving into the kitchen, Emma following, watching while he surveyed the contents of the fridge, no doubt wondering what he was going to rustle up for supper. He did most of the cooking because, to be fair, he was a much better cook than she was. And he enjoyed it, which she didn't.

He picked out some meat, vegetables and cheese for a pasta dish, put them on the worktop. Got out the pasta and the casserole dish before he finally spoke, his voice filled with a forced calmness. 'I'm surprised to hear you say that, because, as you know, when you're self-employed, money comes in chunks, doesn't it?' She knew he was upset with her. Could see the vein on his forehead that only appeared if he was wound up about something. He started chopping an onion with deft, practised strokes, the job done in seconds. 'It's quite hard to keep a steady cashflow.' He glanced up, his jaw set. 'Sometimes we might have to pick up the slack for each other, don't you think? There needs to be a bit of give and take. And you'll be taking time off after the baby, won't you? So keeping the household ticking over will be on my shoulders at that point.'

She cringed, could see she'd sounded mean. Pedantic. He was looking at the bigger picture, at a long-term partnership, and she was seeing another expense after the shock of spending all that money on the plot, and ring-fencing an even larger amount of money for the build.

'I'm sorry,' she said, moving behind him, her arms round his waist while he carried on chopping the vegetables, not wanting to see the annoyance in his eyes. 'Of course I'll pay the deposit.'

She felt his body relax a little and she knew she'd been forgiven, telling herself off for being a bit short with him about money. He was planning to look after them, and now he'd found them somewhere to live. Their first proper house together. How exciting was that? All this effort he was going to on their behalf should not be underestimated or taken for granted. She told herself to broaden her focus and stop sweating the small stuff, because in the greater scheme of things, the deposit for the rental property was not going to break the bank.

While he was cooking, she took some time to study the details for the cottage, wondering how it would feel to actually live in the town they were going to call home. The more she looked at it, the easier it was to imagine herself there. In fact, the sooner they moved there the better, she decided. A fresh start, in a new place, would be exactly what she needed to put the past behind her and turn her attention to their future.

She must have dozed off, because she was roused by the blaring of the smoke detector, making her spring up off the sofa, heart racing, feeling dopey and confused about the sudden noise. Clouds of smoke were billowing from the cooker and before she could move, Sam sprinted into the kitchen, his body wet, a towel wrapped round his waist.

He snatched up the oven gloves, then pulled a burning object from the oven, throwing it in the sink and turning on the taps. The smell was horrendous, like burned plastic, a thick layer of odious smoke hanging in the air. He switched on the extractor fan and Emma dashed to open the windows, coughing as the acrid smoke caught the back of her throat.

He turned to her, a deep frown etched on his brow. 'What the heck is your wallet doing in the oven?'

He looked shocked. But not as shocked as she felt.

'I turned the oven on to crisp up the pasta bake, then went

to have a quick shower and get changed, not imagining there'd be anything else in there.' He gave a frustrated grunt. 'It must have been stuffed at the back where I couldn't see it.'

What *was* her wallet doing in the oven? Her heart was pounding so hard she felt it might bounce out of her chest, making her feel so light-headed, she had to sit down.

'Imagine if you'd been at home on your own,' he continued. 'The whole place could have gone up in flames.'

He was right, it could have been disastrous. Fatal even, if the flames had spread. The exit from the lounge was through the kitchen, and if she'd been slow to react, she could have been trapped.

He came and sat next to her, putting an arm round her shoulders. 'Hey, you're shaking. It's okay, love. No harm done. Except your bank cards are probably melted, so you'll have to get new ones.' He pulled her to him, stroking her hair, kissing her forehead. 'I don't think the pasta's going to be edible, though, and I'm not sure how usable the oven is now with melted plastic all over the shelves.' He sighed. 'I'll order a take-away, sort it out tomorrow.'

She clung to him, scared now. It wasn't the first time she'd done something stupid since she'd been pregnant. Was it hormones? She didn't remember being like this with her first pregnancy, but she'd read that every time was different. Perhaps it was because life was more complicated this time round, her mind on so many things, causing her to be distracted, doing things without thinking.

She'd lost her keys and found them in her bedside cabinet. She never kept them there and only looked out of desperation. By the time she'd found them, she was too late to make the appointment for her first scan, so that had to be rearranged. Fortunately, everything was okay, so it hadn't mattered. Then a pile of Sam's papers had been found in the bin after they'd turned the flat upside down looking for them. It was bin collection the following day and the bag was all tied up ready to take out. Weeks of his work could have been wasted and a big chunk of money lost.

Those incidents had been frustrating, but more recently she'd been doing things that were downright dangerous. Like dislodging the immersion heater cable from its casing in the airing cupboard. She couldn't remember doing it, but she must have pulled it out when she'd gone to get a towel. She'd grabbed it without realising it was there. The electric shock had sent her tumbling to the floor, gasping for breath for a few minutes. Thankfully, she had an antenatal appointment the following day, so she was reassured no harm had been done to her baby, but she had a nasty burn on her hand and felt shaken for the rest of the day.

Now this. Stuffing flammable things in the oven was a whole new level of dangerous. She could see how it might happen, with this tiredness she felt. She'd probably got distracted, thought she was putting something else in there.

After they'd eaten their takeaway and Sam had cleared up, he came and sat next to her on the sofa, took her hand in his. He was quiet for a moment, his mouth opening and closing like he wanted to say something but was working out how to phrase it. 'Look, love... Don't take this the wrong way, but would you mind if I got Faith to check in on you when I'm away? I'm getting a bit worried about you.'

She sighed. 'That's not a bad idea. I'm getting a bit worried about myself. What is happening to my brain?'

He squeezed her hand. 'Things do seem to be getting worse, don't they? Are you sure it's just the pregnancy? I'm wondering if it might be a good idea to make an appointment with the GP and see what they say.' He sounded properly concerned and she wondered if she'd been a bit blasé about her mental health. 'I mean, it's probably nothing, but what if it isn't? What if there's something else going on?'

She swallowed, unnerved. 'I've spoken to the midwife and she doesn't think there's a problem.' There was a defensive note to her voice, uncomfortable with the suggestion there might be something seriously wrong. 'Apparently, it's common to be a bit forgetful. I'm fine, honestly. Nothing to worry about.'

He didn't look convinced, but he left it there. Her mind, however, chewed over his comments like a dog with a bone. Did he think she was going mad? Would that make him have second thoughts about their relationship? More to the point, though, was her own concern that she'd suddenly become a danger to herself.

CHAPTER SIX

Two weeks after the wallet in the oven incident, they moved to Appleby. It had been Emma's idea to go ahead, thinking it was being in Manchester, with all the mental baggage of her past, that was causing her brain to scramble. She didn't feel safe in the apartment any more and had decided a fresh start, a move towards their future life, would be good for both of them. Perhaps her brain wouldn't feel so cluttered in a new place, she reasoned. She could forget about paperwork and emails and messages that needed responses. Put everything on hold while she concentrated on making their baby and keeping herself healthy.

Sam had been delighted and the fact that she hadn't been to see the cottage didn't matter. It was temporary and she could live anywhere for a short time. Anyway, it looked delightful and she was impatient to be gone from the city and out into the fresh air of the countryside.

Since the cottage was furnished, they didn't need to take much, and she'd kept the flat on for an extra month, just in case it all went pear-shaped, and they needed to come back. It also gave her more time to sort through her possessions. While Sam was working, she was going to travel back to Manchester on day trips and gradually transfer everything she wanted to keep into the storage unit where she kept Zach's artwork and other bits and pieces she couldn't bear to look at.

'I'll give you a hand,' Faith had said, when she'd popped over one evening for supper while Sam was away.

'Would you?' Emma heaved a sigh of relief. 'That would be great. My energy is a bit limited at the moment and who knows what I'd end up throwing away without adult supervision?'

They'd laughed, Faith taking it as a joke, but Emma knew there was a big grain of truth in there as well.

The cottage was open when they arrived. It was owned by the farm at the back of the house, their fields surrounding the property. Apparently it used to house farm workers back in the day but now it was a source of extra income as a holiday let. Emma got out of the car and turned in a circle, taking it all in, delighted they had their own private lane to the property. After living in a city, it was wonderful to have so much space to themselves and no neighbours to intrude.

It was a beautiful spring day, although there was still a slight chill in the air. The sky was bright blue, the trees in full leaf, the sound of birdsong music to her ears. The cottage was even nicer in real life than in the pictures, made of red sandstone blocks with a sash window on either side of a central porch downstairs, and a matching pair of windows upstairs. Like a picture a child might draw of a house. At one time there would have been flower beds at the front, but these had been replaced by block paving so there was parking for two cars. A climbing rose was trained up the front of the house, a lavender bush on either side of the door.

A fire had been lit in the wood burner in the lounge area and the place was warm and cosy. Her eyes travelled round the one room that constituted the downstairs of the property. A kitchen to the left, with a breakfast bar separating it from the living room, a small table and two chairs pushed against the far wall, then a squishy sofa and a recliner in the cosy living area. Upstairs there were two bedrooms and a bathroom. Small, but perfectly adequate for the two of them. Maybe a squeeze once the baby arrived, but she wasn't thinking about that now. She wandered around the rooms while Sam started to unpack the car, delighted by the decor and cleanliness. It was very Laura Ashley, all sage green and grey with burned orange accents in the soft furnishings. It would be a lovely first home for them.

Still, the knot of anxiety in her chest refused to loosen.

Having made the decision to move, she'd been increasingly concerned she was rushing into something pretty major without a lot of grown-up consideration. Did it make sense to be building a new house at this moment in time, with a baby on the way? It could be one thing too many, putting pressure on their relationship, and that was the last thing she wanted.

There was a voice in her head telling her it would be prudent to step back and slow things down, and although she loved the excitement of this new adventure with Sam, loved the fact they were having a baby together and they were head-over-heels in love, her gut was telling her she was taking on too much. Especially when her brain was clearly overloaded already. She appeared to be a danger to herself and wasn't that a red flag, a sign she needed to do less, not more?

The day was busy with unpacking and going out to buy supplies, then their landlady popped round to make sure everything was okay. She was a kindly middle-aged woman, with a no-nonsense manner, dressed in mud-splattered jeans and a home-knitted jumper that had seen better days and looked like it might have been made out of oddments.

She'd brought a casserole and an apple pie with her. 'To save you the bother of cooking, dear,' she said, giving Emma a knowing look as her eyes travelled down to her belly and back up. Emma blushed, realising Sam must have told her she was pregnant, thrown by the idea that she knew. 'I hope he's been doing all the hard work?' The landlady winked at Sam, who took the food from her, putting it on the worktop behind him. 'I'm Hilda, by the way. Anything you need, don't be frightened to ask. We're only next door.' She laughed. 'Well, technically, we're round the corner and quarter of a mile up the lane, but you know what I mean.' She gave them a quick tour of the place and showed them how everything worked and then she was off, striding back down the lane, like she had somewhere to be, things to do.

'Isn't she great?' Sam said, putting the casserole in the microwave. 'Perfect timing. We might as well have this now, then we won't have the bother of cooking.' He turned and caught her expression, taking a few seconds before he understood what her disquiet might be. 'You didn't mind me telling her you were pregnant, did you?'

Only Faith and Sam knew about the baby, and Emma felt uneasy about spreading the news more widely. 'I'm not sure I want everyone knowing. Not for a few more weeks, then you're...' She could feel the emotions building, threatening to spill out, her voice wavering. 'You're less likely to have a miscarriage. Otherwise...' She swallowed, unable to carry on with what she was about to say. She hadn't realised she still felt so raw, thought she'd put her miscarriage behind her. 'It's hard explaining to people you're no longer pregnant while you're grieving for the little soul you've lost. I can't do it again.'

A sob burst out of her and she covered her face with her hands, embarrassed to be falling apart in front of Sam. She was normally fully in control, quite practised at pushing things away to the dark corners of her mind where she wanted them to stay. After Zach's accident, people had remarked on her resilience, her fortitude. But they didn't know what was going on inside, couldn't see the anguish eating away at her. That was why she'd hit a crisis, Faith had told her. Bottling it all up. She'd promised herself she would be different with Sam. It didn't make the sharing of her feelings any easier, though.

She felt his arm round her shoulders, pulling her to him, gently wiping away her tears. 'I'm so sorry. I didn't know you'd had a miscarriage. It was stupid of me not to ask if you minded. It just helped us to get this place for a year instead of six months, you see.' He was gabbling, trying to cover his mistake. 'I was trying to make it easy for you and the baby. Otherwise, we might have had to move and that would have been mega stressful.'

She pushed away. Men didn't understand these things because they weren't the ones growing a new life inside them. It wasn't real to them until an actual baby appeared at the end of nine months. A miscarriage wasn't the end of the world because you could have another go, make a new one. They didn't understand how it felt to nurture a baby and then to lose it, to lose your child. It wasn't something she wanted to explain or discuss, because it felt futile. Like trying to explain calculus to a class of eleven-year-olds. She swiped at her eyes, took a few deep breaths, her heightened emotions making her brave, able to say what she'd been thinking all day.

'Sam... I... I don't think I can do this.'

'What do you mean?' He sounded confused, looked horrified.

'The house. Building a house.' She moved away from him, perched on a stool at the breakfast bar, no longer trusting her legs to keep her upright. The sudden surge of emotion had left her feeling light-headed, making her heart race.

'But...' He leant against the worktop, looking completely dumbfounded. 'It's been a long day, sweetheart. I know you're tired and probably hungry. Why don't we have something to eat and then we can talk about it. See if I can put your mind at rest.'

'Don't patronise me,' she snapped.

He held up his hands. 'I'm not. Really, that's not my intention, but I know what you're like when you need to eat. You go all frantic.'

'I am not frantic,' she snarled, enunciating each word, the smell of the casserole making her stomach gurgle in anticipation.

The microwave pinged and he got the dish out, gave it a stir, put it back for a few minutes. The smell filled the air, meaty and delicious. She positively yearned for the meal in a way she'd never yearned for food before she was pregnant, and she wondered if he had a point.

'Okay,' she murmured. But the words didn't want to wait and came blurting out anyway. 'The thing is... I don't think I can deal with the stress of a new-build. I've been watching the programmes – you know, *Grand Designs* – and it never ever goes right. They always spend way more than they budget and I've got a bad feeling about it.' She glanced around the kitchen. 'Why can't we rent this place until we find somewhere we want to buy? Wouldn't that be easier?'

Having vocalised her worries, she realised they'd been gnawing away at her for weeks and she'd pushed them aside, not wanting to acknowledge her misgivings, wanting to go along with the whole new-build dream. Sam gazed at her, his mouth twisting, his face a mask of concentration. There was no doubt he was listening.

The microwave pinged and he dished out the food, brought it over to the breakfast bar, perching on a stool next to her.

He waited until she had almost finished her meal before he spoke.

'I know it seems daunting, building a new house. But it's my job. It's what I'm good at. I've been doing it all my working life and I've made all the mistakes.' His hand slid round her waist, fingers playing with the hem of her T-shirt. 'I design things in a way that makes them less problematic to build. My cost esti-mates have contingencies built in.' His hand moved up her back, rubbing in slow, small circles. It felt lovely, relaxing, and she enjoyed the sensations while she finished eating. 'I'm good at managing budgets and I don't want you to worry about any of that.'

Finally, she put down her cutlery, turning towards him. 'It's a lot of money to commit and... we might not like living in Appleby.' Now she'd started to air her concerns, all the issues she'd dismissed over the last few weeks were queuing up to be voiced. It was fine dreaming about these things, but the reality didn't feel comfortable yet. Coming from a city, she'd thought she would enjoy the lack of traffic and people. But with Sam working away for half the week on his projects, she would be spending a lot of time on her own. She'd never been great at making friends, something that seemed so much harder as an adult, and she already felt a bit lonely when he was away. Faith had been there for her in Manchester, but she wouldn't have her company up here and it was a loss she hadn't considered until now.

'But it doesn't have to be permanent if you don't like it here. We can sell up and move on.' She saw how seriously he was taking her concerns and it made her feel better. He was right and she reminded herself this project was an investment as much as anything else. A way to make the money grow. 'I honestly think this is going to be my best house yet. It will cost virtually nothing to run and with the solar panels and windmill in the garden, plus the heat pump, you could even make money out of the electricity generated.' He smiled at her. 'It's a ground-breaking design. One that could lead on to lots more projects for me. It could be the making of my practice. Then you won't have to worry about working. You can concentrate on looking after our family.'

He was making a good case and she could feel herself starting to waver.

'I promise you won't find another house that's so easy to live in. I know it's daunting but you just have to trust me.' His voice was calm, soothing, his hand working wonders on the knotty muscles in her back. 'I need you to give me the chance to do this for you. Build this house because I love you. Build it for our family.'

She sighed. *Our family*. This wasn't only about her. Still, she felt uneasy. 'I don't know. I think I need to sleep on it.'

His hand stopped massaging and a frown rumpled his brow, his voice hesitant. 'You're not... having second thoughts about us, are you?'

Maybe it took a beat too long for her to answer, because he got up and started clearing the dishes away, his back towards her as he filled the sink. She could tell by the stiffness of his posture, the jerkiness of his movements that she'd upset him, and she slid off her stool, went to stand beside him, her arm round his waist as he scrubbed at the casserole dish.

'I love you, Sam. I do. But this is all happening so fast. It just feels like... there's too much going on. I think that's why I keep doing stupid things. My mind is overloaded with it all.'

He stopped scrubbing, his eyes meeting hers. 'It's happening fast because it's the right thing to do. It's meant to be. Can't you feel it?'

He turned and kissed her, a deep, lingering kiss that told her he meant every word he said. 'I desperately want to do this for us. I love you so much and it's made me realise how much I want us to be a family.' He found her hand, his still wet and soapy, dropped down on one knee, looking up at her. Her heart flipped. 'Emma, my love, will you marry me?'

CHAPTER SEVEN

Emma burst into tears. His proposal was another complication, but it was the ultimate demonstration of his commitment to her. She couldn't speak, gulping down the sobs while her mind told her it wasn't right. Not now, not so soon after Zach. But then she thought of her child and everything Sam could offer, the life they could have together. She loved him, couldn't think about life without him, and she realised there was no decision to be made.

'Yes,' she said, and he grasped her hand tighter, his eyes fixed on hers, a huge grin on his face.

The next morning, Emma woke early, her mind full of wedding arrangements and everything she'd have to do. It felt daunting to the point of overwhelming and the euphoria of the previous evening had morphed into anxiety.

'Let's do it,' Sam said to her, when he turned on his side and saw she was already awake. 'Get married, I mean. The sooner the better. I can't wait for you to be Mrs Barclay. Emma Barclay, that has such a nice ring to it.' She smiled and gave him a delighted kiss, thinking this man was a mind reader, sensing her unease before she'd had a chance to voice her concerns. She didn't want to be a single parent, she needed commitment, and her dream of a larger family still burned strong in her heart.

'Who needs a big wedding?' she murmured, snuggling closer to him, his hand caressing her back. She'd done that once and couldn't contemplate being in the spotlight again.

'Something quick and quiet is definitely my preference,' he said. 'I'll admit my first wedding was sort of unbearable. Alice invited the whole village, I think. And she came from a big family, so there were relatives galore.' He gave a shudder. 'You and me. That's all we need, and a couple of witnesses. It's about us making a commitment to each other at the end of the day, isn't it?'

She loved that he was so focused on the two of them, and she felt utterly cherished. They hadn't been together long and many men would have run a mile from an unplanned pregnancy at this stage in a relationship. She'd prepared herself for that, and knew it would have been a difficult road for her as a single mum, having been brought up in a single parent household. She would have done it in a heartbeat, though, because being a mum was all she'd been thinking about for years now. In fact, since her mum had died, the idea of having her own child had obsessed her to the point where she was buying baby clothes for a child she didn't have. She also had six names lined up, three for boys and three for girls.

Her first pregnancy ending in miscarriage had been a severe blow, and then Zach's accident had appeared to put motherhood out of her reach. Didn't it show you should never give up hope, because you didn't know what was waiting round the corner in life? Good or bad, the surprises kept coming. She kissed Sam again, thinking he was the best surprise, and all her concerns melted away when his arm tightened around her and he kissed her back. Yes, she could definitely enjoy the thought of a lifetime with this man. All her weaknesses were his strengths, and didn't that say perfect partnership? What a team they'd be.

Sam was on the phone as soon as they'd had breakfast and somehow managed to get a cancellation at the registry office, only four weeks away. The time flew by, packing up the flat in Manchester and getting properly settled in the cottage in Appleby. Most of her stuff went into the storage unit, along with some small pieces of furniture that had come down through her family. Her mum's dressing table, a comfy chair that had belonged to her grandma, and a grandfather clock that had apparently been in the family for three generations.

She'd had the storage unit for a while now, having had to clear out Zach's studio and not wanting to throw anything away. His canvases were covered with dust sheets until she decided what to do with them. At some point she'd have to make some decisions, but it could wait until after the baby when everything had settled down. In her experience, things changed so fast; who could predict what the situation would be in a year? She might feel differently about everything by then and have different decisions to make. Most of her art materials went into storage too, the cottage being too small to accommodate additional baggage. Especially when the spare room would have to be Sam's office as well as the nursery. She didn't want to contaminate it with the smell of oil paints and solvents, so she just took sketchbooks, pencils and watercolours. That would do for now.

Sam, she was discovering, was extremely organised. Positively anal when it came to detail. She'd always considered herself an organised person, but next to him she looked ramshackle. And getting worse by the day. Thankfully, he was happy to take over a lot of the domestic paperwork, which was very welcome given her overwhelming tiredness.

He did all the address changes and name changes for her

too. When she'd married Zach, she'd been in full feminist mode and had wanted to be a Ms rather than a Mrs and keep her own name. It was how she was known in the art world. It had taken a while to build up her reputation and following, and she didn't want to risk losing commissions by confusing potential clients with a name change. Now, though, a new name would give her a clear break from the past and a new role for the future.

'I want you to revel in being pregnant,' he said when she apologised for not being able to keep up with his energy. 'You're making a new human. It's a hell of a thing for your body to cope with. You concentrate on that and I'll concentrate on everything else, including organising the wedding.' It was like music to her ears. 'Faith said she'd come and be a witness, so we only need one more and she said she'd find somebody.'

On the day of the wedding, he dressed in his best charcoal suit and she donned a floaty white dress, which she'd bought online and altered to fit round her bump. It was vintage and beautifully made, with tiny pearl buttons up the front of the bodice. On her feet she wore sparkly Doc Martens. Not only were they supremely comfy, but it was a statement about who she was as a person. Still the no-nonsense, arty feminist. Plus, her feet had swollen and she couldn't fit into ordinary shoes. She remembered how she'd bowed to convention for her first wedding, how uncomfortable she'd felt in her expensive dress and high heels. No, this was a time in her life when she was going to be unashamedly herself.

Faith looked elegant in a fitted cornflower-blue suit, her hair in an updo that must have taken hours of work by her hair-dresser. Emma liked the fact she'd made such an effort. She'd pulled a stranger off the street to make up the numbers. An elderly lady who looked all dewy-eyed throughout the cere-mony. It felt reckless, romantic and absolutely right.

They skipped a honeymoon, staying the night in Appleby Castle in the bridal suite. Sam promised he'd take her somewhere special once the baby was born and the house was built and their cashflow had settled down. Then they could relax and enjoy being a family somewhere warm and far away.

The day after the wedding, as soon as they were home, he was planning a trip to see a client.

'I don't want to leave you on your own,' he said with a sigh, 'but we need to get some money coming in if you're not working.'

Emma was out of touch with the state of their finances. Sam had been looking after the money for the past few weeks, while she waited for her new bank cards to arrive. Moving had complicated things because she'd had to wait for an official document to verify her new address.

'Let me look after you properly,' he'd said, taking her hand as they sat on the sofa, her with her legs up on a footstool. 'I'll take on all the jobs you don't like, because I'm okay with the money side of things. When you think about it, managing money is a big part of my job. I can deal with our day-to-day expenses and the money for the build.' He laughed. 'I've always been careful. Even as a child, I was the one with a savings account, who put money aside rather than spend it.'

She giggled. 'I was the kid who was always borrowing off everyone else.' Money had never stuck to her like it did with other people. There was always something she needed, a new aspiration, the next goal to be heading towards. Somehow, what-ever she had in the bank was never quite enough and she had a bad habit of indulging in spending sprees if she was feeling stressed.

'There you go.' He squeezed her hand. 'See, we have to play to our strengths. Let me sort out the finances.'

Her face fell when she realised there was a big stumbling block.

'But I can't change my savings account. It's a bit of a weird set-up because of the compensation payout and the safeguards I put in place for myself.'

'If it's your money, you can amend it, can't you?' He turned to face her. 'How about we set up a new joint account just for the build and you can transfer your budget into there. Then I can get on with everything but I can't go over the amount agreed, can I? And you don't have to worry.' He smiled. 'After all, we're married now, so what's mine is yours and vice versa.' He shrugged. 'I think it's pretty normal for a married couple to have joint accounts, isn't it? We'll set up another one for household bills too. Does that sound like a good idea?'

She chewed her lip. It was a huge amount of money to hand over all at once and she didn't want to do it. Okay, so Sam didn't have money to invest, but he was putting in his time, which would add up to a fair sum if she'd had to employ a professional. She understood that, but it wasn't quite the same. However, refusing would make it seem like she didn't trust him. 'I'll give my account manager a ring tomorrow, see what I can sort out,' she said, effectively putting the idea on hold for now, until she had a better idea.

'Attagirl. It'll speed everything up, I guarantee it.' He patted her hand and stood, stretching. 'I've got a chat with Faith on Zoom now. An informal counselling session. She thought the wedding might be triggering for me, so...' He swallowed and turned away, cleared his throat. 'I'll ask her if she'll stick around for a few days, shall I? So you're not on your own.'

He picked up his laptop and she felt a familiar twinge of jealousy. He was going to talk about losing his deceased wife for an hour. It was good for him, she knew, to sift through his lingering emotions and try and put the trauma behind him. But she couldn't pretend she liked it. She glanced up at him, forced a fleeting smile.

'I'll go upstairs to the office, then I'm not disturbing your programme.' He pointed to the TV, where *EastEnders* was starting.

She nodded and tried to concentrate on the story, but her mind kept wandering, asking her the same question. *Why would he be talking to Faith on Zoom when she was only staying at the hotel in town?* Then another, more disturbing question entered her head. *Was he really calling Faith at all?*

CHAPTER EIGHT

After the wedding, with Sam falling back into his usual routine of half the week at home, half away, life felt a bit flat for Emma. In fact, if she hadn't had the gold band on her finger, she might have found it hard to believe the marriage had actually happened.

She'd given up work when they moved to Appleby, to allow time to settle in and prepare for the baby, but the novelty of having nothing to do was beginning to wear off. She decided to take the opportunity to explore the area with her sketchbook and camera, capturing scenes she could use later for paintings. She was experimenting with watercolours and enjoying getting back to art. It was a relaxing way to while away some time, and the weather was settled at the tail end of summer.

On her third outing of the week, she wandered home, hoping Sam wouldn't be back too late that evening. Tired after her afternoon walk, she settled herself on the sofa for a nap.

The blaring of the smoke detector startled her awake, blinking furiously, heart racing, while her brain tried to work out what was going on. It felt like déjà vu, reminding her of the incident in the apartment. She could smell burning and she clambered off the sofa to see wisps of smoke snaking down the stairs. Without thinking if it was a good idea, she hauled herself upstairs to investigate.

The smell hit her as soon as she opened the bedroom door, the duvet cover smouldering, small flames licking towards the pillows. She'd left her curling tongs plugged in and lying on the bed. How on earth had she done that? Normally, she would sit at the dressing table to curl her hair, using the socket on the wall. Now the tongs were plugged in beside the bed, which was odd because she could have sworn she'd unplugged them and put them away in the bottom of the wardrobe. In fact, she was certain that was what she'd done. She'd only started curling her hair recently, the tongs a present from Sam to cheer her up when she'd been complaining about pregnancy making her hair go straight, and she always put them back in the box when she was finished.

There was no time to think about it now. If she wasn't quick, the whole bed would be on fire. She grabbed the power cable and tugged the tongs off the bed, switched the socket off then dashed to the bathroom and wetted a towel. She slapped at the flames until she was sure she'd put them out, puffing and panting like she'd been doing a cardio workout. The duvet was ruined, but it was the least of her worries.

She sank onto the bed, appalled. The whole bedroom would have been on fire in minutes. Imagine if she'd stayed out longer. She would have come back to an inferno. Her body was shaking, her mind running through all the possible scenarios. What would Sam think when he found out? He already thought she was losing her mind and she didn't want to reinforce that idea in his head. He couldn't know.

The sound of a car pulling into the drive made her look up, and her heart sank. Sam was home. But she might still have time to hide the damage.

Quickly, she pulled the duvet off the bed and bundled it in

the corner, next to her bedside cabinet. There was a spare duvet on the top shelf of the wardrobe – she'd spotted it when they moved in – but the shelf was too high for her to reach and try as she might, she couldn't grab hold of it.

'Emma!' Sam called. His feet clumped up the stairs. 'Emma, what's that smell?'

She was standing on the bottom shelf of the wardrobe, making a final desperate effort to reach the duvet, when he walked into the room. He frowned at her. 'What are you doing? What's going on?' His nose wrinkled. 'Why is it all smoky in here?'

Her shoulders slumped and she stepped down, defeated. There was no escaping the truth now. She was going to have to tell him.

'Christ, Emma. That's the third time you've nearly set our home on fire,' he said when she'd finished. 'It was the candle catching on the curtains a couple of weeks ago, wasn't it?'

How had she forgotten about that? Probably embarrassment putting her in denial. But he was right. It *was* the third time, and every time it happened, she had no recollection of doing the thing that had instigated the fire. She couldn't remember putting her wallet in the oven, or lighting the candle, or plugging in the curling tongs.

'I'll sort this out,' he said, going to the window and flinging it open before coming back and giving her a kiss and a hug. She sank into him, relieved he didn't seem to be cross, more concerned for her welfare. 'You go downstairs and put your feet up.' He stepped away, studied her face. 'You've gone pale, love.' She didn't move and he shooed her away. 'Go on, I can do this. Anyway, it's not good for you or the baby breathing in all this smoke.' She plodded downstairs, her thoughts spinning round the conviction she was losing her mind.

But a voice in her head piped up, insisting there was a

different story and she needed to listen. Telling her that maybe, just maybe, she hadn't done these things at all.

Downstairs was clear of smoke, the front door still open, and she left it to get a draught pulling through. She shivered as she filled the kettle, switched it on and leant against the worktop while she waited for it to boil. Her eyes were drawn to the singe mark on the curtains in the lounge.

Of the three events, it was the candle incident that stood out for her as being the hardest to explain. Sam kept buying her scented candles as gifts, to help her relax, he said. She wasn't a big fan because they seemed to make her eyes water and her nose run, but she couldn't tell him that. He was buying them out of love, and she appreciated the gesture, didn't want to hurt his feelings. The point was, she wouldn't have lit the candle that caught on the curtains. She shivered again, not wanting to think the unthinkable.

The kettle came to the boil and she made a peppermint tea for herself and a coffee for Sam, taking her mug over to the sofa, her eyes straying again to the damaged curtain.

It was a puzzle she was struggling to solve because she had been the only one in the house at the time. She took her mind back to the evening it had happened. Sam had been away and she'd been in the bath. Fortunately, she came downstairs before any real damage had been done. If she hadn't come down when she did, though, it might have been a different story because it turned out there were no batteries in any of the smoke detectors.

Sam had stormed up to see Hilda, incensed at her oversight, but she swore blind she'd put new batteries in before they'd moved in as part of her safety checks. Anyway, the issue had been rectified, and new batteries put in the smoke detectors, thank goodness, or Emma might not have woken up today.

The thought sent another shiver through her body and she took a sip of tea, needing its warmth. Could she have been starting the fires and not remembering? It was still a possibility, but her mind drew her back to the alternative, that it was someone else.

She thought back to the wallet incident in the apartment. Sam had been away as usual. The electrician had been to sort out the immersion heater cable. He'd been in and out, like tradesmen always were, fetching tools and bits and pieces, propping the front door open to make it easier to carry things through. She'd been sorting through her clothes in the bedroom, having a bit of a clear-out while she listened to an audiobook, so she wasn't taking any notice. Anyone could have walked in with the front door open.

She supposed there might be people who'd think she'd moved on too quickly from Zach. He had a strong circle of friends. People she hadn't kept in touch with because it was too difficult. It was the only possibility she could think of, but none of them knew where she lived now. And she couldn't imagine any of them would want to do her harm.

She shook her head, telling herself she was being melodramatic. Nobody else had been around when these last two incidents had happened, so it must have been her. *Did I lock the door when I went out, though?*

She had been relaxed about security since they'd moved, as they lived in the middle of nowhere and there was nothing to steal anyway. When they first moved in, she'd kept forgetting to take her key with her and had locked herself out a couple of times, having to traipse up to the farm to get Hilda to let her in. Since then, Hilda had suggested she leave the door on the latch. And she didn't lock it if she was home alone during the day, just at night. Now, though, she knew she needed to be careful, more vigilant, because this was one fire too many and the next one could be deadly.

She cupped her mug to her chest, feeling cold all of a sudden. A loud bang made her jump. The front door slamming shut. She screamed, tea spilling all over her top, making her jump to her feet, pulling the scalding material away from her skin.

Sam ran down the stairs. 'What is it? Are you okay?'

She stood staring at the door, not sure that she was.

CHAPTER NINE

Emma woke to the undulating murmur of voices coming from downstairs. She was six and a half months pregnant and was supposed to be in her element, glowing even. Unfortunately, that wasn't how pregnancy had worked out for her. The baby was pressing on her internal organs in a way that made her want to pee all the time, so sleep was erratic. She also had sciatica causing shooting pains down the back of her left leg. There were exercises she could do, but her belly got in the way now, so it was almost impossible to get any relief. Lying down helped, but she was frustrated, tired and grumpy. Nothing was working out the way it should.

Thankfully, she hadn't managed to set anything else on fire recently, and apart from a nasty shock when she'd been changing the light bulb in the bathroom, nothing untoward had happened. Hilda had been apologetic and couldn't understand why the bulb had even needed changing as she'd put new ones in all the fittings before their rental agreement had started. Apparently, some wiring had come loose, probably rodents in the loft, she'd said. They tended to come in during the winter, which wasn't much of a consolation because now Emma lay in bed at night listening for the sounds of scurrying feet above her head.

She was starting to wonder if her suspicions that somebody was trying to do her harm had been misguided. However, she had been more vigilant, making sure the door was locked all the time, even when she was at home, and it seemed to have worked.

As she listened to the voices, unable to make out words, she wondered how she was going to start the conversation with Sam about progress on their new house. Or lack of it, which was the main problem. Many a time, in recent weeks, she'd wished she'd never bought the plot at all, then she could have been happily living in a ready-made house by now. Instead, she'd aimed high, and got caught up in a desire to have the perfect home. How stupid was that?

Of course, at the start, she'd secretly hoped it would all happen faster than Sam's planned twelve months. Wanted to believe it would be ready when she was about to give birth and they could move in there with their new baby. The perfect start to family life. How naïve she'd been. It was before she'd watched all the house-building programmes, before she knew anything about the process. Now, instead of living in their new house, they would be crammed into this small cottage, with its spiders and other uninvited wildlife, for many months to come.

She hated spiders, but country cottages were full of the things. And slugs that came up the waste pipes, leaving their trails all over the kitchen worktops. She hated slugs too. Obviously, she'd spoken to Hilda about it, but she'd shrugged and said there was nothing she could do. These things came with the territory. Sam didn't seem to be bothered either, but Emma woke up in a cold sweat with images of her baby's face covered in an army of arachnids spinning their webs, blocking the child's airways; or slimy intruders wriggling into their ears or open mouth. In truth, she didn't want to live here any more. She wanted her shiny new house with its triple glazing, snug-fitting doors, state-of-the-art security system and slug-proof plumbing.

She sighed and heaved herself upright, sitting on the edge of the bed. The room was spinning. Another delightful side effect of pregnancy every time she got up from sitting or lying down. She was seriously reconsidering the number of offspring she wanted to produce if this was going to be the process.

She heard the light tap of footsteps, someone running up the stairs, and Faith appeared in the bedroom doorway, holding a gift-wrapped box. 'Oh, you're awake. Sam said you'd been having a lie-down.'

Emma huffed. 'It's all I do at the moment. This baby is in an awkward position and I get all these niggly pains.' She smiled at her sister-in-law, not wanting to drag the mood down with her moans. 'It's so good to see you. I thought you were working down south this week.'

Faith came and sat beside her, gave her a hug. 'It's been postponed, so I thought I'd head up here and see you two.' She passed her the box. 'A little pregnancy present.'

Emma was curious now. Faith was such a thoughtful friend, never turning up empty-handed. And usually, it was exactly what she needed. She ripped the paper, revealing a TENS machine for pain relief. 'Oh, you angel,' she gasped, opening the box and pulling the machine out. 'The midwife mentioned one of these. Said I should give it a try, but I keep forgetting to order the darn thing. Honestly, my brain is running on a flat battery at the moment.'

Faith smiled sympathetically. 'I hope Sam is looking after you?'

Emma laughed. 'Poor Sam. He's always having to go out and get things I've forgotten when I've been shopping. And I nearly...' She stopped herself from admitting she seemed to keep almost burning the house down or electrocuting herself. She didn't need Faith thinking she was losing her mind too. She noticed the little sideways glances Sam gave her, the way he kept checking up on her, calling her more often to make sure she was okay, arranging for Faith to come and stay over, like she was Emma's babysitter.

Faith rubbed her back. 'Where does it hurt? Shall we give it a try?'

A few minutes later they had everything set up, Emma perched on the edge of the bed with Faith sitting next to her, so she could move the pads if they weren't in the right place. Emma's eyes closed as she felt the machine pulse to life, sending a warm glow into the tight muscles of her lower back. 'Oh... oh, that's lovely.'

'When I was pregnant, these things weren't so widely available,' Faith said, her hands gently massaging Emma's neck. 'I remember it being a godsend when I started in labour. I had a home birth and the midwife brought one for me.' She pulled Emma to her for a quick hug. 'I'm glad it's helping.'

It was the first time she had mentioned having a child and it made Emma wonder if something tragic had happened, because Sam hadn't mentioned a nephew or niece either. She turned, opening her mouth to ask, but then thought better of it, deciding it would be unfair to put Faith on the spot. She hoped that, as their friendship developed, Faith might open up a bit more about her life. Given the time she spent helping others through bereavement, that focus and drive had to come from somewhere. And it seemed likely it came from the pain of her own personal loss.

Emma groaned as the baby wriggled, pressing on a nerve. 'I didn't think pregnancy would be quite so... uncomfortable.' She winced. 'It's getting me down now. And then there's the house...' She gave a frustrated sigh. 'Don't get me started on the house.'

'Sam said there'd been some unforeseen delays on the build.'

Emma rolled her eyes. 'It's one big unforeseen delay. And I can't believe how much money it's taken to get precisely nowhere.' She threw her hands in the air in frustration. 'I mean, he says the site is cleared, but that seems to be it.'

'He was giving me a rundown of the problems the other day,' Faith said, as she adjusted the pads on Emma's back. 'It seems the planning department are being a bit awkward and the foundations are going to need more work than expected. But he has ordered a lot of materials, so those have had to be paid for.' She patted Emma's shoulder. 'He's doing his best, lovely. These things take time and you're going to have to be patient.'

'But he's still dashing off to work with other clients and I said to him we should take priority.' Emma tapped her own chest with a finger. 'His wife and child. He should put clients on hold, not us.'

'But he needs to bring some money in, doesn't he?' Faith said patiently, rubbing Emma's neck in slow, gentle circles as the TENS machine began to lessen the pain. 'It's all a bit of a juggling act for him.'

Emma didn't have an answer. She wasn't working so she did see Faith's point about bringing money in, but surely he could put a bit of concentrated effort in to push the damn project off the starting blocks.

'Anyway...' Faith drew the word out, signalling a change of subject, 'I have some news for you. Good news, I hope.' She stood and came round to sit in front of Emma, her eyes shining, a wide grin on her face. 'I'm moving up here for a while. I thought I might follow you two out to the countryside and have a break from the city. You know, a bit of a refresh. And it means I get to see more of you both.'

'What?' Emma squealed. 'That's wonderful news!' All her complaints about the house were swept away by her delight that Faith would be closer. She wasn't just her sister-in-law, she'd become her closest friend too. A fleeting thought flickered in her mind, a suggestion her low mood might be more to do with isolation and less to do with lack of progress on the house. Had she been deflecting things onto her husband, putting everything on him? Faith's voice snapped her out of her thoughts.

'With your mum not being around, I thought you could use some help with the baby, especially if Sam has to work away.' Faith beamed at her. 'I've reorganised things so I can do my counselling over Zoom, and Debs said she'd carry on with the bereavement support group in Manchester – she runs half the sessions anyway. And I've cut down on the number of guest speaker events I'm going to do.' She laughed, clearly looking forward to the move. 'I can't quite believe I'm doing this.'

'Wow, you're a dark horse. Why didn't you say anything?' Emma could have done with this news weeks ago, then she wouldn't have been so fixated on the house.

'Well, I didn't want to get your hopes up in case I couldn't find anywhere to rent.' Faith gave her shoulder a playful punch. 'And I wanted it to be a surprise. I know how you like surprises.'

Emma flung her arms round Faith's neck, hugging her tight. 'I can't tell you how happy I am about this. Oh my God, it's the best news. Have you told Sam?'

'Yes, I told him I was looking a few weeks ago.' Faith laughed. 'When you got married, actually, that's when I decided to do it. I mean, you two are all the family I've got. Anyway, I moved in today.'

'Today?' Emma squeaked. 'That's... fantastic.'

Yes, it was fantastic, but it was also annoying neither of them had thought she should know what was being planned, treating her like a child who couldn't deal with bad news if it hadn't come off.

She told herself she was being grumpy, banishing her annoyance while she embraced the joy of having a local friend. 'So where are you living?'

'I've got a place in Penrith. An apartment with lovely views over the fields. I decided not to go full country cottage like you guys. As much as I love to visit you here, I do like my creature comforts – a decent supermarket and a few coffee shops and a pub on the doorstep.' Emma thought it sounded like heaven, the country cottage dream having become a little tarnished by the spiders, slugs and rodents. 'But it's only twenty minutes away,' Faith continued. 'Dead easy for me to pop over any time you need me. You know... if you're feeling down or lonely. And if you want to get out for a while, you can come to me and we can amble into town for a coffee or lunch.'

Emma grinned, already looking forward to the fun they could have together. 'Do you know, this is what I've been miss-ing. I had people I could hang out with in Manchester. Here, I haven't met anyone I've gelled with yet.'

'I'm sure there's an antenatal group you could join. Then you'd get to know other mums.'

Emma pulled a face. 'I did try a class for a few weeks, but I didn't want to go on my own. It's on a Thursday, you see, and Sam's always away.' She sighed and Faith rubbed her shoulder. 'Everyone else is there with their partner. It felt a bit... awkward.'

'I'll come with you, if you like? I'd be delighted to. Then I'll get to know some people as well. It's the best way when you have a common interest, something you're all going through together. You won't be the only mum who's bringing a friend.'

Emma felt her shoulders relax. Perfect. A proper friend on the doorstep to help when Sam was away. Perhaps things weren't so bad after all.

Faith turned to her, looking serious now. 'I've been meaning to have a chat with you, actually.' She hesitated, looking uncer-tain. 'Now don't take this the wrong way. But with the fires and the electric shocks, well... I've been getting a bit concerned. There seems to be a pattern with it always happening when Sam's away.' Her gaze searched Emma's face. 'I was wondering... you don't think you're a bit depressed, do you? Wanting Sam to pay you a bit more attention. Is that why it's been happening? Or is it something else? You're not seeing things, are you? I know psychosis is rare in pregnancy, but that doesn't mean it isn't real.'

Emma's breath caught in her throat. *Depressed?* No, she wasn't depressed. Fed up, maybe, but that was all. She dropped her eyes to the floor, resenting the implication she was doing these things to herself. But it was the mention of psychosis that stuck in her head. It sounded serious. There had to be a different explanation.

'Sam's been talking about it,' Faith continued, her voice a low murmur, presumably so he couldn't overhear. 'You know, after what happened to Alice, losing you to a fire is his worst nightmare and I want to put his mind at rest. Stop him worrying.' She patted Emma's leg. 'Thankfully, I managed to persuade him you weren't showing the signs of being a psychopathic arsonist or a pyromaniac and it was safe for him to stay with you.'

Emma's head snapped up. Was she joking? It wasn't easy to tell.

Then Faith laughed and she knew she must be.

Many a true word spoken in jest.

She felt the blood drain from her face. 'Is that what he thought? I'm an arsonist? A... a psychopath?'

Faith tutted. 'No, of course not. Sorry, that joke was in very bad taste. You mustn't take the things I say quite so literally.' She gave Emma a reassuring smile. 'But you two do need to talk about what's happened and why it might have been happening. I mean, he said he was going to talk to you. No point moaning to me about it.' She frowned. 'But I knew he wouldn't. It's too hard, you see. After Alice. He just wants to pretend everything's perfect. Head-in-the-sand mentality.'

'He hasn't said a word,' Emma muttered, her mind racing.

Had he been moaning about her? Was that really what he thought?

That night, after Faith had gone, she decided to ask him. Otherwise she'd be second-guessing everything. And she didn't want to be 'after Alice', like she was second-best. Somehow that hurt more than him thinking she was an attention-seeking psychopath.

She waited until they were getting ready for bed, propped up with pillows while he cleaned his teeth. 'Do you think I'm an arsonist or a psychopath or a pyromaniac?' she asked as he came out of the en suite. His eyes widened, mouth dropping open as he clambered into bed beside her. She watched him, noticed his avoidance tactics, setting the alarm on his phone while she waited for an answer. 'Don't deny you said it. Faith told me.'

Was he shocked she'd asked, or shocked because that was exactly what he thought and he was appalled Faith had reported something said in confidence? He ran a hand through his hair, his eyes on the ceiling. 'What was Faith thinking, saying that to you?'

'She was concerned about my welfare and wanted to know if I'm depressed. She knows there is this unspoken thing between us and we need to get it out in the open. You haven't said a word to me, have you? And how do you think that makes me feel?' She didn't wait for him to answer. 'It makes me feel it's exactly what you think. That I'm not safe to be around.'

He looked at her then. 'Oh, come on. It's not out of order for me to talk to my sister. It's better for me to share concerns with her, let her talk me down, than upset you over something that doesn't make sense.'

She glared at him. 'I'm your wife,' she snapped. 'If there's a problem with our relationship, with me, don't you think you should talk to me about it first?'

He blinked, looked down at his hands, twirling his wedding ring round and round his finger. The silence was electric, making the hairs stand up on the back of her neck.

'I'll admit I've been concerned,' he said eventually. 'All these little fires. It seemed like there was a pattern and it was getting worse as your pregnancy progressed. I thought...' He sighed. 'I thought the two things might be connected.'

She could feel her teeth grinding and loosened her jaw. 'And is that what you think now?'

His Adam's apple bobbed up and down. The unspoken answer was *yes* and it felt like a dagger to her heart.

'No, of course not,' he blustered. 'Everything's been fine these last few weeks. Perhaps it was a flush of hormones and now you're past that stage. And I should have been paying you more attention, I know I should.' He reached for her hand. 'I love you, darling. With all my heart. I was never going to leave you. Please, let's not...'

She couldn't bring herself to answer, hurt beyond words, shaking her hand free from his and turning on her side, putting out her bedside light. It had always been her policy never to go to sleep on an argument, but this had blown her mind.

He thought she was setting things on fire to get his attention, which was insulting to say the least. *What is going on?* She clutched the duvet more tightly round her body, convinced now, more than ever, that all the little accidents and near misses added up to a more sinister picture.

Someone meant her harm. And that someone might be lying right next to her.

Or was her imagination running away with her again?

PART TWO

CHAPTER TEN

NOW

After the call ended, Emma sat in the car, feeling like she'd been punched, her breath coming out in little gasps, her chest tight, as she replayed the conversation over and over in her mind. *I'm his wife,* the woman had said. Sam's wife. And she thought Emma was a stalker. Could this be a misunderstanding of some sort? But however much she wanted things to be different, there was no way she could have misinterpreted the woman's words.

She had alluded to previous conversations with Sam, possible suspicions about Emma being a stalker. It sounded like she genuinely believed she was Sam's wife and Emma was delusional.

She clasped her head in her hands, unable to think past the fact she'd been deceived. Massively, unimaginably deceived.

Unable to move forward, she thought back. It had been terrible these last six weeks, knowing Sam thought she was mentally ill, that he believed all the mishaps were signs of some serious mental health issue or personality disorder. He'd also admitted Faith had moved closer at his request, so she could make sure Emma and the baby were safe while he worked away.

She'd shrivelled up inside when he'd said that to her, embarrassed and hurt that both of them thought the same thing.

There was nothing she could do to prove her suspicions that somebody else might have been involved, and even to her own ears that theory sounded a bit far-fetched. Her idea it might be Sam didn't add up, because he was always away when things happened, as was Faith, so they were in the clear. And she wasn't the sort of person who had enemies, so it was a bit ridiculous to even consider it.

In reality, if the hormones were affecting her memory, then the chances were she wouldn't remember doing the things that started the fires even if she had. There was no getting away from the fact she was absent-minded, but she didn't think she was completely out of touch with reality. There was also Faith's comment about pregnancy psychosis to consider. Yes, she'd googled it, who wouldn't? And what she'd read had set off a whole new flurry of worries. She was going round in circles and not reaching any definite conclusions.

For the sake of marital harmony, she'd had to let it go in the end, thankful her pregnancy was reaching its conclusion and hopeful all the nonsense would stop once the baby was born. Sam had been extra caring and thoughtful and Faith had filled the gap when he wasn't there.

But now she had this bombshell to face. Sam had another wife. She tugged at her hair, struggling to comprehend how she hadn't known, frustrated she hadn't spotted the clues before she'd married him.

Did Faith know? Icy fingers inched down her spine, unease clamping the back of her neck. *She and Sam were so close, how could she not know?* Emma's head ached, her mind blown to a million pieces, and she struggled to even think, let alone work out what she should do next.

It was a while before she moved, her eyes staring through

the windscreen at the hospital car park, people coming and going as if everything was normal, as if nothing had changed.

Sam's other wife. Could that be his first wife, Alice? Perhaps she wasn't dead after all. Perhaps he'd spun Emma a web of lies.

Her hand found her phone and she googled his wife's name, Alice Barclay, finding several newspaper articles about the tragic fire that had claimed her life almost two years ago. Their cottage had stood on its own on the edge of the village, not visible from the main road. By the time the fire was spotted, the whole house was in flames. Her remains had been found the following day, once the fire had cooled enough for the property to be searched. Apparently, she was fond of scented candles, used to have them in every room. That was how the fire had started.

Her heart stuttered as her brain made a connection. Scented candles. Like the ones Sam kept buying for her. *Why would he want them in the house after they'd killed his wife?* And now a candle had nearly started a fire in his and Emma's home. It was one hell of a coincidence, wasn't it?

Unnerved, Emma sat back, lost in thought as her mind raced around, presenting her with alternative theories. *What if the body they'd found wasn't his wife? Was it possible? If they'd only found remains...* She searched her phone for more information. Found a notice about the funeral in the local paper. *They'd buried somebody, but was it actually Alice?*

She wondered how easy it would be to fake your own death. But then, she told herself, there had been a real death, with an actual body. *So, if his wife was still alive, then somebody else was dead.* The thought made her shiver, her mind diving into a cesspit of sinister images that made her heart pound. *Had Sam killed someone and covered it up as his wife's death?*

She felt faint, nauseous. You're being ridiculous, she scolded. Fanciful in the extreme.

But her mind wouldn't stop. *What if he'd killed his first wife, making it look like an accident? And, if that was the case, who was the woman on the other end of the phone saying she was Sam's wife?*

More to the point, where did this leave Emma?

CHAPTER ELEVEN

She could feel her shoulder muscles pulling as she curled in on herself, almost slumped over the steering wheel, wanting time to stop. To go back to the place where she didn't have these suspicions, where Sam was hers and hers alone and she was looking forward to starting their family together.

The longer she sat, the more her thoughts settled. There was only one way to sort this out. She took a deep breath and rang him again.

'Hey, darling.' He answered after the first ring. 'Is everything okay?'

She hadn't expected him to answer so quickly, wasn't ready. She cleared her throat, telling herself to be brave, confront this thing head-on. The most important thing was to know the truth, wasn't it? However devastating it might be. 'Where are you?' she asked, buying herself some time.

He laughed. 'That memory of yours is getting worse, isn't it? I told you last night. I'm in Dumfries, looking at the site for the new client.'

'Who are you with?' It sounded like an accusation, and she

cringed, thinking she needed to tread more gently if she was going to catch him off guard.

There was a beat of silence, and his voice was more guarded when he answered. 'Molly and Jack. My clients. Who else would I be with?'

'You tell me,' she snapped, unable to contain herself.

'I... I just did. What's this about?' His voice held a note of concern. 'Are you sure you're okay? Shall I ask Faith to come round?'

'I am perfectly fine,' she spat, then stopped herself from carrying on, aware she was sounding unhinged. He wouldn't listen to her if he thought she was hysterical. She took a calming breath. *Get to the point.* She made herself slow down and say each word carefully. 'When I called you a few minutes ago, a woman answered. She said...' Her voice hitched in her throat and she had to force herself on. 'She said she was your *wife*.'

Deathly silence, not even the sound of his breath, and she wondered if he'd hung up.

'Sam, are you still there?'

'Yes, I'm here.' His sigh hissed into her ear. 'I'm so sorry that happened. Molly has... let's call it a unique sense of humour. She keeps messing with my phone, sending texts to people and answering my calls.' He gave a frustrated huff. 'No awareness of boundaries, I'm afraid.'

'I'm supposed to believe that, am I?' Her voice crackled with rage.

'Oh, darling, why on earth would I lie to you? She's autistic and she struggles with social norms. That's why her dad, Jack, is building a cabin for her in the garden. So she has her independence but he can keep an eye on her.'

Emma's brain recalibrated her inner narrative in the light of this new information. It all sounded so feasible. She vaguely remembered now, Sam talking about a special needs client, how he was excited to delve into ways to make her life better through architecture and interior design.

She blushed, feeling foolish for throwing such an accusation at her husband. But she also felt a huge wave of relief wash over her. She leant forward, resting her head on the steering wheel. All the adrenaline, all those terrible thoughts had left her feeling exhausted.

'Do you want me to come back now? I will if you need me, but I'm desperate to tie down this specification and get them to sign off on the next tranche of expenditure. Then I get my cut and we have a chunk of money coming in.' He sounded weary. 'We're nearly there with it. I'll only be a few more hours. Back for tea.'

He was right, they did need to secure the money. He'd spoken about it only the other day, how none of the projects he was working on were progressing fast enough and cashflow was looking tight. She knew he was worried. Now she felt bad for interrupting him, throwing terrible accusations at him.

'No, no, you carry on. But can you please keep your phone away from that woman? She gave me a horrible shock and who knows how it could affect the baby.'

'I'm so sorry, love, really I am. I hope you're resting.'

Resting. It was what the consultant had told her to do. As she'd suspected, her blood pressure had been through the roof when they'd checked it at the clinic. She'd been sent home with instructions to put her feet up and an appointment for the midwife to call in to make sure there was nothing untoward going on. Pre-eclampsia had been mentioned and she'd been told to watch out for fluid retention and to call if she was in any way concerned. The last thing she'd needed was a shock like this.

'I'm on my way home now. Anyway, I'll let you get on.'

'Okay. I'll come home tonight, yeah? Should be back for six-ish.'

It was unusual, him offering to come home when he was with clients. The conversation had obviously rattled him more than he was letting on. They said their goodbyes and she set off, feeling jittery and unsettled. At least she didn't have to go anywhere else today and could take it easy now.

As she drove, her mind started to process the conversation with Sam. She couldn't help thinking that if he did have a second wife, he was sharing his time nice and equally between the two of them. That returned her thoughts to scenarios of dead wives and burned bodies and she turned on the radio to distract herself, singing along to the music. Thankfully, it worked, and she pulled up outside the cottage in a more positive frame of mind.

She heaved herself out of the car and let herself in. Dumping her bag on the breakfast bar, she made herself a cup of chamomile tea and took it into the lounge area, flopping onto the recliner, the only seat in the house she found remotely comfortable. She took some calming breaths, shook all her grumbles from her mind and made herself focus on the baby. When all was said and done, the well-being of her child was the only thing that mattered. All the other stuff was her mind playing tricks on her, sending her imagination into overdrive. Perhaps she should make an appointment with the GP, or talk to the midwife about pregnancy psychosis after all.

She felt a jolt as the baby kicked, jarring the mug of tea in her hand. She smiled to herself, reassured that everything was okay, then rubbed at her stomach and was rewarded with another kick. 'You are going to be perfect,' she said, hoping their baby had Sam's skin, which tanned so easily, and his black wavy hair. The brownest of eyes, like chestnuts, spun with gold. A straight and noble nose.

She hadn't asked what sex the baby was, wanting it to be a surprise. It was exciting, not knowing who you were going to welcome into the world – a girl or a boy. Obviously, it would be easier to know because of colour schemes, but she'd bought neutral colours for baby clothes. Just the smallest size for now. She loved looking at baby clothes, all those gorgeous little outfits, and she got up to retrieve her phone from her bag to have a browse while she drank her tea.

The page from the magazine floated onto the worktop and she picked it up, reminded of her earlier concerns. Why she'd rung Sam in the first place.

Her picture on someone else's wall. And she had no idea why.

CHAPTER TWELVE

Emma frowned, smoothing the page out on the breakfast bar while she studied it properly. Within a couple of paragraphs, she found the answer to one of her questions. The house belonged to Marcey Dubois, a retired fashion model who now ran her own company making chic children's clothes. No children of her own, but she adored her nieces and nephews, of whom there were five. Apparently, it was how the business started – making clothes for them.

The article was ripped in two – she must have left a page in the magazine – so there was no more information, but Google would be able to fill in the gaps. She settled herself on the recliner and spent a good hour scrolling through articles about Marcey Dubois, who had a colourful past. Spells in rehab for opioid addiction. Depression. Suicide attempts. That was when she was in her twenties, and she put it down to the pressure of the job. Once she'd retired – not voluntarily, but because her image was too tarnished to model any more – her life took a turn for the better. She found love, and that was all that was needed to catapult her business into the limelight. Her lover was a famous actor. He left her, but apparently it was a blessing in disguise because then she met her soulmate and things had been pretty marvellous ever since.

So, Sam had designed the house and given Emma's picture to this Marcey woman. But why? Firstly, why did he give it to her, and secondly, why didn't he ask Emma if it was okay?

She flicked back to the photograph of her picture hanging on the wall. She could answer the first question, of why he'd given it to his client. It looked pretty spectacular in that setting and Sam had an eye for these things. Aesthetics mattered to him. As to why he'd taken it without asking, well, that would be a question for him to answer when he got home. It would be much easier if she had the evidence to hand rather than catching him unawares on a phone call, and anyway, she was nervous about ringing him again when he was with his client. It could wait.

Seeing the picture again stirred up a lot of memories, and she lay back in the chair, closing her eyes as she was reminded why the painting was so important and why she had to get it back.

Four years ago, Emma had been sitting in the National Gallery in London, gazing at a Rembrandt self-portrait. Her eyes tracked up and down the picture, studying the composition, marvelling at the textures the artist had created. Of course, she never expected her own work to be of this quality, but with each commission she finished, she was striving to improve her technique. That was what this study trip from her home in Manchester was all about. A whole day to mooch around the galleries and work out what she needed to do better.

Of all the wonderful portraits here, this was one of her favourites, although she couldn't put her finger on the reason why. Was it the facial expression, the sense of movement? That was such a hard thing to achieve when you were painting someone, giving the impression there was life bursting out of the picture. It was what she hoped to achieve, but it didn't always work out the way she wanted. There was always room for improvement.

She was so engrossed, she didn't notice a man had sat down beside her until he spoke. 'He was a genuine master, wasn't he?'

She jumped up, startled, her hand pressed to her chest.

'I'm so sorry,' he said, a smile in his cornflower-blue eyes. 'I thought you'd seen me sit down.' He spoke with a gentle Scottish accent, Edinburgh, at a guess. His fiery red hair was short at the sides, long and wavy on top. His face pale with a dusting of freckles over his nose. The most striking thing about him, though, was his magnificent beard. 'Please, don't let me disturb you.'

She gave a hesitant smile, not sure now whether to sit back down or walk away.

'I'm just waiting for Mam.' He grinned, showing a perfect set of teeth. 'She's looking at the Botticelli, but that's not my bag. Picasso's more my thing.'

Intrigued, she sat back down, tucking a stray curl into the headscarf that was tied with a bow on the top of her head. Her hair fell in coiled springs to her jaw and had a mind of its own; at least the scarf kept it out of her face.

'What is it you like about Picasso?' she asked, genuinely curious.

'He broke the rules. Interpreted what he was seeing in a unique way. His paintings are... bold, don't you think?'

She considered that for a moment. 'I think bold definitely covers it, but I prefer realism.'

The conversation had them rooted to the spot for almost an hour until a short, slim lady with spikey pink hair bustled up and put a hand on his shoulder. 'Zach, at last! I've been wandering around this place for ages trying to find you.'

He looked a bit sheepish, put his hand over hers. 'I'm sorry, Mam. We just got talking.'

The woman looked at Emma, her eyes the same blue as her son's. Gave her a beaming smile and held out a hand, which Emma shook, noting the firm, dry grasp of her fingers. A down-to-earth sort of person, she decided. 'I'm Maggie,' she said. 'And I don't want to break things up, but I'm gasping for a cup of tea and a bite to eat.' She looked around. 'Is there a café in this place? I can't remember seeing one.'

Emma introduced herself, then smiled and stood, thinking she could murder a cup of tea herself. She checked her watch. There was still plenty of time before she had to get the train home.

'There's a lovely café downstairs. I'll show you if you like.'

The truth was, she was reluctant to leave. She'd connected with Zach in a way she hadn't connected with a man in years, and it was lovely. It turned out he was a fellow artist, and although they painted in completely different styles, it had been wonderful to discuss art with someone who knew what they were talking about. They'd both done fine art degrees, him in London, her in Manchester, both of them staying in the cities where they'd studied, reluctant to leave their respective artistic communities.

'Will you join us?' Maggie said when they arrived at the café. She glanced at her son. 'I think Zach would be okay with that, wouldn't you?' There was a twinkle in her eye and Emma could see that she was teasing him. Was he blushing? It was hard to tell with his beard covering half his face, but his ears were glowing.

'That would be lovely, thank you,' she replied, sure that Zach was feeling the connection, a sense of excitement stirring inside. She was thirty years old but felt like a teenager, sitting next to him under his mother's gaze. Maggie was fun, though, and she had them laughing with her observations about her favourite paintings.

Time flew by and when Emma noticed that the café was emptying, she checked her watch and realised she had to go if she was to catch her train.

'I'll walk you to the Tube station,' Zach said, jumping up. 'You don't mind waiting here, do you, Mam?'

Maggie laughed and shooed them away.

At the Tube station, he hugged her goodbye and they exchanged numbers, promising to keep in touch. All the way home Emma felt like she was floating on air, filled with the hope she had finally met Mr Right, the man who would father her children. Of course, it was early days, not even a relationship as such, but already she could see them – two girls and a boy, all with his gorgeous red hair. She was pondering on girls' names when the train pulled into Manchester Piccadilly Station.

Children were very important to Emma. They hadn't even been on her radar until the last year, and then a mixture of her biological clock and her mum dying of breast cancer made her realise she was now the only adult in her family, with nobody to look out for her, nobody to connect with. It made her think. Wherever she looked, she suddenly saw babies. Happy couples cooing over their little ones, mums kissing their chubby-cheeked offspring, enjoying cuddles. With every sinew of her being, she wanted to be a mum herself.

However, she wasn't going to have a child with just anyone. It had to be the perfect match. So many of her friends had ended up as single parents, and that was such hard work. She couldn't imagine herself being able to do it and working as well. So, she'd started the search for the perfect mate.

As a project, it had been a challenge. So many idiots, who looked hot, but had no interest in anything apart from football and Xbox. She decided she would change her criteria and go for shared interests, but it threw up a bunch of misfits and she couldn't cope with that either. She'd got to the point of despair. But now she'd met Zach and the thrill was indescribable. She was even more thrilled when he messaged her that evening and they spent a couple of hours on FaceTime, the conversation flowing like fine wine, full-bodied and immersive.

By the time she went to bed, she knew she'd found him. *The One*. He was coming to Manchester the following weekend and she was going to take him to her favourite galleries. She'd never been more excited about anything in her life.

Ten months later, he moved in with her, settling in Manchester as the rent was so much cheaper than London. They both worked day jobs, their artistic incomes being too sporadic to earn them a proper living just yet. He did labouring work for building contractors and she worked as a virtual PA, mainly managing people's social media.

She enjoyed being self-employed, guiding and advising her clients on their social media presence, making beautiful images for them to promote themselves and their businesses. It was a fun way to make a living, and the flexible working hours would fit perfectly round having a family. She'd thought it all through, had the means to earn a living in place; all that had been missing was her soulmate. Now she'd found him, it was all systems go on project have-a-baby.

Unfortunately, nature decided to give them a hard time and her first pregnancy ended in miscarriage. Emma was devastated. But Zach was an absolute star. He held her and comforted her and reassured her, always there when she needed him. And he painted her a picture, an impressionistic image of the two of them bound together by their love. It was red and gold and all the shades in between, an image of warmth and love and togetherness.

That's what the painting meant to her. It should never adorn someone else's wall. It was a love letter to her. To them. And right now, it should be in her storage unit.

'My love for you knows no bounds,' he told her when he presented her with the picture. 'It doesn't depend on us having children. All I'll ever need is you.'

She was fortunate to have him, that was the important thing to remember. This passionate Celtic man with a huge heart and a generous soul. Art was such a powerful medium, she'd thought at the time as she gazed at the painting. How Zach had managed to convey eternal love with minimal brush strokes and a bold use of colour was genius. His talent was there for all to see, his style unique. No wonder he'd been starting to make a name for himself.

His words were exactly what she'd needed to hear at the time, having convinced herself she'd never be pregnant again, and being a mother was all she could really think about.

The picture took pride of place on their bedroom wall, and she vowed to always treasure his gift to her, this token of his undying love, whatever happened.

Then the accident had changed everything, making the picture even more important to her. Quite apart from that, she didn't want other people to see it. There was no way she could leave it hanging on someone else's wall. It had to be kept safe with the rest of Zach's work. His legacy. Their love.

CHAPTER THIRTEEN

It was almost seven o'clock when Sam bounced into the living room with two pizza boxes. The aroma of tomatoes and cheeses and basil filled the room and Emma realised how hungry she was. Time had slipped away as she'd sat thinking about the picture and the past and how she'd come to be where she was now. Life was never straightforward, always raising questions.

He handed her a box. 'Chicken and Mediterranean veg for you. Is that okay?'

She nodded, taking the box from him and opening it up, saliva already filling her mouth. Hopefully she wouldn't feel quite so angry with him once she'd had something to eat, but at the moment she was so livid she couldn't speak.

He got himself a beer out of the fridge, poured her a glass of sparkling water and brought them into the lounge. As usual, he'd chosen a meat feast, and all the oil swimming on the surface made her stomach lurch. She looked away, concentrated on her own meal.

'You're very quiet,' he said, once he'd devoured half his pizza. 'Is everything okay? Come on, tell me how you got on at the clinic.'

Emma gazed at him, trying to gauge if the food had improved her mood. The answer to that was a big, fat no. She was still livid.

She handed him the torn page from the magazine. 'I saw this when I was at the clinic. It was in a magazine I was reading.'

He frowned, took it from her and started to read while he ate. 'Ah, Marcey Dubois. Her house won me a prize. Did I tell you?'

She nodded. 'Yes, you did tell me. But I want to know why my picture is on her wall.' He looked blank. 'The first photo at the top of the article.' She leant over and tapped the page. 'That's my painting.'

He stopped chewing, seemingly frozen in time.

'You took it without asking, didn't you?'

He winced, couldn't look at her. 'I... well, yes, I suppose I did, but I didn't think you'd mind. I mean, it was stuffed away in your storage unit, not seeing the light of day, and it was perfect for the house. And Marcey was happy to pay a decent price for it.'

Emma gasped, thought she might explode, her voice a shrill squeak. 'You *sold* it to her? You can't have. It's not yours to bloody sell.' Who went around selling someone else's property? It was so out of order she could hardly believe he would have done it. 'Zach gave it to me when... well, before he proposed. That painting is priceless to me; it means nothing to the woman you sold it to. It's just a decoration to her.' A whole rainbow of emotions flashed through her mind. The last one being fear. Fear the painting might be lost from her safe keeping. Her voice cracked. 'How could you have done this? You've got to get it back.'

Sam looked confused. 'But I thought it was one of yours. One you'd painted and didn't want. I figured that's why it was in storage and not on your wall somewhere. I mean, I did notice it was different to the style you paint now, but I thought you'd done it as part of your degree or something.' He looked across at her, quite crestfallen. 'I honestly thought I was doing the right thing. Getting a bit of money for the new house. You know everything's gone up in price and it's going to be tight with the budget. Every extra bit of money helps.'

They stared at each other. She could understand his logic. Zach's painting style was so very different to her own, and she couldn't remember if she'd even told him Zach was an artist. It would have been a sensible assumption to make, that it was old work she no longer wanted. But that wasn't the point.

'I want my picture back.' She didn't care that it had put money into their build account. 'It wasn't yours to take, let alone sell.'

He grimaced, worry flickering in his eyes. 'I'm not sure that's going to be possible. She's not the easiest person to deal with.' Then his face lit up with a smile. 'How about this for an idea... What if I get a print of it for you?'

'I don't want a bloody print,' she snapped. 'I want my painting back and I don't want you touching anything else in that unit. It's my stuff and I decide what I do with it, okay? You had no right to go in there in the first place. In fact, why did you?'

'Why did I what?'

'Why did you go in my storage unit?'

He was looking frustrated now. 'Isn't it obvious? I needed Marcey's house to look good for the photo shoot and I'd seen the picture when we were emptying the apartment. It was perfect, exactly what I'd been looking for.'

'Wait a minute. Did you take any other pictures out of there?'

He looked thoroughly uncomfortable now.

'Bloody hell, Sam.' She closed her pizza box, no longer hungry. 'How many did you take?'

He cringed. 'Three. There were three. The other two are on the upstairs landing.' His voice was small, apologetic. 'They were perfect too.'

'Oh, Sam.' She gazed at him. Angry and disappointed and frustrated all at the same time. But he looked so contrite, she knew he understood he'd done wrong. 'You get everything back, and I might, possibly, be able to forgive you.'

She pushed herself to her feet, before waddling to the stairs. It was impossible to be in the same room as him while she felt like this. She stomped up to the bedroom, where she locked herself in before slumping on the bed, shoulders heaving as she sobbed.

A tap on the door. Sam trying the door handle. 'I'm sorry, love. I should have thought to ask, I know I should, but I didn't want you to say no. We'd been looking for artwork for weeks and not found anything. Marcey loved it as soon as I sent her a photo. Please let me in. Let's talk about this, can we?'

The door handle rattled again, but she wasn't sure she was calm enough to have a sensible conversation about something so emotive.

'Please, Emma. Let me in. I've got to go back to Dumfries tomorrow to make some adjustments to the spec and see if I can finally get the design agreed. I don't want to leave on an argument.'

She swiped the tears from her face. She didn't want him to leave on an argument either, not if she was going to be on her own for a while, with time for the bad feeling to fester and grow. She sighed and heaved herself to her feet, unlocked the door, opening it a crack, so she could see him but he couldn't come in.

His face was a picture of apology. He stepped closer to the door. 'Oh, sweetheart. Let me make this right. I promise I did it with the best of intentions. I thought I was helping you to have the home of your dreams.'

She looked into his eyes and felt the familiar pull, the undeniable love she felt for this man. His behaviour was totally out of character, she'd give him that, and she knew she should allow him the opportunity to make things right now she'd made her feelings known. She swallowed, opened the door a bit wider and allowed him to give her a hug. Not easy with the size of her belly. They'd sort of made up, but his misdemeanour was not forgiven.

He passed her a plate with the rest of her pizza on it. 'I heated it up for you.' He ventured a smile. 'Can't have you starving, my love.'

She hesitated, then took the plate. It was her duty to feed her baby, even though she would have liked to refuse.

After he'd left, she munched her way through her food, sitting on the bed, staring out of the window. She needed to talk to someone about the picture incident, how she should deal with it. Above everything else, she needed to talk through her anger, which was burning in her chest, because that sort of emotion was not healthy for her baby. Better out than in, as her mum had been fond of saying when she blew up about things, then moved on. She'd been an expert, but Emma wasn't.

'Emma, how are you?' Faith said, a smile in her voice when she answered Emma's call.

'I've just had a big row with Sam, and he's going away again and I feel bad about it, but I'm so bloody angry with him and would you mind if I talked it through with you?'

'Oh dear, I'm sorry to hear that, but fire away, lovely. Let it all out and I'm sure you'll feel better.'

Emma explained what had happened.

'Am I being unreasonable? I mean, I can understand him seeing a chance to bring some extra cash in, and goodness knows we need it with the cost of this build. But that's not the point, is it? It's my picture, with huge personal value to me, and he should have asked.'

'Absolutely. Don't go giving yourself a hard time. Sam is clearly in the wrong, but he's said he's going to put it right, so you've got to at least give him a chance. Why don't you try and put it to one side until he's home? Then you will have given him two days to do something. I think that's a pretty reasonable approach.'

'But what if he doesn't do anything?'

Faith tutted. 'What have I said about worrying about things that haven't happened and might never happen?'

Emma sighed. 'You're right. One step at a time. Okay. Well, thanks for the pep talk. It's really helped.'

'Go and meditate or something. Get yourself calmed down. It's not the end of the world when all's said and done. Remember his actions came from a place of love.'

'But he crossed a line selling something of mine.'

'Maybe he did, but he thought you'd said you were going to sell the paintings in the unit. I remember you saying that when I was helping you pack everything up.'

Emma frowned, confused. 'It's funny. I don't remember that at all.'

Faith laughed. 'Well, I do. It's clearly a bit of a misunderstanding. Let him put it right and I'm sure things will go back to normal.'

Emma took a deep breath. 'Okay.'

'Anyway, how's the baby doing? Not long now, is it?'

'Three weeks and five days.'

'Are you all right up there on your own? I mean, you could go into labour any time now, in theory. I've got work tomorrow, but I can come over in the evening if you like?'

Now Faith had mentioned it, Emma realised it probably wasn't the best idea to be on her own in their cottage, two miles from the town, now she was in her last month of pregnancy.

'I've got the rest of the week free. I'm going to be working on updating my bereavement course for seniors, so I can do that anywhere. Do you want company?'

She smiled. It was amazing how Faith always knew exactly what she needed. 'That would be fantastic. Thank you.'

'Okay, well I'll be there tomorrow evening. I'll bring us something to eat, so you don't have to bother about cooking.'

'Lovely, I'll see you then.'

'And if you need me, any time, night or day, you ring me, okay?'

'Thank you, Faith. You're a star.'

They said their goodbyes and Emma settled herself on the bed, feeling much better now she'd talked it through. All the anger had seeped away. Faith was a great sounding board, always calm and measured, seeing both sides of the story. If Emma had said she was going to sell some paintings, Sam wouldn't have realised she'd meant her own paintings and not Zach's.

She padded downstairs, where Sam was watching a movie, and snuggled up to him on the sofa, wanting the animosity to be over. Still, she couldn't shake the questions from her head. *Was selling the painting an honest mistake, as Faith had suggested, or was there something else going on? And was the woman on the phone his client, as he'd insisted?* There was so much she didn't know, nothing truly made sense and she was starting to wonder how well she knew her husband.

CHAPTER FOURTEEN

It took her a long time to get to sleep, her thoughts marching around her head, making too much noise for her to settle down. Eventually, though, she fell into a deep sleep, and when she woke the next morning, Sam had already gone. A lukewarm mug of peppermint tea sat on her bedside cabinet, his parting gift.

Her stomach grumbled, and she padded downstairs to organise something to eat. She sat at the breakfast bar, munching her way through a bowl of granola, the whole day stretching out ahead of her. At least Faith was coming over this evening, so there was that to look forward to.

She supposed Faith was a bit of a mother figure to her, being fifteen years older, and she was definitely a lot wiser than Emma, able to make her see sense when she got herself wound up about things. A lovely calming influence. That was Faith. Oil on troubled waters. The ideal personality for her job as a bereavement counsellor.

She was going to be Emma's birthing partner too, which was a comforting thought, Sam being a bit squeamish. Emma wasn't confident he'd be able to see the whole thing through, but Faith would be her rock.

For the first time during her pregnancy, she felt vulnerable on her own. It was too quiet and her mind was stuck on a negative track, feeding her images of fires, and hidden wives, and Sam selling things that were hers. Her leg jigged up and down as she ate, anxiety making her feel agitated and unsure.

It was only eight in the morning and the idea of being on her own all day pottering round the house, with her stupid fanciful thoughts, was not appealing. She needed to get out and about, doing something. *But what?*

She'd left the page from the magazine on the breakfast bar, and as soon as her eyes landed on her painting, she knew what she was going to do. She was going to go and talk to Marcey Dubois, check out Sam's story and make sure arrangements had been put in place to return her picture. If he'd been telling the truth about that, then she could be more certain he was telling the truth about everything else.

With a purpose in mind, she checked the location of the property, tucked away on the Northumberland coast. Then she sorted out her route, which looked straightforward once she got on the A66. Two hours tops, she calculated, and she could stop as many times as she liked. No rush; she could enjoy the scenery, and stop for a drink and a snack along the way. Make it into a fun day out.

It felt exciting, getting out of the house after being at home for the last couple of months, and she had the moral upper hand in this situation, so she felt she was perfectly within her rights to make the trip. She was curious to see the house in real life as well, because she knew their own build was based on some of the ideas in this design. All in all, a worthwhile research trip. Plus, she could bring her picture back, then at least one worry would be extinguished.

. . .

It was the first time she'd been to Northumberland, and she drank in the wildness of the landscape, beautiful moorland with wonderful vistas out over the coast. She'd taken her time on the journey, stopped in a little market town to stretch her legs and have a nosy around. It was almost noon when her sat nav told her to turn off the main road.

She was on top of a rise, admiring the undulating country-side ahead of her, farms dotted here and there. She turned left onto a single-track lane, which ran between two dry-stone walls, with fields on either side. A few hundred yards further along, by a clump of thorny bushes, the track split, and to the right she noticed a big lump of gritstone with the house name carved into it. *The Hollows*. That's where she was headed, although she couldn't see any sign of the house. The land dipped away into a hidden valley, and she supposed it must be at the bottom.

Cautiously she drove on, the track pitted with potholes. It snaked through a little patch of stunted woodland, the trees bent against the prevailing wind, forming a dark tunnel. It wasn't terribly inviting and the surface of the lane had been washed away in places, leaving big stones jutting out.

Keeping the car in a low gear, she carefully navigated the bumpy track, wondering whether this was such a good idea after all. Unfortunately, once she'd committed to it, there was no going back unless she wanted to reverse to where the track divided, and she would have to admit her driving skills were probably not quite up to the task. Better to keep going and hope it improved, she decided, which it did, once the gradient flattened out.

The trees thinned, but still hid the house, until she turned a final corner and could see the roof of the building below her. There was a square parking area, then the track went down a steep slope to the side of the house. She decided to park up and walk down, her feet cramping after all the driving.

A fresh breeze blew in off the sea, which was visible in the

V between the sides of the valley. In front of the house, there was a wide lawn and gravel gardens with beds of grasses, punctuated by seating areas. A little stream bubbled through, twisting and turning between the beds. It was a magical spot, she decided as she plodded down the track, excited to see what the front of the building looked like.

She turned the corner, stopping for a moment to catch her breath, the nip of a stitch in her side making her wince. The house was not a surprise, because she'd seen it in the magazine article, but it looked so much better in the three dimensions of real life. It was hard to say what made the place so attractive, but it was probably something to do with proportions, she decided. It was imposing without being too big, the glass frontage reflecting the surrounding landscape, making it blend in rather than stand out. And the way it nestled against the hillside, giving it some protection from the elements while still enjoying the magnificent view, was a stroke of genius.

Her eyes travelled along the front of the house, taking it all in, until she saw something that made her heart stutter. She walked closer, not able to believe what she was seeing. Next to the house was a double garage, and parked outside was her husband's car. Sam wasn't in Dumfries with his clients, Molly and Jack. He was here in Northumberland with Marcey Dubois. He'd lied to her.

CHAPTER FIFTEEN

Emma turned and hurried back up the slope to her car, unable to think about anything but getting away from this place before she was seen. She had a pain in her chest and was feeling quite sick with the shock of discovering her husband had been lying. Not any small deception, but something huge, like living a double life.

She heaved herself back into the driver's seat, managed to get turned around and drove up the track a lot faster than she'd driven down, not caring about the lumps and bumps and the intermittent clunking of metal on rock. She could hear herself gasping and was afraid she might be on the verge of a panic attack. She'd had one before, when she got the news about Zach's accident, but it had scared the living daylights out of her and she didn't want to go through another one.

She reached the main road, and remembered that she'd passed a village just a mile or so away, where she could stop and gather her thoughts. The nausea grew stronger, and she knew this wasn't caused by shock; it was her body telling her she needed to eat.

Her hand went to her bump, the slow stretch of a tiny foot

arcing across her belly giving her the reassurance she needed. Stress wasn't good for her baby, and for the sake of her child, she needed to calm down. She eased her foot off the gas, taking deeper breaths in an effort to get her heart rate to steady, but it didn't seem to be working.

A building to her right caught her eye and she swerved into the car park of a country pub with a lawned area to the side, set out with rows of picnic benches next to a large conservatory. A sign advertising lunches swung in the brisk autumn wind that was blowing off the sea. This would do.

The car park wrapped around the building and she decided to park at the back, in case Sam drove past and saw her car. It was an outside chance, but she couldn't face him, not until she'd processed what she'd seen and worked out what to do about it.

She parked in front of a low wall that separated the car park from the patio at the back of the pub, set with more picnic benches. Her number plate would be hidden from view, and she decided it would do and hurried inside.

The pub was laid out in a series of booths at the back, with larger tables near the front of the building that could be pushed together for bigger parties. Her head was pounding and she decided against the conservatory, where a group was already settled and having a lovely time by the sound of their raucous laughter. She picked a booth at the back, where the lighting was subdued and the seating was soft.

The place was quiet, and it wasn't long before a waiter appeared, handing her a menu and talking her through the daily specials. She picked the first thing on the list, not bothered about what she was eating as long as it arrived quickly. Then she ordered a bag of crisps to keep her going while she waited for the food to arrive, otherwise she knew the nausea would win and she'd be doubled over in the ladies. The joys of pregnancy. Still, she was nearly there, nearly at the finish line. And if this baby was the only child she ever had, all the anguish about whether she was doing the right thing after Zach's accident, well, it would have been worth it.

She munched on her crisps, sipping her ginger ale while she ran through everything in her mind. It was possible that Sam had come over here to collect her picture, she realised. He'd been well aware she'd been upset about him selling it to some random client just because it would look aesthetically pleasing on her wall. She considered for a moment. Would he really do that? Sacrifice the weekend he was supposed to be spending with his clients to tie down his next job? She wasn't sure he would.

You're being naïve. That's a stupid romantic notion you've got in your head. He'd get the painting shipped. That's what he'd do. No need to collect it in person. The chatter grew louder in her mind, bursting into an angry snarl. *The other woman said she was his bloody wife!* That was the key thing she needed to focus on. Forget the painting. The woman with access to Sam's phone had clearly said she was his wife. No doubt at all about that.

That then begged the question: who had answered the phone? As far as she could work out, it could be any one of three people. His first wife, who wasn't really dead; Molly, his alleged client in Dumfries; or the woman who lived here, Marcey Dubois. She thought back to her research and what she knew about the woman in the article. She'd been jilted, then found her soulmate. *Was that soulmate Sam?*

No, it couldn't be. She couldn't let herself believe that, because if she did, then everything about their life together, everything she'd poured her heart and soul into was a lie, and Sam was working to a completely different agenda.

Her meal arrived then and her focus was purely on shovelling the food into her mouth as fast as she could to try and ease the sickness and get on her way. Just as she was finishing, mopping up the last smudges of gravy with her remaining chips, she heard a familiar voice. Her brain froze. Her heart raced. It was Sam.

Carefully, she put her cutlery down, taking a few deep breaths to try and calm herself. She needed to hear what he was saying and see who he was talking to. Could she risk a look?

The booth had been constructed at right angles to the bar, so she was confident she was hidden from view. She shuffled along the seat and peeped round the edge, saw Sam at the bar with the blonde woman from the article. Marcey. She was stunning in a Marilyn Monroe sort of way, her hair obviously coloured. But she looked pale and fragile without the make-up from the photos, her eyes huge in her face. She was casually dressed in jeans and an oversized mustard jumper that had slipped off one shoulder, showing a white vest top underneath. It was clear she was one of those people who could wear anything and look good. Sam's hand, she noticed, rested on the small of her back. Protective. Possessive.

'What can I get you to drink, darling?' he asked.

Darling? Her breath caught in her throat, and she yanked her head back, her heart skipping a beat. A few moments later, she risked another look, saw them move away from the bar to a table in the conservatory. From where she was sitting, she could still see them, but she didn't think they'd see her in the gloom of her corner. They sat down next to each other on a bench seat by the window. Marcey's hand rested on Sam's thigh. The heat of anger flashed through Emma's body. This was no professional relationship; this was something far more intimate.

She didn't want to see any more. Horrified, she grabbed her bag, shuffled to the end of the seat and made a dash for the exit at the back of the room, hurrying outside and back to her car. She caught hold of her panic, pulled it to a halt and made herself use her brain. Could there be another explanation for this? Was the woman just being overfamiliar with him? The articles had said she was troubled by her mental health, so maybe she wasn't great at boundaries, overstepped the line and...

You're clutching at straws, the voice in her head told her. Think about what you saw. Think about the evidence.

She covered her face with her hands, not wanting to admit to the truth. Sam had looked proprietorial with her. He'd called her *darling*. There were no excuses to be made, no other conclusion to be drawn. Emma's marriage was not the perfect union she'd thought it was. Sam had given this other woman the painting, his body language said he cared about her, there was an intimacy between them that couldn't be denied. And there was the final piece of irrefutable evidence: the phone call.

There was no other explanation: her husband was already married to someone else.

CHAPTER SIXTEEN

Emma closed her eyes as she sat in the car, searching for clues that should have told her everything was not as it should be. Bigamy happened, she was well aware; knew from her Google search that the police investigated around ninety cases a year. She also knew eighty-two per cent of cases against bigamists went unpunished. Seven years in prison was the maximum penalty, but only a few people were prosecuted and many more cases went undetected. A low-risk crime if there was no alternative to get what you wanted. But what was it Sam wanted?

For some reason she'd never imagined it would happen to her, but now she thought about it, the way Sam divided up his week into two neat parts should have been a clue. The fact that he refused to move away from his work pattern, even now she was heavily pregnant, should have been another. A burning disappointment settled in her chest, a despondency weighing her down so her limbs felt leaden and useless. She could hear her teeth grinding. She'd moved away from everything she knew to be with Sam, had taken risks, committed to him one hundred per cent. This was not how her life was supposed to be.

Her phone pinged. The sound of a message arriving. She

tensed, checked the screen. It wasn't Sam. But it was something she would have to answer at some point. She'd wanted to ignore that part of her life for a little while longer, pretend it didn't exist while she had her baby and got herself back on an even keel. Then she could think about how she was going to deal with it.

You could only ignore people for so long before they started making a fuss, wondering where you'd gone, calling friends to ask if they'd seen you. Especially if you owed them.

She'd been sending replies to previous messages, fobbing them off, and it had worked up until now, but she'd foolishly given a deadline, and if things were going to work out how she wanted, she'd have to more or less stick to it.

Her reply would have to wait, though. She had an unforeseen emergency to deal with. One that required her full attention. All she could think about was the fact that her husband appeared to have another wife. One who was already there when she and Sam got married.

Her wonderful reality had been smashed into tiny pieces and she couldn't see how she'd ever be able to piece it back together again. Her hand caressed her stomach, her child responding with a movement. As long as the baby was healthy, it would be okay, though. Wasn't that the most important thing? That was what marrying Sam had been about; the dream of her perfect family.

She gave a strangled howl, laid her head on the steering wheel, a sob caught in her throat. Why would Sam need two wives, for God's sake? Her baby squirmed, prompting a new theory. Perhaps he had married her because he wanted to be a father. Maybe Marcey couldn't have children.

Her mind raced, searching for explanations, looking for another interpretation that she'd missed. Who are you trying to kid? she scoffed, sitting upright and dragging the seat belt over her belly, fumbling to clip it into its holder. It was plain to see what was going on and she needed to face up to it, not try and make excuses. That wasn't going to get her anywhere. She found a packet of tissues and cleaned up her face, blowing her nose, drying her eyes. She gave a final sniff, a shake of the head as if trying to rattle her thoughts into shape. Crying wasn't going to help.

Desolation morphed into a fury that enveloped her. Clamping her teeth together, she slammed the car into reverse. The tyres spun as she took off out of the car park and onto the road that would take her back to Appleby.

With her mind snagged in her raging thoughts, her foot pressed harder on the accelerator, the fields speeding past, faster and faster, her thoughts only of Sam and Marcey.

She would go home and have a good old nosy in the spare room, which Sam had set up as an office, see if she could find anything that would confirm her fears that he was a bigamist. Then she'd have to have a difficult conversation and turf him out. Yes, that's exactly what she was going to do.

She'd got wrapped up in lovey-dovey dreams of the future and her brain had been overruled by her heart. Well, her brain was going to be in charge from now on. Everything he said would be scrutinised, nothing assumed. Her heart was pounding, palms slick on the wheel, her foot pressing even harder on the accelerator. The sooner she got home the better.

Her mind travelled back through their relationship, picking out bits of evidence to prove that he'd been up to no good. Using her in some way. Because that was the only reason for him to bother marrying her when he already had a wife. A wife who lived in the very best of his architectural creations. Prize-winning, no less. Who was gorgeous and talented and not short of money. Her fist smacked down on the steering wheel, a strange buzzing in her ears.

How dare he do this to her. *How dare he?* When she'd given him all her love, had trusted him completely to look after her.

She smacked the steering wheel again, and again, until she was more focused on hitting the wheel than steering the car. The blaring of a horn brought her attention back to the road, and the huge articulated lorry heading right towards her.

She hadn't noticed she'd crept over to the wrong side, hadn't noticed much about the last few miles at all. She screamed and yanked the steering wheel to her left, careened across the road, eyes wide in horror as she realised that she couldn't regain control.

The steering seemed to have a mind of its own, her speed too fast to correct her position, and the stone wall that ran alongside the road was now directly in front of her.

An almighty crash, the windscreen shattered, the airbag inflated, smacking her in the face.

Then everything tipped, and her head banged against the door.

Blackness.

CHAPTER SEVENTEEN

Emma came round to the sound of shouting, the rumble of engines, a high-pitched screaming sound that seemed to pierce her brain. She couldn't move her head, or her body, finding herself stuck on her side. The face of a fireman appeared in front of her, visible through the space where the windscreen used to be.

'Hello, love. We'll have you out in no time, just stay nice and still. There's going to be a bit of noise for a few minutes while we cut you out of there, okay?'

He stood, shouted to someone. 'She's come round.' Then there was a flurry of activity, more firemen using great pincer things to break the car open like a tin of sardines.

She lay still, like she was told, her hands frantically feeling her belly for movement. But there was nothing. Please be okay, she whispered. Please, please don't leave me. She closed her eyes, repeating her prayer, over and over and over. How stupid she'd been. Reckless.

But it was Sam's fault. He'd done this to her. If she hadn't been so worked up about finding him with that woman, she would have been more careful, wouldn't have been distracted, would have seen that lorry coming towards her. She ached. Oh my God, did she ache, every little bit of her, and moving her neck sent a shard of pain right down her spine. But she couldn't think about the damage she'd done to herself. She could only think of the damage she might have done to her baby.

Was that a movement? She adjusted her hands, but still felt nothing. Tears ran down her cheeks, into her mouth. She'd bitten her lip when she'd crashed, could taste the tang of blood.

The noise was so loud she could hardly bear it as the cutters took the roof off the car, a gang of firemen pulling it free. Then the chill of the wind in her hair. A couple of men came and crouched by the window, wordlessly assessing the situation, working out what else they needed to do to get her out.

'You pregnant, love?' one of them asked, and she tried to speak but found she couldn't, had to nod instead, groaning as the pain stabbed at her. She felt sick, dizzy, black dots filling her vision until there was nothing but blackness once again.

She came round to bright lights and beeping machines, a bag of saline swaying from side to side on a stand, her head clamped so it wouldn't move. A paramedic smiled down at her. 'Ah, you're back with us.' He had a sing-song accent. A native Geordie. 'You've had a bit of a car crash. We're on our way to hospital, pet.' He adjusted the saline bag, checking it was flowing through. 'Can you tell me your name?'

She tried to speak but once again found she couldn't, her tongue swollen and sore, her mouth too dry. He passed her a cup of water. 'Can you manage a sip?'

He tipped it slowly and she let the liquid dribble into her mouth, felt her tongue loosen.

'Emma Barclay,' she croaked. 'My baby...' A sob stopped her speaking as she feared the worst. 'My baby.'

He patted her shoulder. 'Your baby is fine, pet, don't you

worry. We'll give you a thorough check when we get you to hospital.'

'Where are you taking me?' She had no idea about the local geography, having only searched for the route to Marcey's house.

'We're going to the Specialist Emergency Care Hospital at Cramlington.' He checked his watch. 'It's not too far. Should be there in ten minutes, I would think. Try and relax as best you can.'

Cramlington? She'd never heard of the place, had no idea where it was. Everything was out of her control and that brought a spike of anxiety. She needed to get home. Needed to find out what Sam had been hiding from her.

Her heart thumped in her chest, every movement of the ambulance creating new discomfort. It took her back to Zach and his horrific accident. How that had all ended. Was that going to be her fate too? She gulped, tried to move her fingers and toes and was glad to find that she could feel every one. It was uncomfortable strapped to the back board but she knew it was a precaution. It didn't mean she'd damaged her spinal cord.

'Am I... am I going to be okay?' Her voice was hoarse and croaky, the vibrations from her vocal cords sending twinges of pain through her neck. Was it broken?

The paramedic gave her shoulder a gentle squeeze. 'I think you'll be just fine. But you need to have a proper examination by the doctor.'

She swallowed, concentrated on keeping still, worried that movement might exacerbate any injuries she might have sustained. She cursed herself for not paying more attention, for being consumed by rage over her husband's infidelity.

Thinking about him was making her blood pressure rise, heat flushing through her body. *It's not good for the baby, calm down.* There was nothing to do but wait. Try and relax, find out what damage she might have done to herself and take it from there.

Four hours later, she had been examined and X-rayed and given the news that everything was more or less okay. Apart from whiplash and some facial bruising. She'd also bruised her shoulder when the car had rolled on its side and she'd been thrown against the door, but nothing serious and it should soon heal.

It could have been so much worse, and the best news was that no harm had come to her baby, the ultrasound showing a healthy heartbeat. She'd also found out she was expecting a boy. So that surprise was ruined, but it was a small price to pay for reassurance that he was healthy.

The difficulty came when she was told she could go home. Because even if she'd been fit to drive, she had no car to go home in. Her heart sank. *How was she going to get back to Appleby?* She could catch a train, but it would take three hours and a change at Carlisle and she wasn't up to that ordeal. She imagined rattling around on the hard seats, having to squeeze her baby bump behind a table. She knew she couldn't put herself through that hell unless she really had to.

She didn't want to ring Sam, because there would be questions about what she'd been doing in Northumberland and she wasn't ready to face him yet. He wasn't due home for a couple of days, and she was willing to keep up the pretence until then and hope by that time she felt a bit more ready for the fight. It was going to be a row and a half when it happened.

In the end, the only person she could ring was Faith. This in itself brought a new concern. *Could she trust her?* Surely Faith must know Sam was already married. They were extremely close and she couldn't imagine how she *wouldn't* know. Still, it seemed like her only option to get home, and she could bend the truth a little.

Faith answered on the second ring.

'Emma! How are you? I was just thinking about you. I was wondering what time I should come over?'

Emma cut to the chase, the nagging pain in her neck making her short on patience. 'Faith, I've had an accident and I wondered if you'd be able to come and get me.'

'Oh no! Where are you?' There was a note of panic in Faith's voice, something Emma had never heard before. 'Are you okay? Is the baby all right? Oh my God, what's happened?'

Emma sighed, rubbed her forehead, not up to a barrage of questions. 'I'll tell you all about it when you get here. I'm really sorry to have to ask you to do this, but Sam is working in... Dumfries.' That was his official line, so she'd stick with it for now until she'd had the chance to run through the whole story. 'I'm in Northumberland. On a day trip. And I had an accident. Car's a write-off.'

'Bloody hell! What...?' Faith stopped herself. Emma heard her take a deep breath, her voice calmer when she came back on the line. 'Okay. Tell me where you are. I'm coming right now.'

Emma breathed a sigh of relief and gave her the information, thanking her profusely before ringing off. At least she'd be able to get home, and although she didn't trust Faith completely, it was her only option. *I don't have to tell her the absolute truth, do I?*

It would take Faith a few hours to get to the hospital, and in the meantime, she needed to do her best to rest and work out what her next move was going to be. She relaxed back against the pillow, her head supported in a neck brace. It was clear she wasn't going to be very mobile for a while, but that didn't stop her brain from working.

Her phone beeped. Another message. She opened it up.

Where are you? Is everything okay? I thought you'd be back in the UK by now.

She thought for a few minutes, a whole new set of possibilities firing through her brain. Perhaps another door had just opened.

CHAPTER EIGHTEEN

It took Faith over three hours to arrive. How the time had dragged, Emma sitting alone on an uncomfortable chair in a little meeting room for the last hour, her mind trudging round the same old circle, coming back to the inevitable conclusion. *Money.* That's why Sam had married her. Thinking back over their time together and the points at which critical decisions had been made, she could see money was the driving force.

She shouldn't have told him she had the funds to spend on a new-build. That was stupid, unnecessary boasting. Done to impress at the time, she was ashamed to say. And on the back of that, she'd given him everything he needed to pull her into this fantasy narrative, this romantic vision, that only he could help her to realise. He'd understood exactly what she yearned for and promised her all that and more.

He was a con man, pure and simple. And she'd been stupid enough to fall for both him and his lies. Once she was home, she knew exactly what she'd be looking for. The bank statement for the build account. She hadn't looked at it for a couple of months, letting Sam deal with all the finances, and he'd been ever so willing to take on that responsibility. She cursed her stupidity. Cursed the trust she'd put in him.

'There you are,' Faith said, as she dashed towards her looking unusually flustered, her face pink, tendrils of hair escaping from the single plait that hung down her back. 'I've been pushed from pillar to post. Nobody knew where you were. I mean, they knew you were in the hospital but they weren't sure where. Thankfully, I finally found someone who said they'd put you in a meeting room. Honestly, what is happening to the NHS? You should be in bed.' She tutted. 'Look at your poor face. And your neck.' Her expression was sympathetic. 'That must be so sore.'

Emma flashed her a ghost of a welcoming smile, never more relieved to see anyone in her life. 'There was an emergency and they needed my bed. They were extremely apologetic about it.'

'It's appalling.' Faith's normally serene face was scrunched in a frown. 'I feel like making a complaint.'

Emma flapped a hand, heaved herself to her feet. 'No, no, please... don't do that.' She winced, the brace holding her neck so straight and upright, her head didn't feel like it was still attached to her body. 'Let's go. I can't bear to be here another minute.' She'd already been in this unfamiliar hospital for what felt like half a lifetime. She waddled towards the exit, Faith hurrying after her, giving her an arm for support.

It was quite a walk to the car park and Emma wished she'd asked for a wheelchair, each step jarring her neck, sending stabs of pain through her body.

'You're very quiet,' Faith said, as she settled her in the front seat of her large SUV, a new purchase, which still smelt of showroom cleaning products. She fussed about with levers to adjust the height and leg room. Tilting the seat back a little so it was at the right angle. Finally, she was satisfied and Emma tried to relax, but the pain in her neck was pretty intense.

'I don't suppose you've got a paracetamol, have you?' she

asked, hopefully. So much of her body was throbbing in time with her heartbeat, she wasn't sure which bit hurt the most. 'They offered me pain relief and I said no because of the baby, but I really don't think I can cope.'

'Oh, love, of course I've got a paracetamol. You poor thing. A couple will definitely do you more good than harm.' Faith flipped open the glove compartment and pulled out a Ziploc bag. 'Emergency supplies,' she said as she opened it and took out a packet. She popped two tablets from the blister pack, handed them to Emma. 'I've got some water for you here.' She unscrewed the lid and passed the bottle across. 'I stocked up for the journey. Something about travelling makes me ever so thirsty for some reason.' She watched as Emma swallowed the pills and washed them down with a few sips of water. 'But they said you're okay? And... the baby?'

'Whiplash and bruising. Nothing too serious. And the baby is fine.'

'But whiplash can cause lasting problems if you're not careful. You'll need to go and see your GP. Get them to refer you to physio.'

Her words wafted over Emma's head as she closed her eyes, grateful to be in a position that didn't hurt quite so much. She heard the passenger door shut, then Faith got in the driver's seat and started the engine. They were off. On the way home. Though how long she was going to be calling that cottage home was another matter. Then again, where else was she going to go at this late stage in her pregnancy? She was in the loop with the local midwives and would be loath to start afresh somewhere new.

Besides all that, she did like Appleby as a place to live. The question, then, was what to do about Sam. How could she share a house with him when he had another wife, when he had betrayed her so completely? She could feel her eyes welling up again and turned her head towards the door, not wanting Faith to see her crying. He doesn't know you know, she reminded herself, and that was her trump card at the moment. *She* had the choices; *she* was in control of this situation.

Faith's voice broke into her thoughts.

'Are you going to tell me what you were doing all the way over here?' She sounded a little cross, a sharpness to her words. 'At your stage of pregnancy, you should not be doing stuff like this. Taking off without telling anyone where you are. Being alone in your car for hours. What if you'd gone into labour and needed help? I mean, phone reception was patchy at best on the drive over here.' She tutted. 'I'm sorry, I don't mean to nag, but I care about you and you've got to think about your baby.'

Emma bit her lip, reminding herself that Faith could not be considered trustworthy. She didn't want to give Sam any warning that she knew what he had been up to until she'd had a chance to investigate their financial situation and had a full grasp of where she stood. *Knowledge is power.*

'I wanted to see his award-winning house, because he's used the design as the basis for ours.'

'Oh, Emma.' Faith gave a frustrated huff. 'I could have shown you a clip on YouTube that they filmed for the awards. You didn't need to come all this way.'

'Yeah, well, I didn't get there in the end, so it was a complete waste of time. And look what I've done to myself. And my car. I'm so sorry I had to drag you over here. I mean, it was a stupid thing to do, but I get cabin fever stuck at home. I needed some-thing to focus on.'

'It was reckless. You could have been badly injured. Or worse.'

'I know. I know. Sam will be fuming. He always says I drive too fast.'

Faith stretched out a hand and patted her knee. 'Don't you worry. I'll be there. I'll make sure he knows it's his fault you were in Northumberland in the first place. Because that's the truth of it. If he hadn't gone back to work, you wouldn't be here.'

Emma managed a weak smile, reassured that Faith had accepted her version of events, hoping that Sam would too.

By the time they arrived back at the cottage, it was almost 11 p.m. Emma's muscles had seized up and she could hardly walk. Faith guided her up the stairs and ran her a hot bath, sprinkling in some fragrant crystals she'd brought with her as a present. She was so thoughtful, clucking over her like a mother hen at times. But we all need mothers, Emma thought as she lowered herself into the steaming lavender-scented water, even if they're not our own.

Her mind floated, her muscles relaxing, and she let herself doze, glad to be able to take the neck brace off while she was in the water. She'd been told to wear it for the next couple of days, when she was up and about; after that, she could use it when her neck was feeling tired and sore. And she had to go and see her GP to get a physio referral to help with rehab exercises. At least she should be on the road to recovery by the time the baby came, but she'd been warned it could take months for this type of injury to heal, depending on ligament and muscle damage. Another complication she had to deal with.

As the water started to cool, she clambered out of the bath, which was no mean feat these days when she was fully fit, but with her shoulder stiff and sore, where she'd slammed against the car door, the whole process was that bit harder. By the time she'd dried herself and pulled on her pyjamas, she was exhausted. Thank goodness Faith was here to help.

She waddled out of the bathroom and called downstairs to say she was going to bed. No reply. Then she remembered Faith saying she had to pop back home to pick up some bits and pieces if she was staying over. She'd sleep on the bed settee in the lounge. It appeared that Emma was home alone for the time being.

Her brain fired up. This was no time to go to bed when she had the chance to snoop in Sam's office without having to explain herself. It was an opportunity she had to take. She shuffled across the landing to the spare bedroom, a room she rarely entered as it was his workspace and he didn't like to be disturbed when he was in the middle of things.

His desk was large and tidy, pushed against the end wall with a view out of the window to the woodland that surrounded the house. A printer sat on one corner, his iMac on the other, leaving room in the middle to roll out drawings. He also had a big drawing board to the left, where he sketched out initial ideas before turning to technology to bring them to life and do all the measurements and whatever else an architect did. To the right was a four-drawer filing cabinet, an in-tray sitting on top. The flat-pack cot lay unassembled on the floor, along with a box containing the pieces for a set of drawers, waiting for Sam to put them together. The bags with the baby clothes she'd bought huddled in the corner, out of place in a room that was still an office. Would it ever feel like a nursery now?

She sat at the computer, turned it on and tapped in the password. She blinked. It didn't work. She thought she must have mistyped and put it in again, but still no luck. She gave a frustrated grunt, banged a fist on the desk. He'd changed it. Now didn't that suggest something suspicious was going on?

They'd set up a new joint account for the build after they'd got married, and her first thought had been to check how much money was in there. But she realised that wasn't going to be possible now because everything was online. The last time she'd looked, he'd logged in and shown her, but she was mortified to realise she had no idea what the account number was, or any of the access details.

Fuming with herself for being so lax about such a large sum of money, she started pulling out the drawers in the desk, looking for anything that might tell her what was going on. It didn't take long to realise there was nothing of interest.

She was thankful she'd resisted Sam's insistence that she transfer the whole amount for the build at the start, deciding instead to move over smaller sums as and when they were needed. So far, she'd put forty-five thousand in there, which was a lot of money to lose.

She turned her attention to the filing cabinet, rattled the drawers when they refused to open. Locked. And that made her wonder why he would need to lock them when there was only the two of them in the house. Didn't he trust her? Or was he hiding something? She corrected herself. Something *else*. He'd already hidden a wife, for God's sake.

Her stomach roiled. In truth, she had a bad feeling about everything now, unable to trust anything he'd ever told her. That's how corrosive a single lie could be. She had evidence now that he'd lied to her. She also knew that he'd taken things that were hers and used them like they were his own – sold them even, the paintings being a prime example. What else had he been up to? She rattled the filing cabinet drawers again, frustrated that she couldn't look inside.

Her eyes settled on the in-tray and she pulled it towards her, taking it to the desk and methodically working her way through. On top was correspondence about the Dumfries project, so he hadn't been lying about that. It did, at least, exist. Various sketches, photocopied plans, with annotations where he was going to make amendments.

Underneath that was a letter about planning permission on their own build. She skimmed it and was about to turn the page over, look at the document underneath, when something registered in her brain and she read it again. Then again. Checked the date. The letter had been sent three weeks ago. Planning permission for their project had been refused. On appeal.

They couldn't put another application in due to objections

by the Environment Agency. The bat survey had identified a number of different species living in the ruins of the house and around the site. There was also an ancient yew tree, thought to date back at least five hundred years, which had a protection order on it and their plans would require it to be taken down. That was it, the project was finished, doomed to the dustbin. Even Emma knew you couldn't argue with bats. They were a protected species.

Her anger erupted into a strangled scream. Why hadn't Sam told her? The application must have been rejected months ago, then he would have had to prepare an appeal and submit that. Weeks would have elapsed and she'd known nothing about the problems. She gritted her teeth, and carried on looking through the rest of the pile.

At the bottom of the heap, she found a bundle of invoices clipped together, with a printout of a spreadsheet at the back. She flicked through, realising these were invoices for work done on the site. The one on top was payable to the demolition company – for demolishing and removing the remnants of the house. She checked the letter from the planning officer again. No demolition work was to take place. But the house had gone, taken down a week before the letter had been sent if the invoice was anything to go by. Sam must have taken a gamble, convinced he'd win the appeal.

Her heart raced as she wondered what the penalty might be for demolishing a house you weren't supposed to. Whatever Sam was playing at, it felt like the stakes were high, dicing with the possibility of harsh fines. Could he be sent to prison? She could vaguely remember a conversation about foundations, and as she racked her brain for clarity, she could hear his voice in her memories, encouraging her to keep away from the site until they had the shell up.

'Some people find the new-build process mega stressful,' he'd said. 'It all looks such a mess at the beginning and it's hard to judge the scale. I don't want to put you off the whole idea. But I know once the walls are up and the roof's on, and we've got the site properly cleared, you're going to love it. With your artistic flair you'll make a fantastic job of the interior design, bringing the place to life for our family.' He'd smiled at her, planted a gentle kiss on her lips. 'Imagine what a legacy we're creating for our children. A house built for them by their parents. How special will that make them feel?'

He'd lifted her feet off the footstool, taken them in his lap and started to give them a gentle massage. She'd closed her eyes, enjoying the sensation of his touch, deciding that she loved the idea of creating a legacy for their children.

'I don't suppose I need to come down to the site at the moment, then?'

'No need at all. Your priority is making our baby and keeping yourself nice and calm and healthy. You'll just have to trust me to get on with it.'

She sighed. 'It's taking so long, though. I honestly thought we'd have something built by now.'

His hands slid over her skin, gently kneading away the aches and pains. 'You'll be amazed at how quickly it all comes together once we get going. Like I said, leave me to it and prepare to be pleasantly surprised once the baby is born and you're ready to come and have a look.'

He'd gently lifted her feet, placing them back on the footstool as he stood. 'Okay, m'lady. You have a doze while I go and make us something to eat.'

She'd blinked her eyes open, half asleep already, and given him a smile before letting her lids close. She was going to do as he said, let him do the architect bit while she concentrated on making their baby. A perfect allocation of duties.

She had trusted him completely. *What a fool.*

Her mouth twisted as she remembered her contentment, the love she'd felt, that illusion now shattered. She flicked through the papers. Bills for groundworks. Concrete deliveries. Blockwork. An invoice from a roofing company for trusses. Slates. Insulation. On and on they went. But there was something about these invoices that was bothering her. They were all printed on A4 paper. All the same size. The same typeface. That didn't seem right. When she got invoices for her art supplies, every company seemed to work with a different system. Nothing was the same size, or the same quality of paper, or print size come to that.

Her breath caught in her throat as she realised what she was looking at. *Are these fake invoices?*

The question popped into her head out of nowhere, but she had to consider it. From her extensive viewing of *Grand Designs*, even she knew they weren't ready for half of these materials, that having them on site now would mean they were in the way. *Maybe the house hasn't been demolished after all...*

She looked at the spreadsheet, which suggested that invoices totalling two hundred and seventy-three thousand pounds had been paid. She swallowed, knowing that couldn't be true, because she'd only put forty-five thousand into the account. He must have prepared these in advance, ready to ask her to transfer more funds. It seemed like an awful lot of money at this stage of the build, especially when she knew the fittings and fixtures could be the most expensive items. Then there would be all the tradesmen to pay. If these invoices were anything to go by, Sam would be asking for much more than the budget they'd agreed on.

She could hear her quick, shallow breaths, feel her heart pounding, panic starting to set in. Sam was scamming her.

The door banged downstairs and she heard footsteps, the sound of the door closing again. The clunk of bags being put down on the worktop. The TV being turned on. Faith was back.

Quickly, she scooped all the paperwork up and bundled it back into the in-tray, returning it to the top of the filing cabinet.

She stifled a groan as she leant against the wall, easing out her neck.

Footsteps running up the stairs. She'd been too slow, and before she could get out of the room, Faith was in the doorway. Heat travelled up her neck as she searched for an excuse, a reason for her to be standing in Sam's workspace.

'I don't suppose you have any idea where Sam might have put the assembly instructions for the cot, do you? I've had a quick look, but I can't seem to find them.'

Faith's eyes travelled from Emma, to the cot and back again, a frown creasing her brow.

'What on earth are you thinking? Now is not the time to be putting a cot together. Come on, let's get you to bed. It's almost one o'clock. You must be shattered after the day you've had.'

She put an arm round Emma's shoulders, guiding her across the landing to her bedroom, helping her to get the pillows sorted so her neck was comfortable. She looked down at her, the frown still on her face.

'How are you feeling, lovely?' Her head cocked to one side as she studied her. 'You're looking a bit peaky. Can I get you another painkiller? It's ages since you had that last one. And would you like a hot chocolate or something to help you sleep?'

Now Emma's body had cooled after the bath, she felt pulverised, like someone had been over every muscle with one of those meat tenderiser mallets.

'Yes, please,' she murmured, watching as Faith hurried out of the room and back downstairs. A few minutes later she reappeared with a steaming mug and a couple of pills in her hand. Emma swallowed them down with a sip of chocolate, glad that it was at drinking heat. Faith was right, she was exhausted, but she didn't expect to get much sleep, not after everything she'd discovered.

Faith sat on the bed, watching her drink, lost in her own

thoughts. When Emma finished the last drop, she took the mug from her.

'I think you'll have a good night's sleep now,' she said, a small smile playing on her lips as she left the room, switching the light off as she went.

Emma settled herself in the least painful position she could find, the strange expression on Faith's face playing on her mind. A creeping realisation made her eyes open wide. Were the tablets she'd swallowed really painkillers? But her eyelids felt heavy, and moments later, she was asleep.

CHAPTER NINETEEN

It was after eleven by the time Emma woke the next day. She couldn't remember the last time she'd slept all the way through the night, let alone till this late. There was no way nature would have allowed her to sleep this long and she wondered what Faith had given her. It was either sleeping tablets instead of painkillers, or she'd put something in her drink.

She could hear the mumble of voices in the room below, then she heard a burst of a theme tune she recognised and realised it was the news channel. Faith always had it on in the background, although she never seemed to actually watch it.

She clambered out of bed, wincing as she walked to the en suite, each step sending waves of pain through her body. She caught sight of her face in the mirror, a dark shadow of a bruise across her forehead and the bridge of her nose. Another on her cheek. They must have been caused by the airbag, but she looked like she'd been beaten up. Her body felt like it too. The collar was still on top of the vanity unit where she'd left it yesterday and she put it on, grateful to have the weight taken off her neck.

Gingerly, she made her way downstairs, hoping the pain would diminish once she'd started moving about a bit and her muscles got going. Faith was in the kitchen, the smell of bacon making Emma's mouth water as she watched her crack a couple of eggs into the frying pan.

She smiled at Emma. 'Good morning, sleepyhead. I hope you're up for this. I've been waiting for you to wake up and I'm starving. I'm sure you must be too.'

She looked cheerful, Emma thought, which was the exact opposite to how she herself was feeling. The burden of yesterday's discoveries about Sam was weighing heavily on her mind, not to mention the fact she thought Faith might have drugged her the previous night. You can't trust her, she reminded herself, not sure what Faith knew about Sam's other wife, or the suspected financial irregularities. But she had to try and act normal, as though there was nothing wrong. Not easy. Not easy at all.

She sat at the dining table, where Faith had already laid out cutlery and glasses of orange juice. 'It smells wonderful,' she said before taking a big glug of her juice, hoping the sweetness would give her energy a quick boost.

'I've done the full works, so it can be brunch.'

Emma watched as she started assembling their plates of food, adding beans and mushrooms and sausages to the bacon and eggs. Quite a feast, and she couldn't wait to tuck in.

'I do appreciate you looking after me, Faith. And coming to get me yesterday. I can't believe what an idiot I've been.'

'No worries at all. Honestly, you're family.' Faith brought their plates over and sat down at the table. 'Of course I'll look after you.'

They ate in silence, Emma unable to think of a single bit of small talk to fill the void. It felt unnatural, awkward, as usually they chatted away to each other. But Faith was quiet too, lost in her own thoughts, which made Emma nervous. *What is she thinking about?*

A noise made Faith turn towards the kitchen. 'Is that your phone?'

Emma stopped chewing and listened, could hear the muffled ringtone coming from her bag, where she'd left it on the breakfast bar the previous evening.

Faith stood. 'Let me get that for you.'

Emma knew from the ringtone that it was Sam. Her heart skipped. She wasn't ready to talk to him, not sure yet how she wanted to play things, her mind sluggish.

Faith pulled the phone out of her bag and answered. 'Hi, Sam, how's it going? What? Yes, well, it wasn't the plan, but there was a bit of an... incident, let's call it.' She listened for a moment, her jaw tightening. 'I'll let Emma tell you. But you really shouldn't be leaving her on her own at this stage of her pregnancy. The baby could come at any time.' She was silent for a moment, nodding. 'Yes, I suppose you're right about that. Anyway, I'll put her on.'

Emma frowned as she took the phone from Faith's outstretched hand. 'Hello,' she said, not able to think of anything better.

'Hi, darling. How's everything? It sounds like there's been a bit of a problem. I'm just checking in to say I should be finished tomorrow, but it's likely I'll be home late. It's been one hell of a tedious trip, I can tell you.'

'Tedious? Really?' she snapped, then clamped her mouth shut, afraid if she spoke again everything she knew would come tumbling out in a stream of accusations. And that would make her vulnerable.

'So, what was the incident Faith was talking about?'

The bare facts, she told herself. Short and sweet. 'I had a car crash yesterday. It was stupid of me. I wasn't concentrating and swerved to avoid a lorry and ended up in a ditch.'

'Oh my God, love! My God, are you okay? Is the baby okay?' Panic sharpened his voice, raising it a couple of octaves. 'Where were you?'

'Northumberland.'

A deafening silence filled her ear, his voice uncertain when he spoke again. 'What? Why on earth were you over there?' He sounded flustered now, as well he might.

'I thought I'd like a day trip, fed up of being stuck here on my own.'

Static burst down the line as he gave a frustrated sigh. 'Darling, honestly... Look, I'm going to come home. Right now.'

Emma's heart sank. She'd been hoping for a bit of time to herself to process everything and get her ducks in a row before he got back. She hated confrontations, but there was one almighty one coming. It was inevitable and she needed to have a long, hard think about what outcome she was looking for, test how she felt about everything. It wasn't straightforward with their child about to be born; she had to think about what was best for her son as well.

'No, no need to do that,' she said quickly. 'It's okay. I'm fine. Faith's here looking after me. You stay in *Dumfries* and get your work finished.' She couldn't help the emphasis on Dumfries, knowing that's not where he was. She glanced at her sister-in-law, hoping she hadn't picked up on it, but she just gave her a thumbs-up.

'No, I'm coming home. I'll be there as soon as I can.'

'Okay, well, I'll see you later.'

'I need a quick word with Faith if you could put her back on. I'll be back in a couple of hours tops, okay?'

She handed the phone to Faith, thinking she'd got the tone all wrong. Snappy rather than delighted that he was coming home early. It was going to be hard, but she had to keep up the pretence that everything was normal for a few more days while she got herself organised, armed herself with the facts and sorted out a Plan B.

It would have been handy if she'd been able to contact the bank so she knew exactly what had happened to the money in the build account, instead of jumping to conclusions. She might have got it completely wrong. But it was the weekend and that would probably have to wait until Monday now. Still, she was convinced she was right. Maybe she should make Sam open the account in front of her, show her the transactions. Yes, that's what she'd do.

The fact that he'd deceived her not once, but twice had opened up a wide gulf between her and her husband. Could she still love him after he'd done this to her? A double betrayal. There couldn't be a future for them together when the trust had been smashed to smithereens. It was a question of how to free herself from this mess and get her money back.

Nobody took her for a fool and got away with it. Nobody.

Her body was aching with the effort of sitting at the table, so she went to the recliner in the lounge while Faith finished her conversation with Sam. As she picked up the remote to turn the TV off, she noticed something that made her turn up the volume instead. A reporter was standing in a muddy lane. There was something about the place Emma recognised. The caption said *Alnwick, Northumberland.* With a start, she realised that's where she'd been the previous day. She looked closer, recognised the fork in the lane, the granite block with *The Hollows* etched on it. She could hardly breathe as she listened.

'The fire was reported by a neighbour. Emergency services were soon on the scene and a woman was rushed to hospital.' A picture flashed on the screen of the same hospital Emma had been in the previous day.

'Unfortunately,' said the reporter, 'Marcey Dubois, the

world-renowned clothing entrepreneur and former model, was dead on arrival.'

Her heart leapt. The baby kicked. Marcey was dead. What a coincidence, she thought, her fingers twisting the hem of her jumper. Two relationships. Two fires. A chill crept down her spine, a coldness slithering into her joints, making her shiver. Her brain froze on a single thought. *I guess he thinks I'm next.*

CHAPTER TWENTY

Faith rushed into the room, staring at the TV, but the news had moved on to a report on fuel prices. 'You saw it?'

Emma nodded, still feeling dazed.

'Sam just told me,' Faith gasped. 'He was watching the news earlier and he saw the report on the fire at the house. Marcey Dubois. You know, the woman who has your painting.'

Emma wondered how Faith would be expecting her to react. She cleared her throat, palms slick with sweat as the idea she was in danger lodged in her brain. 'I saw it. I can't believe it happened.'

Faith squeezed her eyes shut, gave a little shudder. 'What a horrible way to die.'

'Dreadful,' Emma agreed, thinking it had nearly happened to her three times already. *Will he be successful next time?* Christ, she was going to have to think fast, get herself out of this situation. Sod the money, she had to go.

'No news on what caused the fire yet,' Faith added, her eyes glued to the screen in case an update came on.

Emma wondered if it would be scented candles setting fire to curtains, wallets left in ovens, curling tongs on beds, or whether Sam had thought of another way to start a fire that didn't look suspicious. Something electrical, no doubt, judging by her own catalogue of near misses. She was shocked by the turn of her thoughts. Could she really believe Sam was a murderer? He was such a gentle soul, so softly spoken and thoughtful, it was hard to reconcile the person with the act.

It might not be him, she told herself. Don't jump to conclusions. But then, she reasoned, it was better to be safe than sorry, and given the lies he'd already told her, she didn't trust her husband as far as she could throw him. She clearly didn't know him at all, had been taken in by the persona he'd created for her.

Faith grabbed the remote and switched off the TV. 'You don't need all that doom and gloom in your head, do you?' She turned to Emma. 'I know Sam said he was on his way home, but he's had a change of plan. He's gone to see what's happening at Marcey's house.' She folded her arms across her chest, frowning. 'That was his finest achievement, designing and building that house. He wants to see what damage has been done and whether your pictures are still there. I said I'd stay with you until he got back. It'll probably be tomorrow now.' She glanced at the door and grimaced. 'Thing is, I'll have to pop home and feed the cat, grab a few things, then I'll be right back, okay?'

Emma gave a small shake of her head, regretting it instantly as shards of pain stabbed at her neck. That said it all. He was more worried about his masterpiece burning down than he was about his wife being in a car crash. Not to mention poor Marcey being killed. That seemed to be of no consequence. The coldness of it scared her more than anything else.

'I'll be fine,' she said, letting out a long breath, relieved that she was going to be on her own so she could start to work out what to do next. 'I can't believe what's happened.'

'I know. Poor Sam's in shock.' Faith leant against the wall, her frown deepening. 'I don't think he'll mind me telling you this, but Marcey caused him so many problems during and after the build, and she still owes him a chunk of money. A big chunk. Like tens of thousands.'

'Wow. He didn't mention anything.'

'Well, he was embarrassed that he let the woman play him like she did. It was always one more thing she needed then she'd pay up. Just one more thing.' She cocked her head, gazed at Emma for a moment. 'Don't be too hard on him, though. He's got himself in a bit of a mess, love, that's the truth of it and he didn't want to bother you with the details. He's been trying to sort it out in his own way, but it seems to have backfired.'

'Bit of an understatement if ever there was one,' Emma scoffed. 'How convenient that a troublesome woman has just died in a fire.'

She cursed her stupid mouth. She should never have said that. Should never have voiced her suspicions. Faith was giving her a strange look, fire sparking in her eyes. It felt threatening, and Emma shrank back in the chair, fear gripping her shoulders like two hands were pressing her into the seat, keeping her there.

'Now don't go speculating on things like that.' There was gravel in Faith's voice, a determined set to her jaw. 'It's nothing to do with Sam. That woman was mentally unstable. She's been stalking him for months. I don't think I'm talking out of turn when I say she suffered from delusions.' She paused. 'I was Marcey's therapist for a while.'

Emma's jaw dropped. 'When? When were you her therapist?'

Faith shrugged. 'Oh it's a few years ago now. She'd broken up with her husband and was devasted. It took a while to make any progress, she was hell-bent on self-destruction, but eventually we had a breakthrough. And that breakthrough was the idea she should build herself a new home. Be like a phoenix rising from the ashes.' She gave a sad smile. 'She'd had a difficult upbringing, issues with an absent father, and she did tend to throw herself at men. A bit clingy. That house was her baby, her everything. More important to her than anything else in the world. She'd made it happen, you see. It was a thing of beauty, much admired in architectural circles.' She sighed. 'Unfortunately, she developed an unhealthy attachment to Sam and indulged in these fantasies, which to her became real. Very difficult for Sam to manage, and she could flip from being this lovely bubbly personality to a mean, vindictive witch if she didn't get her own way.'

Her mouth twisted from side to side. 'I know I'm breaching patient confidentiality here, but you need to know this. She gave Sam a black eye once. Another time she broke a finger when she slammed a door on his hand. That's how unstable she was. And she started telling everyone she was his wife.' She gave a mirthless laugh. 'I can tell you that didn't go down well with Alice.'

Emma whistled under her breath. *That sort of puts a different complexion on things. Does this mean Sam isn't a bigamist after all?*

Christ, everything was so confusing. What she wanted was for Faith to go away and leave her alone. Give her some peace and quiet so she could think.

Pain burned in her neck, throbbed in her shoulder, but she daren't ask for a painkiller in case Faith decided to give her those knockout tablets again. How difficult it was to be in the company of someone you didn't trust and pretend everything was okay.

But maybe she'd read this all wrong. Maybe giving her a proper night's sleep had been an act of kindness, not something to be concerned about. In truth, she wouldn't have slept much at all left to her own devices. Really, Faith had only ever been kind to her and she wondered if this was her brain twisting things again, making her see threats that weren't there.

Her mind felt like a battleground of conflicting ideas, not knowing which to follow. A bit of time alone was what she needed to sort through everything and decide what she should believe, otherwise she'd drive herself mad.

'Look, please don't take this the wrong way... I appreciate you fetching me from Northumberland and staying over to look after me and cooking and everything. But... I need space to sleep and recover. With the greatest respect, I don't need a babysitter; what I need is to be alone.'

Faith looked shocked. 'But I promised Sam I'd keep an eye on you.'

Emma swallowed, told herself to stand firm. It was the right thing to do. There was no way she was going to relax with Faith in the house. 'I don't want to fall out with you, but I'd like some time alone. Sam will be home tomorrow. It's not for long. He's stocked the freezer with ready meals, so I've got plenty to eat.' She could feel her pulse pounding in her head, even the sound of her own voice jarring. She wanted quiet. Then she could maybe string a set of coherent thoughts together. 'Why don't you go home, look after your cat, have a nice relaxing day, then I'll see you tomorrow. And I'll call if there are any problems, okay?'

Faith's voice was incredulous. 'You want me to leave?'

Emma struggled to her feet, deciding if she had to shove Faith out of the door then she would do it. 'Yes, I would very much like you to leave if you don't mind. I'm going to take some paracetamol and then I'm going to bed.'

'I can get those for you.'

'No, no, I can manage.' She headed towards the kitchen, where she'd seen a packet of painkillers on the worktop.

Faith put a hand on her shoulder, making her stop. 'I'm sorry if I've upset you.'

Emma relented, putting her hand over Faith's. 'Oh, you haven't. It's the shock. I'm feeling... overwhelmed, I suppose.' She grimaced. 'And everything hurts and I just want to go to sleep. But I find it hard to sleep during the day if there are other people in the house. You know, I end up listening to all the little creaks and bumps and I can't relax.'

Faith squeezed her hand, pulled away, her face clouded with concern. 'You've had such a rough time. I completely understand you want a bit of space.' She shrugged on her coat, picked up her handbag from the worktop and slung it over her shoulder. 'You ring me if you need anything, okay?'

Emma forced a smile. 'I will. Thank you.'

She watched Faith close the front door behind her, watched from the window as she got in the car and drove away. Then she locked the door.

I should be safe now, shouldn't I?

Her phone beeped. She picked it up from the worktop, her heart giving a flip when she saw who it was. It was no good, she'd have to reply. A holding message that would keep them happy until the baby arrived, then she'd be able to get her mind round the situation and decide how to sort it. Quite how she was going to do that she had no idea, but her current situation meant it was probably a good idea to keep her options open.

She started typing, keeping as close to the truth as was feasible:

I'm so sorry I haven't replied. Connection has been rubbish out here. Had a car crash, and I'm a bit the worse for wear I'm afraid. So that's delayed my plans until I'm fit to travel. Hope you're doing well. Speak soon. Love Em x

She read it through again, satisfied it was vague enough, and pressed send. At least she wouldn't have to worry about that for a little while.

She sat on a stool at the breakfast bar, her chin cupped in her hands, feeling emotionally drained as she thought about the sender of the message. Honestly, why was life so complicated? There were always things you thought you knew, but then they turned out to be completely wrong. Assumptions made that were later blown apart. Decisions made based on false perceptions that changed the whole course of your life.

Unfortunately, there was no going back, no changing what she'd done. Until a couple of days ago she'd been more than happy with the path she'd chosen. That was before she realised her choices were based on lies. It was impossible to know what to do for the best with the baby due any time. All she wanted was for things to stay calm and uncomplicated for a few weeks, so she could have her baby and then work out the best way forward. She gave a derisive laugh. *Calm and uncomplicated.* As if that was going to happen.

She'd discovered that you couldn't step out of one life and into another, even if you moved to a different part of the country. Now everyone was digitally connected, there was no getting away from who you used to be. And decisions made in the past would come back to bite you in the present.

PART THREE

CHAPTER TWENTY-ONE

Zach was tired but happy after his physio session. There was a new member of staff who had taken a particular interest in him and knew what to say to get him motivated to try a bit harder. It was funny how one person could light a spark that gave you the will to go on. Of course, he would never walk again, but the damage at the top of his spine hadn't been as bad as they'd first thought, and now, more than a year after his accident, he was gaining more strength and movement in his arms.

It had improved to a stage where he could use a wheelchair on his own. He had an electric one with a little joystick as a control, and after years playing video games, he'd learnt how to use it in a matter of minutes. There was nothing wrong with his brain, no damage at all in that respect, thanks to the hard hat he'd been wearing. But in a way it had made things more difficult to accept as he was aware his accident was the consequence of someone else's failings. Scaffolding that hadn't been erected properly. Still, at least they'd admitted liability and compensation had been paid quickly. Enough to make sure he could always be looked after properly.

Having that little bit of independence, the ability to move

himself about, meant his life wasn't confined to his bedroom any more. He could take himself down to the communal lounge if he wanted, find someone to chat to, or even go outside for a motor round the gardens.

He'd enjoyed this summer more than any other time in his life, noticing all the little things now he had time to stop and look properly, nowhere else to go, no deadlines to meet. He'd watched the ducklings on the pond, growing into adults. Made friends with chaffinches and robins, who'd come to the seating areas looking for crumbs from staff lunches.

Noticed so many different insects on the plants, skittering across the surface of the water, hanging in the air, buzzing around his head, landing on his skin. And the flowers. He'd never taken much notice of flowers, except to see them as blasts of colour. Now he'd studied the shape of the petals, seen that some of them were decorated with delicate patterns, like veins, and observed the way nectar appeared in different blooms. Nature was remarkable and for the first time in his life he was properly enjoying it.

He saw his accident quite differently now, and after a year of talking to the psychologist, he had more or less embraced his new reality, letting go of the bitterness that had initially eaten away at him. Of course, there were always going to be good days and bad days, but even the roller coaster of emotions had evened out a lot. On balance, he'd say it had made him into a nicer person. The arrogance had gone, replaced by humility and gratitude. He could take a joke, he'd learnt to have fun in different ways, and be thankful for all the little pleasures in life.

He'd also learnt to give Emma space to come to terms with their new situation.

It hadn't been easy, and at first he'd resented the fact that she'd decided to go away for so long when he wanted her there beside him. But Emma was a free spirit and there was no way he could take that away from her. He also had to remember she'd been through trauma too, her life changed completely. It was going to take time for her to accept her new reality.

There was no rush. He knew she had a lot to digest, especially her disappointment that he'd never be able to father a child. That had been her obsession ever since he'd met her. In fact, he'd often joked that it wasn't him she wanted, but his gene pool. Almost seven months ago, when she'd said she wanted to take time out to travel to India to visit ashrams, practise yoga, meditate and refresh the artist in her, he hadn't tried to stop her. But then, at that point, he was pretty immobile and in a depression. He'd thought he was dying. Or as good as dead. It took a while for him to realise that he was the one limiting his potential. With application and determination, his life could be much better and more fulfilling. When his attitude changed, his body started responding and now he was more mobile than he'd ever thought he could be.

Thinking back, he'd been so immature before the accident. A man child. But now he felt he'd grown in so many ways and he couldn't wait for Emma to get back and see the difference. All the things she used to go on at him about, he'd fixed. And in that way, the accident was a bit of a blessing. He was comfortable with himself now instead of constantly berating himself for being such a stupid arse. He felt calm, peaceful and it was a nice place to be.

It had to be said that, in terms of peace of mind, the compensation payout helped a lot because he had no need to worry about money. With his recent improvements, it would be feasible for them to find a bungalow to share, get it converted to meet his needs and still have plenty left to put towards help with his care. At last, he and Emma would be together again. Husband and wife. The thought brought a glow to his heart. It was all he wanted and the thing that kept driving him on, making him push himself harder at his exercises.

Hopefully Emma would be in a similar place of acceptance

after her ashram visits. It sounded like she was having a good time, although he didn't hear from her often, due to reception issues. He was getting a bit worried now, though, because he hadn't heard from her for at least a week. He sent his usual message a day, but he knew she wouldn't get a signal in some of the remote places she was visiting so he just had to be patient.

He hadn't told her about his physical progress yet, or the much-improved prognosis, wanting it to be a surprise when she arrived. Emma loved a surprise and this was the best one he could imagine. He couldn't wait to see her face light up. She'd still think someone else was typing his messages for him; that he couldn't talk properly or even move much. The last time she saw him, he couldn't get out of bed, had to be fed and washed. Everything done for him.

She wouldn't believe the way he'd changed and the excitement was almost unbearable. He'd be able to hold her again, feel her lovely springy curls, stroke her soft skin, kiss her velvet lips.

When Emma had left, he wasn't sure the doctors were expecting him to live very long as there were internal injuries as well as external and it all depended on infection control and how well his broken body could heal. There were so many unknowns, his care team had been cautious in their predictions.

Looking back, he could see it was a lot for Emma to take in and he couldn't blame her for deciding to go off on her own for a bit. Part of him did feel that their marriage vows, the *for better or worse, in sickness and in health* bit, sort of suggested she should have stayed around to give him the moral support he needed, even if she couldn't do much in terms of hands-on care. The thought of spending the rest of his days in a specialist care home, however nice it was, had dragged him into depression for a while.

Once his voice had recovered, though, and he'd started having more extensive conversations with the psychologist, he'd found a ray of hope. She was a jolly, upbeat person, full of energy and positivity. She was also full of solutions and wise words, having worked with many young people like him who thought an accident had basically ended their useful life.

She'd given him a video of case studies, other people with spinal injuries who'd been able to make the best of their lives. He couldn't believe all the things they were doing, how happy they seemed, especially those, like him, who had access to a good rehab team and the right wheelchair. Who knew what was going to be possible for him in the future?

Now, tired but satisfied after the physio session, he lay back on his bed and opened up his iPad. His eyes widened. *A message from Emma!* He clicked it open, scanned the few sentences, then read it again, horrified to learn she'd had a car crash. In a previous message, she'd said she was on her way home, although she was travelling overland so she couldn't be definite about exactly when she'd be back. With this latest setback it looked like she'd be later than he'd hoped.

He couldn't bear the thought of her being injured and having to deal with things on her own. He felt so helpless, so diminished as a man, her life partner, supposed to be there in her time of need. What on earth could he do, though?

You've got a brain, he told himself. Work it out.

A few minutes later, he had the answer. He sent her a message:

Oh my love, that's terrible news! I hope you're okay? Remember we have travel insurance that will pay for hospital treatment and they will bring you home! Looks like we can be together sooner than we thought. I miss you so much. Love Z x

CHAPTER TWENTY-TWO

The kettle boiled at the same moment as Emma's phone pinged with another message. Her heart sank when she read it. Instead of telling him about the crash giving her more time, it had actually done the opposite. *Bloody insurance!* Why hadn't she thought of that? She threw her phone on the worktop in disgust. Her brain was so overloaded, there was no room for her thoughts to gather themselves into sensible solutions.

With a heartfelt sigh, she made a cup of tea, taking it over to the recliner with a packet of biscuits.

It was hard to escape her own hypocrisy. Here she was sending messages to a secret husband while berating Sam for keeping his own secrets. How the heck had she got herself in such a mess? And how was she going to get herself out of it? At least she had a day to work through her options before Sam got home.

The situation with Zach was all based on a misunderstanding. Or maybe she hadn't been listening properly. After his accident she was in shock, not computing anything properly at all, and there were so many different doctors talking to her, using terminology she didn't understand. All she could see was her husband, her dreams of a family, broken in a way that could never be mended. Her future taken away from her by someone else's negligence. It was a hard blow to bear.

She remembered sitting by his bed, holding his unresponsive hand, staring at the tubes and wires that snaked in and out of his body. Her mind filled with the bleeping of the machines, slow and steady, often the only outward sign that he was alive.

A man approached her, the consultant who was in charge of his care. She listened while he gave her an update, his final sentence making her bow her head and weep. 'There is only one way this is going to end,' he said, and she nodded, understanding in that moment that her life had changed for ever. Her perfect husband was not going to be part of her future.

She'd assumed the doctor meant Zach was expected to die. And even though he seemed to rally a bit once he was moved from the hospital to the specialist centre, to her he looked close to death, his skin so pale it was almost translucent. Reliant on machines to keep him alive. Unable to communicate except in the most basic way.

She was grieving for him even though he was still alive, because it couldn't be long until she was saying her last goodbye. Mentally, she'd descended into a terrible dark and lonely place. Then she'd scared herself with suicidal thoughts, attended the bereavement group and met Sam.

The connection was instant, and initially it was a welcome distraction from her visits to her disabled husband. Sam was supposed to be a diversion, not her future. But she fell for him so hard she couldn't think about anything except the possibility of a new chance at life. Her dreams of having a family, being a mum, were suddenly and unexpectedly reignited. Yes, there was an overlap with Zach, but she'd thought it was only a matter of time before the situation would sort itself out.

Once she found out she was pregnant, she'd had to invent the trip to India so nobody at the spinal centre would notice her changing shape. Then Sam had asked her to marry him, and the dream was there, laid out for her to take. How could she resist?

Of course it was wrong, terribly wrong. But she loved Sam with all her heart, and he was her future, not Zach. It was too late, at that point, to confess she was already married, and anyway, what would Sam think of her if he knew the truth?

Then she started getting Zach's messages, his updates, and she could tell he was getting better not edging towards death, but by that time she was committed and she had no idea how to solve the problem. So, she didn't do anything. She sat on it, kept sending holding messages because there was nothing she could do until the baby was born and she didn't look pregnant any more. Then she could go and visit him, assess the situation and her feelings and have a cold, hard think about what to do.

She loved Sam, but she'd loved Zach first and there was something about their relationship that she found hard to let go of completely. If there'd been an easy solution, she would have done something sooner, not let it drag on, but there was no simple way to solve the predicament she'd found herself in. Here she was, married to two men, living a double life, Zach's compensation money spent on a building plot and disappearing fast from the account. She was a criminal in more ways than one, even if none of it had been intentional.

Seeing the painting in the magazine had been a horrible shock. She couldn't risk anyone else spotting it and showing it to Zach. How would she explain *that* away? The picture that embodied their love on someone else's wall. He couldn't know about Sam until she knew what she was going to tell him, how she wanted the future to unfold in a way that would be best for her and her child.

She pictured Sam with Marcey in the pub, the way he had his hand on the small of her back, her hand on his thigh like it was the most natural thing in the world. He'd called her *darling*. She couldn't dismiss that as unimportant. Even if they weren't actually married, she was obviously his girlfriend. They were in a relationship, whatever label you wanted to put on it, and that on its own was a betrayal.

Her mind was skipping all over the place, reminding her that Sam's first wife had died in a fire, as had Marcey, and she herself had had some near misses. It didn't feel like a coincidence.

She decided to see if there were any updates on the Marcey situation. She opened her laptop, started to google. A lot of the news sites were rehashing stories about Marcey's life, but she knew all that. There was nothing new on the fire, but then if it was an ongoing investigation, she supposed the police wouldn't be giving anything away.

Next, she looked up Sam's first wife again. She found a few articles, pictures of buildings she'd designed. She'd seen all that before as well. Then she found something new – her obituary.

Apparently, Alice was the daughter of a wealthy local family, her parents having died the year before when their boat had exploded on Lake Windermere. *A family beset by tragedies*, the obituary lamented. A talented young life extinguished too soon. Emma winced at the choice of words. Survived by her husband. Everything in Alice's estate would have passed to Sam. So what had happened to all that money?

Her brain went into overdrive. Alice's wealth certainly presented an excellent motive for murder, didn't it? And was the death of her parents really an accident?

She carried on scrolling, another headline catching her eye. *Husband suspected of murder in local architect death.* Her breath caught in her throat. Nobody had mentioned that, had they?

She studied the article. Apparently, Alice had suffered from an eating disorder since she was a teenager and this had ruined her chances of having children. She was prone to depression. Sam had been interviewed several times, even kept in custody for the maximum amount of time allowed, but eventually they'd had to let him go. No evidence had been found linking him directly with his wife's death, and an inquest found that all things considered, it was an accident.

Emma wasn't so sure. Sam was a clever man. A man who was apparently desperate for a family. Would that desperation lead him to kill a wife who could never be a mother to his children? It seemed an extreme reaction. She dug a bit further, found more from the local reporter. Alice had a substantial life insurance policy. It was clear why the police had thought Sam had a motive to get rid of her. But she had to believe the police had carried out a thorough investigation and they must have been satisfied they couldn't charge him.

That doesn't mean he didn't do it.

The thought scared her so much she could feel goosebumps prickling her skin. Where had the insurance money gone? she wondered. Because Sam always appeared to be running on empty where his finances were concerned. Another puzzle.

The noise of a car engine made her glance out of the window. She was alarmed to see Sam's car pulling into the drive. She gasped, confused, sure that Faith had said he wouldn't be back until the following day.

He jumped out of the driver's seat and hurried up the drive, glancing over his shoulder, as though he expected to find someone racing up behind him. The door handle rattled, then she heard his key turn in the lock.

CHAPTER TWENTY-THREE

Sam burst through the door, locking it behind him. He looked flustered, dishevelled, his hair sticking up all over the place. A smell of smoke came inside with him, probably on his clothes, she thought, if he'd been to the scene of the fire.

His eyes met hers and his expression changed to one of horror as his bags dropped to the floor.

'Darling! You poor thing,' he exclaimed, hurrying over to her and crouching by her side. 'God, look at your poor face. And your neck.' He put an arm round her shoulder, leaning forward for a kiss, which she didn't return. She wasn't sure he even noticed. 'What were you thinking, driving all the way over there in your condition?'

His eyes met hers and she looked away, not sure how to respond. 'I... I just needed a trip out. I was going stir crazy stuck at home alone.'

There was a beat of silence, awkward and tense, and Emma wondered what Faith might have told him. She had a terrible sense of foreboding, a darkness filling her mind, and with all her suspicions buzzing round her head, she didn't want him anywhere near her. What she wanted was to get the hell out of there, and find somewhere safe while she decided what she was going to do next.

He stood and fetched a blanket, tucking it round her like she was an invalid, while she pondered on his reaction to her injuries. The way he had blamed her, shoving responsibility back in her direction. If he hadn't sold paintings that didn't belong to him, to a woman he called *darling* and obviously had a relationship with, the accident wouldn't have happened. She wouldn't have been anywhere near Northumberland and she wouldn't have been driving in a state of shock.

But he didn't know anything about that, didn't know what she knew.

She took a deep breath. It would be best to bide her time, see what other information might come out before she said her piece. Because once she started, all her suspicions would pour out in an unstoppable flood and whatever he might say in his defence, at that point, she knew she wouldn't be listening. What she needed to do was ask the questions and listen to the answers. Then she could make a rational decision on what to do next. This fear she felt hovering in her chest might be irrational, might be based on assumptions that weren't correct. That was her hope, because the alternative was unbearable.

He shrugged off his coat and hung it up, went into the kitchen and flicked the kettle on before rummaging in the freezer for something to eat.

'Faith said she'd come over later and bring something for tea,' she called, not able to face the thought of another ready meal. With a start, she understood what that meant – there would be two of them and one of her. She gulped, the feeling she was in danger returning so strongly, it was like a physical presence in the room, pressing on her chest, making her hot and uncomfortable.

Sam's back was towards her and she watched as he made them cups of tea, taking his time, thank goodness. It gave her a moment to smother her emotions. She needed to be alert, her mind firing on all cylinders.

'I've got so much to tell you,' he said as he brought the drinks into the lounge. 'I didn't want to raise your hopes, but I went to see Marcey about getting the pictures back. I thought if I saw her face to face, I'd have a better chance of persuading her to return them.'

Emma frowned, already spotting a flaw in his excuse. 'Well, that was good of you, but you said you sold them to her. So, she wasn't going to give them back, was she? You'd have to buy them. Or maybe you didn't sell them to her in the first place?' She was trying to keep her voice even, but it was a struggle.

Sam sat on the sofa, next to her chair, putting his tea on the floor. 'Ah, well, it was... complicated.'

'I suppose it was.' Anger coiled in Emma's chest like a cobra waiting to pounce. She caught his eye, noticed the hint of a smile on his lips, like he was amused by a secret joke.

'I saw you together.' The words burst out before she could stop herself, and she clutched the blanket tighter as she waited for his reaction.

He stared at her, his mouth dropping open. His silence was unbearable, her anger getting the better of her.

'The thing is, you told me the person on the phone, who said she was your wife, was your client in Dumfries. Remember?' She paused. 'And that was a definite lie, because the person who told me she was your wife sounded exactly like Marcey did in real life.'

'You saw us?' His voice was hardly more than a whisper.

'I did. After I'd been to Marcey's house and seen your car in her drive. I went to the pub and walked in with her.'

'Oh my God.' His Adam's apple bobbed up and down.

'Exactly what I thought. Oh my God, why is my husband calling this woman *darling*? And why is this woman telling me that she is my husband's wife? And why is he here and not in

Dumfries where he said he was?' Her voice was getting shrill, her heart pounding in her chest. 'So many lies, Sam.'

'She. Is. Not. My. Wife,' he said, carefully enunciating each word. 'I only have one wife and that's you.'

'Ha!' she scoffed. 'I'd like to believe you. But every week you go away. Always the same days, regular as clockwork. I believe what she told me – that you were married. But she's dead now, so'

'Stop it!' he shouted, jumping to his feet, red patches blooming on his cheeks. 'Stop this nonsense.'

He paced up and down the room, one hand tugging at his hair. 'Emma, you don't understand... Marcey was a nightmare to deal with. I got into the habit of going along with whatever fantasy she was living in. My priority was getting the house built.'

Keep calm, keep thinking, Emma told herself. 'Yeah, right. But that was finished a long time ago. Before we met. So why are you still seeing her?'

His eyes dropped to the floor as he paced. 'Yes, you're right, it was a while ago. But you see, the problem is...' He grimaced, twisting his wedding ring round and round his finger. 'She hasn't paid me the last tranche of money.' He sighed. 'It's a large amount, because she only paid half the invoice. There were things she wasn't happy with.'

Emma was caught off guard, his explanation having a ring of truth about it. Hadn't Faith said something similar? *But you can't trust her either.*

She blinked, her argument trapped in a dead end for a moment before her brain took her back to her starting point. 'Why would she say she was your wife, though? And why accuse me of being a stalker, saying you'd told her that's who I was?'

He came and sat next to her again, his elbows resting on his knees, his voice pleading. 'You didn't know her, but anyone who did would tell you that was typical. Always projecting her own actions and feelings onto others.' He glanced at her. 'I swear to you she was nothing to me. Nothing but a client. Who unfortunately had considerable mental health issues. Which I ignored, because I desperately wanted the job.'

His eyes closed for a second, like he couldn't bear to be in this reality, wanting to be somewhere else. There was a note of regret in his voice when he spoke. 'I wanted to build my design. I knew it would be stunning. Knew it could launch my career. So I was willing to put up with her crazy behaviour.' He sighed, his head sagging between his shoulders. 'Maybe I was the deluded one. Believing it could possibly work out okay.'

Emma frowned, still unsure about his version of events. 'So why didn't she pay you? Was she broke?'

Sam gave a derisive laugh. 'God, no, she was loaded. It was her way of keeping me coming back. Always stringing me along, you know: if I did this one last thing for her, she'd be able to pay my invoice.'

Emma was quiet, his words going round in her head. Her husband seemed to have an answer for everything, but it all seemed too slick. *He's lying. Again.*

CHAPTER TWENTY-FOUR

Her heart was going at an alarming pace, a surge of adrenaline making her feel light-headed. She told herself to get a grip, not to jump to conclusions, but a normal person would have taken Marcey to court over unpaid bills and sorted it out that way.

'How do I know that you're telling me the truth?'

His demeanour changed, his head snapping up as he glared at her, indignation raising the pitch of his voice. 'What? You think I'm making it up? Don't you trust me?'

She hesitated, not sure how close to the truth she should go. *Why* would *I trust him?* That was the question she was asking herself. There were other grievances to air yet. Not least regarding the invoices for the house. And how the fire at Marcey's house had started. She took a sip of her drink, needing its warmth.

'You lied to me, Sam. And it's been a difficult couple of days, and my neck hurts, and my shoulder, and...'

His expression softened then.

'I'm sorry,' he sighed. 'I know I haven't handled things well, but I didn't want to bother you with my worries when you need to keep your stress levels low and concentrate on looking after yourself and our baby.'

She huffed. 'I can't concentrate on anything when I think you're married to someone else.'

He pinched the bridge of his nose, clearly frustrated. 'I'm not sure what else I can say to convince you, but I can run off copies of the invoices for the money she owes me if that would count as proof? Other than that...' he shrugged, annoyance clipping his voice, 'I'm not sure how you can prove you're not married to someone.'

Emma studied her drink, knowing that whatever he showed her, she wouldn't believe it was real. Not after she'd found that bundle of fake invoices for their own build. She'd hit another dead end.

She stared at him for a moment, her eyes glued to his, trying to work out what his expression meant. Defiance? It certainly wasn't contrition. She cleared her throat, her voice shaking when she spoke. 'I need to ask you... Why did you go back to Marcey's house instead of coming home to me?'

His eyes dropped to the floor. 'I had to see for myself what had happened. I didn't believe it. I mean, I'd been with her a couple of hours earlier. I couldn't understand how it had happened so quickly.'

'And how was she when you left?'

He grimaced. 'I'll be honest. She wasn't too happy with me. I'd asked for payment of the invoice and she'd refused, and I said I was going to take her to court to get my money. And I told her I wanted the paintings back, that I'd take them as part payment. Then I told her our working relationship was over.' He made an emphatic slicing motion with his hand. 'That was it. I was finished with her manipulating me.'

He sounded real, the emotion genuine, but he'd lied before and she hadn't been able to tell. She felt thoroughly discombobulated by the whole conversation. 'You had a row?'

'Well, yes, I suppose you'd call it that.'

'And... did you speak to the police? Tell them you'd been with her?'

A look of horror flashed over his face. 'God, no. Why would I?'

'Because people will have seen you together,' she spluttered, unable to understand his logic. 'She was well known. There were other people in the pub.'

He frowned. 'I'm not known locally. That was the first time we'd been to the pub. It's just reopened after a refurb. Nobody there would recognise either of us because she didn't tend to go out locally.' He shook his head, dismissive. 'I don't think it'll come back to me. The police think I just turned up after the fire, when they were at the scene. I told them I was popping in on my way past. Said I was the architect and I'd wanted to see how the house was settling into its surroundings. I think I covered my tracks.'

She stared at him, his words stirring her uneasiness once again. 'Why would you need to cover your tracks?'

'Because...' He threw his hands in the air. 'Oh, for God's sake, Emma, what's with this never-ending stream of questions?'

He glared at her and she shrank back into the chair, as unwelcomed connections were made in her mind. Nobody had mentioned foul play with regard to the fire at Marcey's house. *But they hadn't said it was an accident either.* The police obviously didn't have Sam in the frame for arson, she reasoned, or he wouldn't be here now. And he wouldn't have gone back yesterday, would he?

His phone rang and he turned his back on her as he answered. 'Faith,' he said. 'No, I didn't. Yes, that's right. I did exactly what you suggested. What? Yeah, I'm home now.' Silence for a moment as he listened, then he turned and glanced at Emma, a frown on his face. 'Okay, yeah, I'll go and check.'

He ended the call and headed up the stairs and into the

office, and with a jolt, she knew exactly what Faith had told him. That she'd found her snooping. In an instant, the call from Faith had changed everything. For a little while, she'd felt in control of the situation, but now she had no idea what Sam's reaction would be.

Fear sat like a knot in her chest, her husband no longer a benign presence. She pulled the blanket up to her chin, sure that everything had been ruined. Whatever he might say, whatever explanation he gave, she wouldn't believe him. The trust was gone.

She chewed at her lip, fighting back tears, appalled at the way her life had fallen apart so quickly, the knowledge that her husband had told her lie after lie. Everything she'd learnt about Alice and Marcey rushed back into her mind, ramping up the feeling of dread, the conviction that she was in danger.

She jumped up from the chair, heart pounding, her mind suddenly clear. She had to get herself to a place of safety, and Sam had just given her an opportunity to get away. He'd left his car keys on the worktop. There was just her hospital bag to grab from the bedroom, then she could take his car and go.

She crept up the stairs and into the bedroom. The bag with everything she'd need for the birth of her child was packed and ready to go, stashed in the bottom of the wardrobe, and she leant in and grabbed it, swung it over her shoulder.

When she turned, Sam was standing in the doorway.

'Going somewhere?' he said, his body blocking her exit.

CHAPTER TWENTY-FIVE

Her heart leapt up her throat. She couldn't speak. She glanced towards the window, so small a pregnant woman wouldn't be able to squeeze through, and knew there was no way out. She would have to use her wits to buy some time while she figured out her next move.

She flashed him a desperate smile. 'Nowhere. I'm not going anywhere.' *Well, not yet, anyway.* 'I thought I'd put my hospital bag downstairs so it's ready when I need it.' She was gabbling now, but couldn't stop. 'You know I went to the clinic and they stressed how important it is not to leave things until the last minute, and my blood pressure was sky high and they're a little bit worried about the baby, so I thought I should, you know, just do what I was told for once.' She gave a self-deprecating laugh, which turned into a gulp, and then she was coughing and pain shot up her neck, so sharp it made her cry out.

'Come and sit down,' he said, reaching for her hand and leading her to the bed.

She couldn't refuse, couldn't fight him in her condition, deciding her best course of action was to play along for now.

Dread swirled in her stomach as she caught the expression on his face, tight-lipped and determined, as he sat beside her, a coldness in his eyes that she'd never seen before.

'Have you been going through my in-tray?' he said, quietly.

She swallowed. She thought she'd got away with it, but knew that in her rush she hadn't put the papers back as tidily as she would have liked. Her mind went into overdrive. Lie or confront, those were her two options.

'We've got a lot to talk about,' she said, trying to delay the inevitable conversation while her brain caught up.

He nodded, standing up and looming over her as she cowered on the bed. 'We do. And you can start by telling me what you were doing in my office.'

There was a challenge in his eyes, his hands fidgeting by his sides, fingers curling into fists. The tension coming off him was palpable, and for the first time in their relationship, she felt nervous in his presence.

'I wanted to know what was happening with the build and where the finances were up to. But I realised I couldn't get on the computer as I don't know the password and I don't even have the account number. I was looking through the papers to see if there was a bank statement.'

She thought that sounded reasonable and glanced up, saw his mouth twist with annoyance. 'But I told you not to worry about that, I'm taking responsibility.'

'Yes, well, it's a lot of money and I do worry about it. Then I thought the paperwork from the bank might be in the filing cabinet somewhere, but it's locked. And I thought, why would you lock it?'

There was the slightest pause before he replied. 'I've got confidential client information in there. That's why I lock it.'

'But I'm not going to tell anyone anything about your clients, am I? And there are things in there that are mine, like the bank papers, so I need access.'

He grunted. 'You only had to ask me and I'd get whatever you wanted.'

'You're hiding things from me.'

He laughed, a forced levity that was clearly false. 'No, darling, I'm not. Locking the filing cabinet and password-protecting the computer is force of habit. Normal business practice.'

'Okay,' she conceded. 'But what about the letter which says we've been refused planning permission. You haven't said a word about that and it's dated three weeks ago.'

His eyes narrowed, a defensive note to his voice. 'I'm sorting it out. It's not a problem. Planning committees can be awkward sometimes, but I've never been turned down for planning permission. There's always a way through if you're patient.'

Was he right? She wouldn't know, having no direct experience of the building process before now. She was starting to feel less sure of herself.

'What about the pile of invoices at the bottom of the in-tray?' He blinked. 'They don't look real to me.'

He stared at her. She stared back, and she knew she'd landed a hard punch because, for once, he didn't have a ready answer. He ran a hand through his hair, his jaw clamped tight as he walked away from her then spun on his heel and walked back. His face darkened. 'What do you mean?' There was a hard edge to his voice, anger in his eyes, and she knew she'd gone too far.

She cursed her stupidity. Now was not the time for another confrontation. Now was the time to make him think everything was okay, make him relax, wait for him to go to the loo and then run away. That was all she had to do, but no... she had to go looking for answers. At the worst moment, her terrier-like instincts had blinded her to the thing she needed to do most.

She closed her eyes, took a deep breath. Adrenaline coursed round her body, making her heart race, bringing clarity to her thoughts. 'I'm so sorry, sweetheart.' She heaved a big sigh. 'I'm not feeling myself. I'm in so much pain with my neck, I honestly can't think straight.' She opened her eyes, gave him an apologetic smile. 'You know what I'm like. I can't blindly accept things. I've never been able to do that. You know this about me, don't you?'

His gaze didn't waver, and she wasn't sure he believed this change in her demeanour. Her act wasn't working. She rubbed at her temples, wincing.

'I know you've been worried about money and I wanted to see for myself how we were doing, see if there was anything I could do to help. You know, like transfer some more into the build account.' Would the mention of more funds win him over? No, not by the thunderous look on his face. She was feeling more desperate by the minute but couldn't let him see that; had to keep up the pretence. 'And I wanted to see how the house was progressing.' She held up her hands. 'I know I shouldn't have been rooting around in your office, but it was the only way I was going to find anything out, because you just give me generalities. You always say everything's fine. But I know it isn't.'

'For God's sake, Emma.' He threw his hands up in frustration. 'I can't do this. This pregnancy has affected your reasoning big-time.' He jabbed a finger at her. 'You don't listen to what I'm saying and now you're accusing me of... what? I'm not even sure where your mind is going with this. You've already accused me of having another wife and now you think I'm *stealing* from you?'

He said it like it was the most outlandish accusation she could have made but that's exactly what she'd been thinking.

He turned and left the bedroom, slamming the door behind him, making her jump. She heard his footsteps pound down the stairs, then a moment later the front door slammed shut as well.

Emma was shaking, feeling jittery in the extreme. She went

to the window, could still see his car on the drive, but there was no sign of him. He must have gone for a walk, she thought, to clear his head.

She blew out a breath, relieved it was over in one way, though in another it had left her feeling that her worries had been justified. He'd had no sensible explanation about his relationship with Marcey and she'd caught him out with the invoices. She'd been right that they were fake. And his whole demeanour had changed now everything was out in the open. There was no doubting he was furious with her and who knew what he'd do in that state.

Come on, get out!

With a start she realised this was her chance, her opportunity to go. She grabbed her bag and hurried downstairs, only stopping to pick up her laptop and put that in as well. All her work was on there, so it had to come with her if this was the end. If she wasn't coming back.

The thought brought a surge of emotion, tears stinging her eyes. It wasn't supposed to be like this, but there was no point wishing things were different. She had to put the safety of herself and the baby first.

Her phone had been on the worktop, but it wasn't there now and a frantic look round the lounge told her it was nowhere to be seen. *He's taken it.* Why would he do that? Her mind answered immediately. *So I can't ring for help.* Her unease ramped up another couple of notches. A scan of the kitchen told her he'd not only taken his keys, but he seemed to have taken her set as well.

The fear was building, the sense of danger making it hard to breathe. *Get the hell out of here.*

She grabbed the door handle and turned. But it wouldn't open. She tried again, thinking it was stuck, tugging with all her might until realisation dawned. He'd locked her in.

Her mind filled with thoughts of flames snaking up the

curtains, wooden beams crackling and spitting, smoke filling her lungs. She banged on the door, her fists hammering the wood until they were bruised and sore, screaming at the top of her voice. But all she could hear in response was silence.

CHAPTER TWENTY-SIX

Emma stopped shouting. It didn't seem like Sam was going to respond, and who else would hear her anyway? The house was in the middle of nowhere, the neighbouring farm a good quarter of a mile away. She had to use her brain. That's the only thing that could save her.

Her breathing was ragged, her heart racing so fast it was making her body shake. Despite his loving words, just minutes earlier, his insistence he was putting their family first, his actions didn't match those sentiments. She was thoroughly convinced he intended to do her harm. Why else would he lock her in and take away her phone? She took a few deep breaths, felt the baby wriggling inside her, changing position. It was a weird sensation and she had to stop for a moment, hold onto the worktop. In the silence, she heard Sam's voice outside. She crept to the front door and peered through the letter box, could see him pacing up and down, talking on the phone.

He was agitated, she could tell that much, his voice getting louder as he argued with the person on the other end of the call.

'Look, this is not the time to have a bloody existential discussion. I don't care about what I should and shouldn't have done.

Or what we did or didn't agree. We can only deal with the here and now and I need you here to help me.'

Silence while he listened.

'Faith. Just stop it. Please. For once can you stop asking questions, stop lecturing me and just come and help.'

More silence. More pacing.

A murmured 'Thank you. Right, I'll see you in about half an hour then? And I promise I'll make it up to you. This is the last time. The very last time, okay?' He stopped pacing. 'Yep... yep. See you soon.'

So now she knew they were in this together, whatever *this* was.

The main thing she'd learnt from the conversation was that he'd called Faith over for reinforcement. She'd also learnt that it wasn't the first time she'd jumped in to help him out. Perhaps she'd helped him kill Alice and Marcey? It didn't bear thinking about. She ran her tongue round dry lips. It could only be bad news for her, couldn't it? If it needed both of them to do whatever they were planning to do.

Bile forced its way up her throat as murderous images came to mind, and for a moment she thought she was going to be sick. Her hands folded into fists, and she clasped them to her chest as she willed herself to stay strong. It was time to take action, not crumble.

Somehow, she had to get out of the house before Faith arrived, find a way to persuade Sam to open the door. Then she could lock him in or something, take the car and go. Driving would be a struggle with the neck brace, but she could take it off for a short time and deal with the pain if it meant she could get to safety.

Her body ached all over after the car accident, her shoulder throbbing now, in time with her neck. She wasn't going to achieve anything feeling like this, and she rummaged in her bag for the packet of painkillers, swallowed a couple down. There wasn't time to wait for them to work, but hopefully they would make her getaway a bit more manageable.

The baby wriggled again and her hand went to her stomach. She would do whatever it took to protect this life growing inside her, however much pain she had to go through.

And that gave her an idea.

She gathered her hospital bag and handbag and put them on the worktop, so they'd be the first thing Sam would see when he came in. Her heart was racing so fast by now she was starting to feel light-headed, sweat beading on her forehead.

Keep going, she told herself. You can get through this, just keep going. Despite her pep talk, her heart was still thundering in her chest, her breathing rapid and uneven. She felt on the verge of being consumed by panic, her mind full of what ifs. *What if he wouldn't open the door? What if he set light to the place? What if he burns me alive?* A sob burst from her throat and she staggered to the front door, started banging on it again. 'Sam!' she shouted. 'Sam! The baby's coming.'

At that point, she realised she wasn't prepared, and she turned, searching for a weapon, something she could use to knock her husband over so she could grab the keys and escape. Her eyes settled on the wine rack, sitting on the worktop next to the fridge-freezer, and she grabbed a bottle, held it behind her back with her good arm, while she rested her bad arm on her stomach. She called to Sam again and bent over as if she was having painful contractions.

No response. He obviously couldn't hear her. She bent to the letter box and peered out. There he was, at the end of the driveway. 'Sam!' she shouted, as loud as her lungs could manage. He turned, looked towards the door. 'Sam! I'm in labour. The baby's coming!' Then she gave a loud scream and watched him run up the drive towards the house.

Quickly, she got into position, leaning against the wall, puffing and panting as she heard his key turn in the lock, saw the door start to open. As soon as he was through, she lashed out with the bottle. She'd been aiming for the side of his head, but her swing was mistimed and she ended up catching him at the base of the skull. The force of the blow sent him staggering forwards, arms windmilling as he tried to stop himself from falling. But his feet were wet and slipped on the tiles.

She watched him lurch forward, his head hitting the corner of the breakfast bar before he landed on the floor with a sickening thud.

Her hands flew to her mouth as she stared in horror at the pool of blood starting to form around his head, growing by the second as it inched across the tiled floor. Her eyes traced from where he lay to the worktop where he'd hit his head, noticing a spray of crimson, the point of impact clear to see.

Her stomach lurched. This was not what she'd wanted. The intention had been to knock him over, but now... She took a step closer, bending down to get a better look. His head was turned to the side, eyes wide open. Not blinking. A trickle of blood emerged from his nose, tracking to the corner of his mouth. There was no movement in his body. No rise and fall of his chest. Nothing at all.

Sam was dead.

CHAPTER TWENTY-SEVEN

She gulped, hardly able to breathe, her brain paralysed. This couldn't be happening. It wasn't real. *How can he be dead?*

Tentatively, she reached out a hand to feel for a pulse, then realised that was a bad idea and snatched it back to her chest. Fingerprints. DNA. Evidence. She had to be careful not to incriminate herself. On its own, this looked like an accident. If he was found now, she reasoned, with the blood splatter on the worktop, they'd think he'd tripped, and banged his head. Which he had, of course. No third-party involvement. An accident.

The word was a balm to her soul and she clutched it to her. *An accident.* She hadn't *killed* him. She wasn't a *murderer*. Yes, she'd hit him, but the rest of it wasn't her fault. If he hadn't been walking about outside and come in with wet shoes, the soles slipping on the tiles, this wouldn't have happened.

His eyes seemed to hold an accusation and she couldn't look at him a moment longer. It was so hard to grasp, that one minute he'd been rushing in to help her and the next he was... gone. A sob lodged in her throat, catching her unawares, and before she knew what was happening, her body was heaving with grief, wave upon wave, pouring out of her in anguished howls. Whatever Sam's intentions, whatever scam he was involved in, she had loved him. There was no way to deny that. For a time, she'd cared for this man more than any other human on the planet. He was still the father of her baby, still part of who she was now and who she would be in the future.

Tears dripped off her nose and she straightened up, everything shifting and swirling for a moment while she wrestled her emotions under control. She sniffed, wiped her face on her sleeve. This was no good. She was a long way from being safe, a whole new set of problems to think about now.

Get a grip.

A switch seemed to flick in her brain as she swung from grief to flight mode. Her pulse whooshed in her ears, adrenaline firing through her body. Stick with Plan A, she told herself. Faith could be here any minute. Christ, for a while there, she'd forgotten Faith was on her way. Now she was filled with a new urgency.

Carefully, she inched around Sam's body, slid the wine bottle back into the rack and gathered her bags from the worktop.

Her eyes flicked towards his body again, her stomach roiling at the pool of blood, still spreading across the tiles. Oh, God, she whimpered. I killed him. I didn't mean to kill him.

An accident, she reminded herself. He slipped, remember.

She hurried towards the door. If she could get away before Faith arrived, there would be no evidence she had anything to do with Sam's death. It was only if she was still here that it would be incriminating. The idea that she might be able to distance herself from this tragedy, this terrible accident that had befallen her husband, sent a new flush of adrenaline round her body. She dashed outside, the cold air hitting her like a slap in the face. But the chill wind was better than the claustrophobic heat of the kitchen, the distinctive smell of death.

A wind had sprung up, rattling the branches of the ash trees that surrounded the house, shushing through the limbs that stretched up into the night sky. She didn't feel alone, had the idea that she was being watched, the hairs standing up on the back of her neck.

There's nobody here, she told herself, glancing over her shoulder, light from the open doorway pooling on the drive. She could see Sam's shoe, just the toe, but it was enough to make her gag, and she rushed to the hedge, unable to stop herself from being sick.

Sam's dead. Would that reality ever be less horrifying?

Reminding herself that she needed to hurry, she wiped her mouth on the back of her hand and made her way to Sam's car, tried the door, but it was locked. She needed the keys. They'd be on the key ring with the house key. And that was... still in Sam's hand. In the house. Probably covered with blood by now given how much his head had been leaking.

She groaned with frustration and slammed her palm against the car. *Dammit!* She was going to have to go back inside. The thought of looking at Sam's dead body one more time made her stomach heave again, but it was her only option and she just had to get on with it.

She crept through the doorway, nervous and jittery. It was important not to disturb the scene, or leave anything that would make the police think this was not an accident. Her eyes scanned Sam's body as she tried to keep the contents of her stomach down, telling herself she could do it. She could prise a set of keys out of a dead man's grasp, no problem.

Unfortunately, it *was* going to be a problem because he was lying on the hand holding the keys. Of course he was. Sod's law dictated that would be the case. She took a deep breath and crouched beside him, gingerly feeling under his body for his hand. It was still warm, his fist clasping the keys. For a moment, she thought she was going to vomit again as she carefully unwrapped his fingers, trying not to look at him as she worked. This was the most awful thing she'd ever had to do in her life.

The keys were sticky with blood, and she couldn't help leaving a smear on the floor when she pulled them free. She took a paper tissue from her pocket and made an effort to wipe it away. Then she wiped the keys clean as best she could, stuffing the bloody tissue into Sam's trouser pocket. Not great in terms of leaving no evidence, but she hoped it would seem like he'd had a tissue in his pocket when he fell. That would have to do. She had to go.

Adrenaline spiked in her veins as she hurried outside again, closing the door behind her, aware that she only had minutes to make her escape. Sam's car was a typical bachelor car; low and sporty, completely impractical for family life but fun to drive. He'd said he'd think about changing it, but they'd decided in the end to keep it, as hers would do for family outings and she liked going out for a drive in his car herself. As a passenger. She'd never actually driven it.

She opened the door and threw her bags on the passenger seat, then squeezed herself into the driver's seat, her belly pressing against the steering wheel. It took her a few minutes to work out how to put the seat back, but once she'd done that, she couldn't reach the pedals properly and certainly not well enough to drive. Her heart sank as she realised this wasn't going to work.

Getting out of the car was harder than getting in, it being so low to the ground, and she whimpered with frustration as she floundered. She couldn't pull hard enough with her damaged arm to lever herself out, and every movement sent stabbing pains down her neck. She was stuck, helpless. Like a cork in a bottle. Tears of frustration streamed down her face, the nightmare refusing to end.

Headlights lit up the sky, and for a moment she thought

they were going past the cottage. Then she saw the white reversing lights come on and the vehicle backed into the drive, parking in front of her, blocking her in.

It was Faith.

CHAPTER TWENTY-EIGHT

Emma's mind went blank, all reasoning deserting her as Faith opened the car door and climbed out. *Oh God, what can I say?* The main priority was to keep her out of the house, make sure she didn't see Sam's body.

'Emma?' Faith moved towards her, clearly puzzled as to why she would be in the driver's seat of Sam's car. 'What are you doing out here? Are you okay?'

Emma's mouth was so dry she couldn't speak, and she made another desperate effort to get out of the car. She cried out in pain as she tweaked her shoulder, and Faith moved closer, her hand outstretched. 'Here, let me help you out of there.'

Emma grasped her hand, and after a couple of tugs she was finally able to free herself, thankful for the extra few moments to gather her thoughts. She ran her tongue round dry lips, clear now what her strategy was going to be. It was the only thing likely to work, and even then, it was a long shot.

If she'd thought before that her heart couldn't pump any faster, her body was determined to prove her wrong, and she found herself panting. But that was okay. In fact, it was perfect.

'I think... I think I'm in labour,' she gasped, hands clutching at her belly. 'I've got my bags, but Sam can't get the car to start. That's why I was in the driver's seat, trying to get the engine to turn over while Sam fiddled about.' She grabbed Faith's arm and squeezed hard as she bent double, letting out a loud groan. 'Thank God you're here. Can you take me to the hospital, please?'

Was that a bad idea? She started second-guessing her instinct to get Faith away from the house at any cost, her body reminding her of the fear she'd felt earlier, the overwhelming feeling that she was in danger. It was too late now, though. She'd have to think of something once they were in Faith's car, but for now, her goal was to make her turn around and walk away from the house.

'Oh my God.' The shock was plain to see in Faith's eyes. It was obvious this wasn't what she'd been expecting, and Emma could almost see her brain working as she reacted to the change of plan. Faith glanced at the house, then back at Emma, who gave another low groan, her hand squeezing Faith's arm so tight she heard her gasp. 'Right, um... well, yes. Of course. Let's go then.' She started to help Emma towards her car, then hesitated, looked at the house again. 'There's plenty of room in my car. Not like his silly thing. Sam can come with us.'

'No!' Emma shouted. 'No, he told me to go with you. He's gone up to the farm to see if they can come down and give him a jump start. Battery's flat.' She puffed out a few breaths, keeping up the pretence. 'Anyway, the midwife said labour takes ages the first time. He's going to follow us over. I don't think he'll be far behind. Hilda rang and said they'd be down soon.'

Faith seemed to accept what she'd said at face value and helped her round to the passenger side of her car. It was a fancy SUV with a tow bar on the back. Rugged, dependable and safe. Why she needed a vehicle like that was a question Emma hadn't liked to ask, but now it seemed like a godsend. Something she could easily climb inside. And out of again should the need arise.

Faith opened the passenger door for her, throwing her keys onto the driver's seat while she went back to Sam's car for Emma's hospital holdall and handbag.

Don't you dare get in the car with that woman, a voice in Emma's head shouted. She hesitated halfway between sitting and standing, not sure whether to carry on. But it was the only option, and Faith seemed genuinely determined to get her to hospital rather than do her harm. She sat down, her jaw set as she closed the door, silently urging Faith to hurry up so they could get the hell out of there.

'Ew, what's this all over your bags?' Faith said as she put Emma's luggage on the back seat. Then she went quiet, holding out her hands, which were now streaked with blood. She looked pale and appalled. 'Oh my God, Emma, are you bleeding? Shouldn't we get an ambulance?' She opened the door, reached for Emma's arm, ready to help her back out of the car. 'Come on, let me get you inside.'

'No, it's fine. I'm fine. It's normal. Anyway, your car will get me to hospital faster than an ambulance.'

'But I'm not a medic. What if it gets worse on the way? I won't have a clue what to do.' Her voice was getting higher, her speech more frantic, her eyes wide. 'You could die. The baby could die. No, Emma, I'm not taking that risk.' She beckoned for her to get out of the car. 'Come on, let's call an ambulance and wait. At least then they can tell me what to do, and you'll be more comfortable in the house than in the car.'

Emma reacted on instinct, pushing Faith's bloodied hand away and slamming the door shut, then pressing the central locking button. Faith hammered on the window as she watched Emma reach over to the driver's seat and pick up the keys. 'What are you doing?' she screeched, looking horrified as she understood Emma's intention. 'Open the door.'

With much grunting and puffing, Emma shuffled herself over the central console and into the driver's seat. It wasn't an easy manoeuvre with her huge belly and a neck brace, but necessity pushed her on through the pain, the urge to escape consuming her thoughts. *You're not safe with her.*

Faith was at the back of the car, trying to open the boot, when Emma found the button to start the engine. Thankfully the driving position was more upright in this vehicle, and she managed to adjust the seat so she could fit behind the wheel and reach the pedals. There was a buzzing in her head, adrenaline fizzing through her veins, her focus on one thing and one thing only. Getting away.

She rammed the car into gear, her foot stamping on the accelerator. But she'd never driven this make of car before, and instead of surging forward, the car shot back. There was a shuddering bang as she slammed into Sam's car behind her. The car jolted, and there was a crash as the back window shattered in a hail of glass, a few shards even pinging off the back of Emma's headrest.

Her heart thundered in her chest, her palms slick with sweat as she tried to turn round and see what had happened. But her neck wouldn't let her, so she angled the rear-view mirror instead, gasping when she saw Faith's body slumped halfway through the back window, limp and still, her legs dangling out of sight.

She froze in disbelief, her mouth hanging open as she looked for signs of life. It had never been her intention to hurt her. She'd just wanted to take the car and get away. Her chest was so tight she could hardly breathe, the dismay at what had happened freezing her brain. She looked again to make sure she wasn't imagining things, recoiling at the sight of Faith's inert body, covered with a layer of shattered glass.

Oh my God, what have I done? I've killed her.

PART FOUR

CHAPTER TWENTY-NINE

Time seemed to stand still as she sat in the driver's seat, her eyes closed, as if not seeing the result of her actions would make it go away. But the images played on repeat in her head until she couldn't bear it any longer. She had to move, do something, anything to stop seeing the carnage she'd caused.

She clambered out of the car, stood on the driveway, wondering what to do. Contact the police? Explain that two people were dead because of two separate accidents? Even to her own ears, it sounded unlikely, even though it was true. With no witnesses, she'd obviously be the prime suspect, and how could she prove her innocence? She didn't think she could. Anyway, if the police were involved, there was a strong chance they'd discover she was a bigamist.

No police.

Panic fluttered in her chest, her breath visible in the cold night air. She shivered, her eyes flicking between the house and Faith's car. Her only choice, she realised, was to run away. She grabbed her bags from the back seat and turned to leave, before realising she'd left way too much evidence all over Faith's car. She found a pack of antibacterial wipes in her bag and methodically cleaned every surface she might have touched, both inside and outside the car, carefully keeping her eyes averted from Faith's body. Once she was satisfied all evidence was removed, she stuffed the pile of used wipes in her holdall and picked up her bags again.

For a moment, she stood on the driveway, the wind swirling around her, whispering through the trees like an audience of appalled bystanders murmuring about what she'd done. Accusing her. She bit her lip, a high-pitched whimper filling her ears. How had this happened? Look at this place. This pretty little cottage, the lights still on. From the outside it looked like a cosy home, not the site of a murder. Bile rose up her throat and she swallowed it down. Double murder, the voice in her head corrected.

Her breath hitched in her throat, tears rolling down her cheeks. It was unbelievable how everything had changed so dramatically in the space of half an hour. Unreal. Worse than the worst nightmare she'd ever had. But it *was* real and she had to deal with it, work out what she was going to do next. And standing here on the site of a crime scene was not a good idea.

She took a deep breath and started walking down the lane to the main road. Think of the baby, she told herself. Owning up to what she'd done and going to prison was not the best option for her child. She had to do better for both of them.

The main thing was to get as far away as possible, then work out how to establish an alibi. There was no time to stage a burglary or try and shift the blame to anyone else. The trick would be to take herself to another place and pretend she'd been there all along. Nowhere near the cottage.

In her rush to leave the house, she hadn't thought to grab a coat, and the night air was cold and damp with drizzle. A shiver ran through her as she trudged towards the road, willing her brain to think. CCTV was the first thing that popped into her mind, making her groan. It was everywhere, she'd have to be careful.

An idea made her stop. She had no phone, because Sam had taken it from her, but she did have her laptop. She got it out of the bag and opened it up, relieved to see she was still close enough to the cottage to access the Wi-Fi. She ordered an Uber from the market square in the middle of Appleby to take her to Penrith station. She could work out her next move once she was there. The driver wouldn't know where she'd come from, or even whether she lived locally. It was dark, and she was sure they wouldn't take much notice. She'd go to Penrith, change her clothes, then maybe she could risk getting on a train. Or maybe not if she felt the risk of being spotted was too high. One step at a time, she cautioned. She'd have to make it up as she went along.

She squared her shoulders and set off again, singing a marching song she'd learnt as a child to keep her going and take her mind off everything she'd done. After a mile, she had to stop for a rest, sheltering behind a large tree, out of sight of the road. More than anything, she wanted to lie down and go to sleep. Yearned for this to be over.

The Uber was ten minutes late, and by the time it arrived, Emma was shivering uncontrollably. She realised this hadn't been her best idea, but she wasn't sure what else she could have done. She'd been banking on the driver not taking much notice, but instead her appearance would prompt all sorts of questions. Her hair was hanging in damp clumps, her jumper soaked through, her feet squelching in her trainers. At least she'd had decent footwear on for walking, but if she didn't get warmed up soon, she'd be on her way to hypothermia.

The driver was a stern-looking woman with a square face and blonde hair scraped back into a high, straggly ponytail. She got out to put Emma's bags in the boot, but Emma held onto them, wanting to keep them close in case she had to make a hasty exit for some reason.

'Suit yourself,' the woman said, opening the back door for her, watching while she shuffled inside.

Emma had removed the neck collar because it was too eye-catching, but her head now felt insecure, the damaged muscles and ligaments screaming at her every time she moved. It was impossible to avoid the odd grunt of pain as she got herself settled, her wet bag sitting on her lap.

The driver peered in at her, frowning. 'You been waiting long, love? You're looking awfully wet. Don't worry about the upholstery, these waterproof covers are marvellous. Wipe-down.' She laughed then. 'Mind you, I wouldn't want you having the baby on the back seat.' She put a hand on Emma's shoulder, her face softening as she looked at her through the open door. 'Off to the hospital, are we?'

Emma's mind screeched to a halt. A pregnant woman going to hospital, what would be more normal than that? She could ask to be taken to the maternity unit and then wander back out again when the Uber had gone. But it would make her memorable, wouldn't it? And... CCTV.

'I'm going to stay with a friend in Penrith,' she said, her teeth chattering so hard it was a struggle to speak.

'Oh, I'm so sorry. Have I got that wrong?' There was concern in the woman's eyes, a frown creasing her forehead into a series of waves. 'It's just the way you were wincing when you got in, I sort of assumed you were in labour.'

'Sciatica,' Emma said, staring ahead of her through the windscreen, hoping that would be an end to the conversation. 'I'm not due yet.'

She clamped her jaw tight, trying to control the shivering, unwilling to engage in any more of this conversation. She'd only say something she didn't mean to, give away a little clue. Best to be quiet and then hopefully the woman would take the hint and stop asking questions.

The driver shut the back door and got into the front, pulling on her seat belt and clicking it into place. Then she turned and looked at Emma. 'Are you sure you're okay, love? I mean, it's late, it's winter, it's raining and you've been standing outside without a coat.' She sighed. 'That doesn't seem like a normal thing to do. Especially not in your condition.'

Emma pressed her lips together, determined not to speak, thinking she'd played this all wrong, but it was too late now. After an interminable minute of silence, the woman gave a little shake of the head, started the car and pulled out of the parking spot onto the main road. Emma shoved her hands under her armpits, hoping that would help to thaw out her numb fingers. Her toes were frozen too, so much so that she couldn't even wiggle them. The shivering wouldn't stop, the clattering of her teeth all she could hear. She was sure the driver must be able to hear it too.

'I'll turn the heat up, shall I?' A rhetorical question apparently, as she didn't wait for an answer. She fiddled with some controls and a fan started up, sending a welcome blast of warm air into Emma's face.

She closed her eyes, enjoying the heat, her body still convulsed by bouts of shivering. Water dripped off her hair and down her neck, and she realised that travelling anywhere while she was in this state was not a good idea. Still, she had a spare set of clothes in her hospital bag that she could change into once the opportunity arose. And a towel to dry her hair. In fact, she could do that now.

While the driver concentrated on the road, Emma rubbed her hair dry as best she could, which was a big improvement. Then she changed her top, which was not easy with the car moving, and she couldn't help a couple of groans when she jarred her injuries. It was worth the pain, though, and with the heater on full blast, the air in the car was nice and warm now. She shoved the wet clothes into a carrier bag she'd packed for her laundry while she was in hospital and settled back in her seat. Okay, so her legs were still wet, but she could find a public toilet and get her joggers changed for dry ones and she'd be all set.

Rain splattered against the windows, the car tyres sloshing through puddles as they drove. It was coming down heavier now, the wind stronger. She chewed at her lip, worried that she was underdressed for the weather now it appeared to be turning into a storm. And if she got wet again, she had no more dry clothes to change into. No coat for warmth. As soon as she stepped out of this car, she'd feel that chill. The thought of it made her stomach churn.

Ten minutes later, the car pulled up outside Penrith railway station. The woman turned in her seat, giving Emma an appraising stare. 'That's a nasty bruise you've got on your face there, love. And I couldn't help hearing you moan while you got changed. That bruise isn't your only injury, is it?'

'I was in a car crash,' Emma said.

'Right,' the woman said, clearly not believing her. 'Well, here we are. This is where you wanted to be dropped, isn't it?'

Emma hesitated, trepidation holding her back as she stared at the sheets of rain.

'Are you sure you don't want me to take you to hospital? Get those injuries checked out?'

'No. No.' However unsure Emma was about what she was going to do next, she knew she didn't want to be anywhere official. Then she'd have to give her name and she'd be in the system, and that meant the police would find her. 'I can't. My... my husband...' Oh God, why did she have to say that? She was feeling nauseous now, sure she was going to be sick.

'Forgive me if I've got this wrong,' the woman said, softly, 'but are you running away from your husband? Is that what's happening.'

Emma waited a beat while she considered her options. 'Yes,' she murmured, because that was the truth. He might be dead, but she was still running away from him and the consequences of her actions. An image of Faith's lifeless body grew sharper in her mind. Tears rolled down her cheeks, a sob catching in her throat. None of this was her fault. It was them. Ganging up on her. Who knows what would have happened if she hadn't acted in self-defence. She'd probably be burning to a crisp at this very moment. The thought made her sob even harder, the hopelessness of her situation too much to bear.

The woman shook her head, anger in her eyes. 'The bastard. I knew there was something wrong. And I know exactly how you feel, because I've been through it myself. Let me tell you, getting away from scum who'd abuse a woman, especially when they're pregnant is the best decision you've ever made.' She hesitated, rubbed at her forehead. 'Look, why don't I take you to the women's refuge? They won't ask questions, but they will look after you, give you a bed for the night, and get you warmed up. How about that? It'll give you a bit of space to decide what to do next, and nobody will know you're there unless you want them to.' She gave a reassuring smile. 'They're really lovely people.'

Emma's sobs hiccupped to a halt. At last, the universe was giving her a break. It was the perfect solution, for tonight at least. Tomorrow was another day and she could start afresh, dry and warm and thinking straight. 'Thank you,' she gasped, wiping away her tears. 'Thank you so much.'

The refuge was housed in a big old Victorian building, which didn't look like it had been decorated in a while. But it was cheerful and homely, with three sofas grouped round an open fire in the communal living room. There was a dining room at the back and a kitchen to the side.

She changed into her dry joggers, and Laura, the manager of the place, wrapped her in a colourful knitted blanket and sat her in front of the fire with a mug of hot chocolate.

'You're a much better colour now,' she said, as she took the bag of Emma's wet clothes. 'I'll stick these in the wash, shall I?' She had wispy brown hair, big hazel eyes and a ready smile that showed her front teeth were missing. Emma nodded, so grateful that she was being looked after. And washing her clothes, getting rid of any blood specks, what could be better? 'Thank goodness Denise was your Uber driver,' Laura continued. 'We couldn't have you out there on a night like this. Where were you going to go?'

'She was very kind,' Emma said, gazing into the fire, feeling safe for the first time in a couple of days since she'd found that magazine article at the antenatal clinic. 'To be honest, I didn't know where I was going. I just had to get away. That was my priority.'

They sat and chatted for a while, talking about babies and pregnancy and all the associated aches and pains, until she could feel her eyes closing. It was late now and everyone else seemed to have gone to bed. Laura showed her to a first-floor room, with a single bed, a chest of drawers and an en suite. Simple but adequate for the one night she was planning on being there.

'You can stay as long as you want,' she said. 'But we can sort out the details tomorrow. You get yourself to bed and I'll see you in the morning, okay? Come down whenever you want. There's tea and coffee in the corner of the dining room. And there's always hot water in the urn and milk in the fridge underneath.'

Once Laura had gone, Emma sat on the bed, stiff and sore and absolutely ready to lie down.

People went missing all the time, she told herself as she lay on the sagging mattress, trying to find a comfortable position. It was hard to find someone who didn't want to be found. Thousands of people every year went astray, and she could be one of them. Reinvent herself.

How many of them were wanted for murder though?

That was different to just going missing. That was absconding. Dereliction of your duties as a responsible citizen. What she should have done was call the police, tell them exactly what had happened. But she hadn't done that and now it was too late. She was going to be on the run for the rest of her life.

Another idea sparked in her brain, and she nodded to herself as she let it develop, a sense of hope blossoming in her chest. *Perhaps I do have options after all.*

CHAPTER THIRTY

Emma was up early, unable to rest in an unfamiliar room lying on a mattress that offered little support to her pregnant body. Her idea had developed overnight, as she'd gone round and round her situation countless times in her head. It kept drawing her back and she'd come to believe it was the best solution on offer. She went to find Laura, who was in the utility room, next to the kitchen, putting a wash on.

'Ah, good morning,' Laura said, with a smile, switching the machine on and wiping her hands on her apron. 'I take it you didn't sleep too well?' Her eyes travelled over Emma's face. 'Nobody does their first night, but you'll get used to it.'

Emma tugged at the hem of her top, pulling it down over her belly. It was too small now, but it was the only spare she'd brought with her. 'I've been thinking.' She bit her lip, dithering now over whether this was the right thing to do, even though it was the only answer that made sense. Be brave, she told herself, clearing her throat to speak. 'I need to go back. Get some of my things.' She tugged at her top again. 'I only brought my hospital bag with me.'

Laura raised an eyebrow, folding her arms across her chest as she leant against the worktop. 'You sure? Is it safe to go back?' The tone of her voice, her whole demeanour, spoke volumes. She thought it was a terrible idea.

Emma looked away, unable to stand the scrutiny. She knew her suggestion was counter-intuitive. Not many battered wives would be hurrying home after they'd found a safe place to be, but she felt she had a valid excuse, a good reason to have to go back – to pick up some vital things. She shrugged. 'Well, I don't know, but there's a chance he won't be there. He might be on site.'

'On site? What does he do?'

'He's an architect. We're supposed to be building a new house. That's what the row was about. The fact that nothing seems to be happening.' She pulled an apologetic face. 'Do you think... Could someone come with me?'

Laura nodded, frowning. 'Okay... I don't suppose it'll take long if you're just nipping in to get a few things. I've got a couple of jobs to finish off this morning, but if you can wait until lunchtime, I can pop over there with you. Help you sort out what you need.' She jerked a thumb over her shoulder. 'I put your clothes through the wash, by the way. They're in that basket by the wall. They can go in the tumble dryer if you need anything straight away.'

Emma looked down at her bare feet, unable to hide her relief. Her clothes and shoes washed. All evidence removed. 'I could do with my trainers. I haven't got any other shoes, you see. I only packed a pair of slippers.'

'Well, the drying room is through there.' Laura pointed to a door behind them. 'If you stick them in now, they'll be ready by the time we set off. In the meantime, if you need anything, we've got a cupboard full of clothes on the first-floor landing. I don't suppose there's many maternity things, but have a root through if you like. Pick out a few things in case you change your mind.' She gave Emma a knowing look. 'You might decide you're not ready to go back inside the house when we get there. Especially if your husband is home.' She put a hand on her arm, gave it a gentle squeeze. 'And that's okay. Whatever you decide to do, it's okay. I've been through it myself. I know the decision to leave is a struggle. I get it.'

Emma gave a weak smile, her nerves already on edge. 'Thank you. I'll see what I feel like when we get close.' She squeezed her eyes shut, gave a big sigh. 'I honestly never imagined he'd be like this. He was fine until I got pregnant.'

Laura huffed. 'Unfortunately, it's a familiar story.'

Emma nodded. 'I really do appreciate all your kindness.'

'No worries, love. Got to look after each other, haven't we?' Laura put an arm round her shoulders, gave her a quick hug. 'Now then, what would you like for breakfast?'

Emma took a couple of rounds of toast and a mug of peppermint tea back up to her room, managing to avoid most of the other residents. There was no way she was going to sit in the hustle and bustle of the dining room, people looking at her, trying to strike up a conversation, asking questions. It would be better to stay anonymous for the time being, until she could see how things were going to pan out.

She ran through her plan in her head, testing it yet again, to make sure it was the right thing to do. With Laura as her witness, she would 'discover' the scene of the crime for the first time, pretending she had no idea how such a terrible thing had happened. Sam must have had a row with his sister, she would surmise, some sort of altercation that had ended in violence. Theirs was a volatile relationship. Then he must have slipped when he went inside, banging his head on the worktop. She could point out the evidence, make a convincing case for the scenario she'd created.

Unless someone else has found it first and called it in.

In which case, the police would see her shock and horror at discovering what had happened. Her fingerprints would be everywhere because she lived there. Her narrative would be convincing because it wasn't too far from the truth, apart from blaming Sam for driving into his sister. Neither death was murder, both had been accidents, and surely the forensics would draw that conclusion anyway? Hopefully, time of death wouldn't be too clear, and she could argue that it must have happened after she'd left.

Who would believe a heavily pregnant woman, with whiplash and a damaged shoulder, wearing a neck brace, could have caused anyone any harm? Yes, it was a bold move, but she was quietly confident she could pull it off. She had to.

The alternative, of course, was to run away, but that idea had little appeal. She'd lose everything. All her money, her comforts, her life, and she'd have to spend her days in hiding. That was no way to live, always looking over her shoulder, scared that someone would find her. It was no way to bring up a child either, constantly moving around, living in a web of lies and deceit.

The baby kicked, reminding her of another reason why running away wasn't an option. At some point she'd have to go to hospital to give birth, provide her name and NHS number. *Guilty people run away.* Instead, going back home, to the scene of the crime, as if she was expecting everything to be normal, would make her look less suspicious.

She nodded to herself as she sat on the edge of the bed, chewing a nail while she waited. *They'll never find out what I've done. Never know the whole truth.*

By the time they set off to Appleby, Emma had the neck brace back on, not only because it was too painful to get into a car without it, but more importantly because it supported her claim of being a battered wife. For the same reason, she hadn't made any attempt to cover up the dark smudges under her eyes or do anything with her limp and straggly hair.

The weight of what had happened the previous day seemed to have caught up with her, making her limbs feel leaden. How could she ever live with the guilt, the knowledge that people had died because of her actions? They were accidents, she kept reminding herself, the words sounding hollow now and doing nothing to change her anxious state of mind.

'I hope you don't mind me asking... but what happened to you?' Laura asked when they'd set off towards Appleby. 'Your neck. Did he do that?'

Emma looked down at her hands, knotted together in her lap. Hmm, that question had caught her off guard. How close to the truth should she go? Not very close, she decided, as hurting herself in a car crash did not make her a battered wife. And if she wasn't a victim of domestic abuse, then she wasn't eligible for Laura's protection. She decided not to answer, gazing out of the window at the fields and the fells rising in the distance.

Laura didn't press for an answer, putting the radio on to fill the silence, for which Emma was grateful.

Her mind took her back to the previous night, to the terror she'd felt, the absolute certainty that she was in danger. It had been so real, she'd had no choice but to act to protect herself and her baby. He'd locked her in, for God's sake. Now she'd never know the truth, but whatever his intentions had been, his actions had led to this horrific situation. And she was determined to navigate her way out of it.

Serves me right, she thought, watching the scenery flash past, fields of cows and sheep, lined with hedges and dotted with trees. This was karma getting her back for abandoning Zach. She'd never been more aware of her own duplicity. But as much as she might deserve to be punished, her baby surely didn't. Whatever happened next had to be in the best interests of her son.

They were getting closer now and she steeled herself for the grisly scene she knew they were about to encounter. Her pulse pounded, whooshing in her ears, as she imagined what Laura's reaction would be.

Calm down, calm down, she repeated silently while trying to do the breathing exercises she'd learnt at antenatal classes.

'You okay, love?' Laura glanced at her, concern in her eyes. 'Do you need me to stop? Or we can turn round and go back to Penrith if you like?'

Emma flashed her a quick smile. 'No. No, I'm okay, just a bit nervous, but I've got to face this. And I need my things.'

'Okay, but you say the word and I'm stopping, all right? We can do this another day if it's too soon.'

Emma clasped her hands together, feeling her bravery diminish each time Laura said they could turn around. There's no backing out, she told herself. You have to do this. 'Thank you,' she murmured, with a heartfelt sigh 'But I want to get it over with, then I can start thinking about the future. Hopefully he won't be there, and I can be in and out without having to see him.'

Laura reached out and patted her knee. 'I admire your courage, love. It took me months before I could think about going back. Mind you, he'd thrown all my stuff out by that point, so your strategy is probably right.'

The lane up to the cottage was quiet. No sign of any police cars. No ambulances or flashing lights. Generally, few people used the lane. Apart from the postman, it was just Hilda's family at the farm, if they were moving sheep, or doing something in the fields beyond the house. There was a strong chance the scene would be exactly how she'd left it.

She closed her eyes as they got nearer, not daring to look.

'Is this it?' Laura asked, bringing the car to a halt. Emma kept her eyes closed. *Just one more minute.*

Finally, she squinted, taking a quick look, gasping as she took in the scene.

CHAPTER THIRTY-ONE

The house looked completely normal. A cute little cottage surrounded by trees, like the first picture she'd ever seen of the place. The driveway was empty. The lights were off. She swung her head from left to right and back again, checking she hadn't missed anything.

The cars had gone. Faith had gone, or her body had. Did that mean the police had already been here? But then... wouldn't it be a crime scene? There would be police tape all over the place, people in white outfits traipsing around looking for forensic evidence. That's what she'd expected to see. *So, what the hell is going on here?*

She twisted her hands together in her lap. Had it really happened, or had she actually gone mad, imagining it all? Pregnancy psychosis. She remembered the symptoms included hallucinating, seeing things that weren't there.

'Emma?' Laura prompted.

'Yes,' she said, shaking herself out of the whirlwind of her thoughts. 'This is it.' She gazed at the house, thinking it was too weird, so different to what she was expecting she couldn't actually grasp what might have happened.

'It doesn't look like anyone is here, does it?' Laura swung the car into the driveway and pulled to a halt. 'Shall I go and knock?'

'Oh, would you? Now that we're here, I'm feeling a bit shaky.' Which was an understatement. And she didn't want to have to look at the dead body of her husband.

But maybe, just maybe, it hadn't happened at all.

If the cars weren't here and Faith's body wasn't here, was there a chance that Sam's body wasn't here either? She swallowed, not sure what she wanted to find. Either her husband was dead, or she was seriously mentally ill. In fact, she should get Laura to take her to hospital, explain that she was imagining terrible things and needed to be in a secure place until the baby was born, for both of their sakes.

'Course I will,' Laura said, already getting out of the car. 'Won't be a tick.'

She strode up the driveway to the front door, pushed the bell, her hands dipping into her pockets to protect them from the icy wind. She waited, rocking backwards and forwards on her heels, then rang the bell again, casting a glance towards the car.

Emma could feel her heart beating so fast she could hardly breathe. Her hands were clasped so tightly they ached. She couldn't imagine how Laura would react when she saw what must be on the other side of the door. Nausea stirred up the contents of her stomach once more as she relived those terrible moments from the night before. The sound of Sam's head against the worktop, the thud when he'd hit the floor, the red of the blood oozing from his wound. His lifeless, staring eyes. She gulped. *Don't think about it, stay strong.*

She shook her head trying to rid herself of the memory, focusing instead on Laura, who was now trying the door handle. The door was opening, and after another glance over her shoulder, Laura went in.

Emma chewed at a fingernail as she waited, time seeming to stand still.

A few minutes later, Laura came back out and hurried to the car, got in the driver's seat, rubbing her hands together and blowing on them to warm them up. 'By God, that's a chilly wind. The good news is the place is empty. He's not there.'

Emma's jaw dropped. *How could that be?* 'Empty,' she echoed, the suspicion of psychosis getting stronger by the minute.

Laura frowned, peered at her. 'Are you sure you're okay, love? You're looking a bit peaky.'

Emma stared at the house. 'I'm fine. I'm just... nervous and... well, you know...'

'I think you'll be okay to go and grab some of your stuff. I'll stay by the door and keep watch in case he comes back.'

Emma nodded. Had her mind played out some weird paranoid dream? In which case, perhaps things weren't as bad as she'd imagined. And if Sam walked through the door, well, it wouldn't be a problem. She took a deep breath, felt her shoulders relax. Perhaps everything was going to be okay after all.

She clambered out of the car and made her way up the drive, hanging back a little to allow Laura to go in first. The citrus tang of the lemon cleaner she used on the floors hit her as she walked into the kitchen. Her eyes scanned the room, noting how spotless it looked. Someone had obviously come in and given the place a good once-over. She wasn't up to doing much in terms of housework at the moment and Sam didn't seem to notice, so she'd been a bit lax in that department, thinking she'd pay for someone to come and do a deep clean in a couple of weeks, before the baby was born. Perhaps Sam had organised it already.

It was very confusing. Something was wrong about all of this, but she was struggling to work out exactly what it might be.

'Everything okay?' Laura asked, a puzzled frown on her face as she watched Emma tiptoeing around the room.

'I'm... I'm not really sure,' Emma muttered. 'It's ever so clean, isn't it?'

Laura laughed, a proper guffaw, and it was a few moments before she could stop. 'I think that's a first. A victim of domestic violence worried that her house is too clean.' And off she went again in another fit of giggles.

Emma was too preoccupied to join in. She stood at the bottom of the stairs. 'Did you go up?'

'Yes, I checked everywhere. It's not like it's very big, is it? No sign of your husband. Honestly.'

Gingerly, Emma climbed the stairs, her neck objecting at every step. The bedroom door was open and she pushed it right back, in case Sam might be hiding behind it, but the room was empty.

That was when she understood exactly what was wrong. The room was emptier than it should be. The wardrobe door was open, the hangers cleared of Sam's clothes. She pulled open drawers, checked his bedside table. Everything of his had gone. There was no sign that he'd been here. She checked in the spare room. No computer, no papers. It had all been packed up and moved. Not that there'd been much stuff to start with, only the bare minimum, as many of their possessions were still in storage.

How odd. How very, very odd. She heard Laura's phone ringing, could hear her talking, then the sound of her feet on the stairs.

'I'm sorry, love. There's a bit of an emergency. I'll have to dash off, see if I can get it sorted. You better come with me and we can come back later.' Her eyes scanned the room. 'Looks like your fella's done a runner, doesn't it?'

'It does look like he's gone,' Emma said, distracted. 'How long will you be?'

'An hour tops? But we need to go right now.'

'I think I'll be okay if you want to leave me here. Then I can sort through what I need and be ready to go when you come back.' She gave Laura a hesitant smile. 'I need a moment to myself. You know, to get my head round it all, make sure I've got everything.'

Laura shook her head. 'I'm not happy leaving you on your own.'

'Please, you go and I'll be waiting for you when you've finished. I need a bit of... closure. Then I can leave for good.'

Laura's phone rang again and she looked flustered, torn.

'Well, I can't make you come with me, but I'd strongly advise—'

'I'll be fine if it's only an hour. Like you say, it looks like he's cleared out and gone.'

Laura answered her phone. 'I'm on my way,' she said, before turning back to Emma. It was clear from her face she thought it was a bad idea. 'What if he comes back?'

Emma grimaced, shook her head. 'Look around.' She pointed at the wardrobe, the empty drawers left half open. 'He's taken all his things. I don't think that's going to happen.'

Laura looked flustered, obviously worried about whoever had been on the phone. She pulled a card from her pocket, handed it to Emma. 'Here's my number. Make sure you lock the door when I leave, and if there's any problem, just ring me, okay?' She turned and dashed downstairs. Emma heard the car engine start, and then there was silence.

It was only when Laura had gone that Emma realised she couldn't ring anyone if she wanted to. Her phone had been on Sam's body somewhere. And she didn't even have the laptop now because she'd left it at the shelter. Along with her bag for hospital. She also couldn't lock the door, because Sam had grabbed her keys when he'd locked her in.

She pulled a suitcase from the back of the wardrobe and started sorting through her clothes – whatever had happened, she couldn't stay here, and this might be her only chance to pack her things. She'd figure out the rest later.

The bang of the front door closing startled her. It only seemed like minutes since Laura had left. The quick thud of feet coming up the stairs made her stand up straight.

Faith was standing in the doorway, her face black and blue, blood crusted round her nose and lips, a big lump on her forehead. Her hair was dishevelled, strands falling over her face where they'd come away from her plait.

'The wanderer returns,' she said with a ghoulish smile as she walked into the room, her teeth rimmed with blood. 'I think we have a bit of catching up to do, don't we?'

CHAPTER THIRTY-TWO

Emma screamed, the shock of seeing Faith making her heart almost explode out of her chest. The baby squirmed, startled by her cry. There was nothing she could do, no way to escape and Faith was supposed to be dead. Her head felt like it was being squeezed in a vice, and to her horror, she found she couldn't move, her body frozen in place.

Faith walked towards her, a benign smile on her face, but Emma knew it couldn't be real given the circumstances. It was like the smile you might see on one of those dolls in a horror film, fixed and unmoving, more sinister than any other expression she could imagine. She took the suitcase Emma had just opened and put it back in the wardrobe. 'It's okay. There's no need to go. I've sorted it all out.'

'I... I don't know what you mean,' Emma stammered as her pulse pounded, her body breaking into a cold sweat. There was scared and then there was terrified, and she now knew exactly what that felt like. She shuffled backwards, away from Faith, until her bottom hit the wall.

'You pulled a bit of a stunt there, didn't you?' Faith said, still smiling, which Emma found confusing, not to mention revolting, given the state of her face and the blood round her teeth. She leant against the wall, closed her eyes, hoping she was asleep and this was part of a nightmare that hadn't quite ended. Or another hallucination, a symptom of the psychosis she must surely be suffering from. Both of which would be preferable to Faith actually being real. She couldn't bring herself to open her eyes to check.

The touch of a hand on her shoulder made her gasp, her pulse rate shooting skywards. 'You had me fooled that you were going into labour.' Faith gave a weird laugh. 'And look what you did to me.'

Emma could feel the heat of her breath on her face. 'I'm so sorry,' she whimpered, her eyes still tightly shut, no intention of looking at Faith if she could avoid it. 'I didn't mean to hurt you. I... I put the car in the wrong gear and it shot backwards before I could stop.'

She had no idea what Faith had planned for her, but she knew she was completely defenceless, unable to move away even if she wanted to. *Is this the end?* She started to shake, tears trickling down her cheeks while she tried to work out what to do, how to save herself and her child. Her instinct was to plead for forgiveness and hope Faith took pity on her. It was her only chance. Finally, she forced herself to open her eyes, trying not to show her revulsion.

'Look... I know it was an accident,' Faith said, her eyes never leaving Emma's. 'I know you wouldn't knowingly hurt me. We're sisters now, aren't we?' She blinked a few times, wiped strands of hair off her face and tucked them behind her ears. It was clear from her voice that she was struggling to keep her composure. 'I understand you didn't mean to kill Sam. I mean, I don't know exactly what happened, but to me, it was obvious he hit his head on the worktop.' She cocked her head to one side. 'Did he slip?'

Emma felt so breathless she couldn't speak. So it *was* real.

Sam *was* actually dead. A weight settled in her chest, emotion blocking her throat as she wished she'd listened to Laura and left when she'd asked her to. She'd never imagined that Faith was still alive, not when her body had looked broken and lifeless. *Why didn't I check?*

'I can see that the whole thing would be upsetting and frightening,' Faith continued. 'But there was no need to run away. I want you to know that I don't blame you.' She swallowed then, her facade starting to crack, her voice with it. 'We can grieve for Sam. We must.' She pulled a tissue out of her pocket, blew her nose. 'But we can't forget that you're about to have a baby. And your health and well-being have to be our top priority.' She gave a shuddering sigh. 'There's nothing we can do to bring Sam back. But we can make sure that his child has the best possible start in life, can't we?'

Emma gulped in a breath, as though she'd just resurfaced after swimming underwater, relief washing over her. It was okay. Faith understood. She wasn't out for revenge. And she wanted to make sure the baby was safe. Whatever weirdness was going on, Emma didn't feel her situation was quite so precarious now.

She watched Faith walk over to the window, gazing out over the driveway. 'So... who was in the car?'

Emma wasn't sure what to say. Was the truth the best option, or should she make something up, try and bluster her way out of this? Truth, she decided. It was time for the truth, then she didn't have to keep track of a web of lies. That was exhausting as she knew only too well after the last year with Sam, trying to pretend Zach didn't exist.

'She runs the women's refuge in Penrith. She's coming back soon; in fact I thought it was her when I heard the door bang. She had to sort out an emergency and left me here to pack a few things.'

'Women's refuge?' Faith turned, looking incredulous, a deep groove between her eyebrows. 'Were you frightened of Sam?'

'No, no, not directly. It was the Uber driver making assumptions. She saw the state of me, jumped to conclusions and took me to the refuge. I didn't know where else to go, what to do. I was in shock, you see. Traumatised. I wasn't thinking straight, so I went along with it.'

Faith's silence was hard to read, making Emma gabble on.

'I never accused Sam of anything. I didn't. But... he did give me a scare.' Her chin quivered, her voice wavering. 'I'd found out some things that were bothering me about the build, and he got all worked up. I've never seen him so angry. He stormed out and locked me in the house.'

Faith was nodding along as she spoke. 'Ah, so that's what happened. I got a garbled phone call last night and couldn't make out what on earth was going on. That's why I came over. I was worried for you, I really was.'

Emma re-examined her thoughts on Faith. Had she read her wrong? She was definitely listening and sounded genuinely concerned. *Is she on my side?*

Emma continued with her story, welcoming the chance to be able to tell someone what had happened. Someone who knew the ending if not the beginning. 'After Marcey died in the fire, and knowing that Sam's first wife had also died in a fire, I convinced myself he was going to burn the cottage down with me in it.'

Faith's eyes grew round as she listened, Emma's narrative speeding up as she relived her ordeal.

'I panicked. He told me he went back to the scene of the fire so the police would think he'd just arrived, not been there earlier, and that scared me, you know, the fact that he wasn't being honest with the police. I thought it made him look guilty. And when he locked me in, I got myself all worked up because I knew I couldn't get out of any of the windows in my condition. If he set fire to the place, I'd be trapped.'

Faith's expression changed then, that familiar look of compassion in her eyes.

'Oh, Emma, love, that must have been terrifying for you. But I think you got him all wrong. The problem with Sam was he was a pushover. Women could twist him round their little finger and that got him into all sorts of trouble.' Her voice was soft and gentle, back to the woman Emma knew and loved. 'But I can promise you he had nothing to do with the deaths of Alice and Marcey. That's your imagination taking over, nothing more.'

'How can you be so sure? It seems like'

Faith held up a hand, stopping her mid-sentence. 'I know it wasn't Sam, okay? He wouldn't harm a flea.' She pinched the bridge of her nose. 'I'm sorry, but I don't think rehashing Sam's mistakes is going to help. It's not going to bring him back, is it?' Emotion clouded her face then, her chin starting to shake. A sob escaped from her throat, then another, until she was leaning against the wall, keening, a noise so raw that it set Emma off too.

She was crying for Sam and the love she'd had for him, for the life they should have had together. But she was also crying in despair at the complicated mess her life had become, at all the mistakes she'd made. It was a while before her tears came to a shuddering halt.

She'd been so wrapped up in her own misery, she hadn't noticed that Faith had left the room. A few minutes later, she reappeared with mugs of hot chocolate and a packet of biscuits.

'I feel better for a good cry,' she said, with a smile that looked surprisingly genuine. She'd given her face a wash, scrubbed the blood from her teeth, and looked sad rather than scary. 'What about you?'

Emma nodded. 'I'm so sorry.' It was utterly inadequate, but she couldn't think of anything else to say.

Faith handed her a mug and they sat on the bed for a while, deep in their own thoughts, sipping their drinks and working their way through the packet of biscuits.

'I'm going to tell you a secret,' Faith said after she'd finished her drink, brushing biscuit crumbs off her lap. 'Even Sam didn't know the truth.' She took a deep breath, looked Emma straight in the eye. 'Sam was my son.'

CHAPTER THIRTY-THREE

Faith watched Emma's mouth drop open. Yes, she thought, it would be a bit of a shock. She gave her a moment to let her words sink in, let Emma work out exactly what she'd done to Faith's world.

'But I don't understand how that's possible. You must have been too young...' Emma's voice tailed off as she gazed at Faith, her disbelief written all over her face.

'You're right. I was far too young to be a mother. Almost fifteen when I had him.' Faith flapped a hand. 'It was a childish mistake, because that's what I was at the time. A child. Experimenting.' She looked down at her hands, fighting back the flood of emotions that always accompanied the memories. It would be easier not to explain. She didn't owe Emma anything. But she wanted her to know. Needed Emma to feel her pain, to trust her. 'My parents were Catholics and totally against abortion, so my mum and I went away for the last few months of my pregnancy under the cover story we were going to look after an elderly relative. When we came back, my mother said the baby was hers, so I could finish school.'

Her body shook as she suppressed a sob. 'My parents said I

could only stay at home if I promised never to tell Sam the truth. Never tell anyone. And I didn't. He knew me as his sister, and the older he got, the more impossible it was to tell him, even after our parents died. Because that would mean I'd lied to him his whole life and he would have hated me. So,' she sighed, 'I had to settle for that.'

Her voice cracked then. 'I never thought of him as a brother, though. He's always been my child. My only child. And now... now he's gone.'

She stood, not wanting to bawl her eyes out again. There were things to do. So many things. And not much time. She gathered the mugs, turned to Emma.

'You have a rest, love. You're looking ever so pale. It's been a nasty shock for both of us.'

Emma yawned, but looked like she might try to fight her tiredness, her eyes blinking furiously. Faith smiled as she watched, knew she was fighting a losing battle. Within a few moments, she'd keeled over onto her side, her eyes closed. Perfect. There were more than enough sleeping tablets crushed into her hot chocolate to keep her out of action while Faith got on with her long list of jobs.

She looked at Emma's sleeping body, despising every molecule of her being. In truth, she'd never been Emma's biggest fan, had always thought there was something about her that didn't quite ring true. As a trained psychologist and bereavement counsellor, she'd learnt to spot when clients were holding back, and she'd seen that in Emma. But it was only when she'd found Emma's phone on Sam's body that she'd come to understand what her secret was. She'd tapped in the PIN number, something she'd seen Emma use many times, committing it to memory for future snooping purposes. And there it was in her messages. Some fella called Zach professing his love.

She'd scrolled through hundreds and hundreds of messages, trying to understand exactly what she was seeing, the context, the timeline. And once she'd gone back far enough, right to their wedding day, the shock had stopped her in her tracks while her brain struggled to match the content of the messages with the actions of the Emma she knew. The Emma who was committed to Sam and building their future. Never had she let the facade drop.

Who would suspect a woman of being a *bigamist*?

It had never occurred to her, the label being solely applied to men in the stories that she'd read and heard about. She wondered how she'd missed the signs. Surely there must have been clues during the time they'd known each other? It was silly to blame herself, though. It wasn't her fault she'd been deceived. It was Emma's fault for being so devious.

Emma's face looked peaceful in her drugged sleep. Beautiful, even though her curly hair had become straighter with pregnancy, her face softened with the extra weight she'd put on. When Faith had first met her, she'd seemed like a gentle soul, and it was that which had drawn her to her. Yes, she was a bit floaty, living in a dream world half the time, idealistic, but she was pleasant enough company. Harmless. That had been Faith's assessment.

Never in a million years would she have thought her capable of such deceit, such betrayal. Imagine... having another husband. She couldn't comprehend how that had happened, how she hadn't guessed something was amiss earlier. But then she hadn't been looking. Why would Emma go to a bereavement group if she wasn't bereaved?

Faith gazed out of the window as she pondered that for a moment, thinking back to when they'd first met, their initial conversation. She could see now that maybe it was her fault after all. She'd connected dots that weren't there. Emma hadn't said that her husband was dead. She'd said he'd had an accident. Her mother was dead, and her unborn child, so there was definitely grieving going on there. And she supposed with her husband having such a serious accident, she was probably grieving for the life she'd lost as well.

She tutted, annoyed with herself. No, more than annoyed, she was raging. But could she take all the blame when Emma had been such an accomplished liar? She didn't think so. Emma could have put her straight, could have clarified right at the start, but she didn't, which meant the deception had been deliberate.

As she thought through everything her sleeping daughter-in-law had taken from her, Faith wanted to wrap her hands round her neck and squeeze the life out of her. Right now. Just be done with it. She took a step back, worried that she might act on impulse. It was not the right time. If she was going to get anything out of this situation, patience was key.

It was clear that she'd underestimated Emma, taken a lot of things at face value. The woman was an accomplished manipulator. She'd made Faith believe she was something she wasn't, and now she'd have to be on her guard to make sure there was no trickery for the next few weeks. Once the baby was born, she wouldn't have to deal with her any more, but until then she needed her to be compliant.

She retrieved the screwdriver from the office, picked up the bolt she'd taken off the garden shed and started to attach it to the outside of the bedroom door, humming to herself as she worked. Once all the screws were in, she gave it a try, shunting the bolt backwards and forwards in its housing. A lovely fit.

Emma wouldn't be going anywhere if Faith didn't want her to, but no need to alert her to the security fittings yet. She slid the bolt back, opened the door slightly so she could hear when she stirred. *It would be ages yet.*

CHAPTER THIRTY-FOUR

Faith decided she could relax for an hour. She'd earned it after all her hard work. Time to make herself a snack and decide what to do next.

There wasn't a lot in the fridge, so she'd have to make do with cheese on toast, washed down with a super-strength cup of coffee to keep her brain awake after a night with no sleep. Surprisingly, she wasn't as tired as she'd thought she would be, after all that lifting and moving things and then the cleaning. Amazing what adrenaline could do.

She sat on the sofa, gazing out of the window as she ate, watching the long limbs of the ash tree blowing in the wind.

In her mind, she relived the moment when she'd come round the previous night, half her body slumped in the boot of the car, covered with shards of glass, her head thumping like someone was playing drums on her forehead.

Thank goodness for the tow bar. It had hit the bumper of Sam's car and saved her legs from being crushed. And because her car was brand new, it had all the top-end safety features, including glass that shattered easily so that pedestrians wouldn't be hurt so badly if there was an accident. That premium price she'd paid had literally saved her life.

With a pounding heart, she'd wriggled out from between the two vehicles, unscathed apart from bruises to her thighs and face. A possible broken nose. She'd known something terrible had happened, could feel it in her gut. Why else would Emma behave like that? And the blood on the bag...

She'd gulped. *Where was Sam?*

Hoping that she was wrong, that she'd find the house empty and Emma's tale about him going up to the farm had been true, she'd staggered up the drive and pushed open the door of the house. Her legs had buckled when she saw him, her son, her lovely, only son lying in a huge pool of blood on the floor.

Nothing could prepare you for a moment like that. The shock of it, the disbelief, the wanting it not to be real, but the terrible knowing that it was.

She'd dashed over and knelt beside him, feeling for a pulse, but she couldn't find one. His face was so pale, his skin starting to cool, his eyes staring into space. Her Sam was dead. Gone. Never coming back.

The realisation had taken her breath away. She'd felt dizzy, thought she might faint, and she'd spent a little while hunched up on the floor, rocking as she sobbed. Staring at his body, hoping that he might move, that she'd got it wrong.

Eventually, her survival instincts had kicked in. There was no getting him back, she'd reasoned, and she had to think about her future. Right now. No time to lose. She couldn't let everything she'd worked for her whole life drift away from her because of that woman.

She wasn't too sure exactly what had happened. She could see that he'd hit his head on the worktop, the splatter of blood clearly marking the spot. Whether he'd tripped, and it was an accident, or Emma had hit him wasn't clear.

But however angry she was with Emma, Faith couldn't

press charges. What she was sure about was the need to keep the police out of her affairs.

She couldn't have the police finding her and Sam's secret bank accounts. Almost two million stashed away in there now. That had been their target and they'd so nearly reached it. So very, very close. Nobody else was getting that money. Nobody.

Sam would have wanted her to carry on. He'd want her to achieve their dream of a life with no need to work. Living in a beautiful newly built property up in the Highlands of Scotland, where nobody would bother them and they could be free from interference for the rest of their days. Sam's greatest project of all. She could still do that. She had the house designs all ready to go and could have it built in his memory. His legacy, something to remind her of him every single day as she lived in his wonderful creation. And maybe something more if she played her cards right.

Dragging her mind back to her current situation, she'd wondered about Emma. She'd obviously run away, but would she go to the police? If it had been an accident, Faith had reasoned, Emma would have been calling an ambulance, not running away. And if she'd killed Sam, she wouldn't be coming back. So the job, then, was to clear the place up, hide any evidence and get herself as far away as possible. Fast as she could. Then she could reinvent herself under a new name, something fitting for the next phase of her life.

It was when she'd been moving Sam's body that Emma's phone had dropped out of his pocket. And then she'd been sidetracked for a good half-hour, working out what the heck was going on with the messages from Zach. At that point, her hatred for her daughter-in-law ramped up to new heights. But she couldn't dwell on it, not then. There were things to do, her rage fuelling her when she thought her body couldn't do any more, removing all traces of Sam from the house and making sure the place was spotless.

Now, as she finished her coffee, she looked around the downstairs room, proud of what she'd achieved. Mind over matter. Compartmentalising. More than one person had called her a cold bitch over the course of her lifetime, but sometimes that could be a virtue. Only she knew the pain in her heart, the place where the love for her son would always be alive.

She'd hidden Sam's body on the new-build site. Made it look like a pile of stones from a crumbling wall had fallen on him. She'd watched enough *Silent Witness* programmes to know about lividity and how the blood settled in a body once it was dead, so she made sure to position him the way he'd been on the kitchen floor, finding just the right sharp stone to rest next to the wound on his head, then covering him with a few other random stones to make it look realistic.

In reality, nobody had any cause to go on the site. There were fences round it, signs to warn of danger. It would be some time before his remains were found, if ever. Of course, it pained her that she couldn't give him a proper burial, but he was gone, he wouldn't know. What she'd left on that site was human flesh, not her son. Not the essence of him. Anyway, there was no alternative, so she had to live with it. Maybe she'd have her own little memorial service when all this was over and she was settled somewhere else.

Poor Sam. She allowed herself to think about her son for a moment, to treasure his memory. He'd loved her so completely she'd never felt the need for a relationship other than the one she had with him. He was her pride and joy, her whole universe, and he'd trusted her absolutely, never taking decisions before asking her advice. Until he'd met Emma. Things had changed then, and instead of feeling like she was trotting through life on a trusty steed, she was suddenly wrestling to control an unruly mustang that wasn't quite broken in properly.

She sniffed, blew her nose and wiped the tears from her eyes. No point crying about it now; that wouldn't bring him back. She stirred herself, aware that if she sat for too long, she'd probably fall asleep, and there were still things to do. She'd moved all Sam's belongings to her apartment, stuffed into bin bags. Those had to go to the tip now, then she was done. She checked the time and huffed, annoyed that she was probably too late to do it today.

Her eyes rested on her damaged car on the drive. Getting that mended would be a priority too. Nowhere round here, though. She'd have to go further afield. Carlisle, maybe. Hopefully it was the sort of job she could get done while she waited, which was not a problem now she could lock Emma in.

She yawned and stretched, taking herself into the kitchen to make another drink. Or perhaps she should have a nap while Emma slept. Her brain might work a bit better then, ready for this evening.

A knock on the front door made her tense. She spun round, her heart missing a beat as the door opened.

CHAPTER THIRTY-FIVE

A woman's face peered round the kitchen door. 'Hello? Emma, are you there?' Her eyes widened when she saw Faith. 'Oh, I'm so sorry just barging in, but I thought Emma was here alone.' She walked towards her, looking wary but holding out a hand. 'I'm Laura, from the women's refuge in Penrith.'

Faith's brain spun into action, the caffeine mixing with adrenaline and making her feel like a speeded-up version of herself. She gave the woman one of her warmest smiles and shook her hand, noting it was sweaty and hot. 'I'm Faith. Emma's sister-in-law.'

Laura looked puzzled. 'She didn't mention any relatives. Said she shared the place with her husband, Sam.'

'Oh, dear.' Faith sighed. 'Poor Emma, she's not taking his death very well at all.'

Laura's eyes widened even further, her voice going up an octave. 'He's dead?'

Faith nodded, gave another heartfelt sigh. 'That's right, so sad. But I think she's in denial. She keeps flipping between knowing he's dead and thinking he's alive.'

Laura blew out a breath. 'Was it sudden? That's when it

seems to pull the rug from under the partner's feet. It's different if you've had time to come to terms with it a bit.' She gave a sad shake of her head. 'Poor girl. I thought her story didn't quite add up.'

'And then we were in a car crash a couple of days ago, which didn't help.' Faith pointed to her own face. 'As you can see, neither of us got away unscathed.'

'Well, I didn't like to say anything...' Laura rubbed at her forehead, clearly confused.

Faith lowered her voice, as though she didn't want to be overheard. 'The truth is, she's not been herself. We were on an outing and a lorry forced us off the road. Emma suffered whiplash and a bruised shoulder, but I have a feeling she might have a bit of concussion as well. She's been behaving erratically for the past couple of days. I was so worried when she went missing, I was out all night looking for her, then when I came back, she was asleep on the bed.' She laughed. 'Honestly, I was so relieved.' She pointed upstairs. 'She's still asleep now.'

Laura seemed on edge, glancing up the stairs and back to Faith, a frown cleaving a deep groove between her eyebrows.

'You can nip up and have a look if you want to be sure.'

She blushed then, looked embarrassed to be caught out not believing what Faith was telling her. 'No, no need for that. I'm glad she's safe and there's someone looking after her.'

'Yes, I'm going to stay for a while, at least until the baby's born, so you don't have to worry.' Faith gave what she hoped was a reassuring smile. 'I think the midwife is popping over tomorrow to check everything is okay.'

Laura seemed to relax a little then, her hand releasing the car keys she'd been grasping, letting them swing from her index finger. 'Well, that's good. The thing is... She left some clothes and her hospital bag at the shelter. I don't suppose you'd be able to pop by and pick them up, would you?'

Faith nodded, gave her another smile. 'Of course. No

problem at all. I've got to come to Penrith tomorrow anyway to get the car fixed. I'll call in after the midwife has been.'

Laura studied Faith's face, then glanced at the stairs again, her mouth twisting from side to side. 'I *will* pop my head round her door if you don't mind. Then I can say goodbye if she's awake.'

Faith was wondering if this woman was ever going to go. Her heart was racing and she had to stuff her hands in the pockets of her jeans so it wasn't obvious how much she was shaking. 'Help yourself. Would you like a cup of tea or coffee or something?'

'No, thanks, I better dash. There's always too much to do and I need to get back.'

Faith turned and filled the kettle as Laura climbed the stairs, hardly daring to breathe. Would Emma still be asleep? She should be, given the amount of sleeping tablets she'd dropped into her drink. She crossed her fingers and waited.

It was only a few minutes before she heard the clump of feet on the stairs. 'She's out like a light,' Laura said. 'I'm sure she didn't sleep well last night, so I'll leave her to rest.' She smiled at Faith. 'Would it be okay to call in another time? It would be good to have a chat before I close her file.'

Faith dried her hands on a tea towel. 'No problem at all. Any time. I doubt we'll be going far given the state of us at the moment.'

'Right, well, I'll be off,' Laura said, finally, and it was all Faith could do to stop herself from bundling the silly woman out of the door. 'And I'll see you tomorrow. I'll get her stuff ready and put it in my office for safe keeping.' She gave another quick smile. 'I could do with her room, so it's all worked out for the best.'

Faith walked to the door, held it open. 'I'm so sorry she troubled you, and thank you for looking after her. I'm extremely grateful. She's the only family I've got now my brother's... gone.'

'No trouble. Honestly, she was in a bit of a state, but it all makes sense now.' Laura glanced up to the ceiling. 'I hope she feels better once the baby is born. At least a bit of her husband will live on in him.'

'Him?' Faith picked up on the word immediately. *Could it be true?*

'Yes, she said she'd just found out she was expecting a boy.'

Faith beamed. 'I didn't know. How lovely.' Her heart swelled with joy. *Wasn't that perfect?* She could call him Sam and he would be her little boy all over again. Images flashed through her mind of her and the baby. She could see it so clearly, and this time she could be a proper mother. The only mother the baby would know – he'd never be aware that Emma had even existed.

CHAPTER THIRTY-SIX

Faith closed the door and leant on it, burying her head in her hands as she let out a long, relieved breath. Thank God Emma was still asleep. That was a close one, and a reminder she had no time to waste. It was essential to speed things up.

She grabbed her phone and started googling ways to induce labour. Because that was going to be the game-changer. The moment the child was born, she could be out of here, never to be seen again. But until then, she was stuck here just as much as Emma was.

Twenty minutes later, she had a shopping list, and she dashed into town to get everything together before Emma came round and the shops shut for the night. She had to get castor oil, raspberry leaf tea, evening primrose oil and chilli. All of them were supposed to bring on labour, and although she knew nothing was scientifically proven, she trusted women to know what might work to hurry their child into the world. A little bit of everything should do the trick, she decided.

She got back feeling out of breath but satisfied, having tracked everything down. So far so good. Quickly, she unloaded her shopping and hurried up the stairs, startled at first to see no Emma on the bed. Then she heard the toilet flush in the en suite. She waited, but Emma didn't appear.

She tapped on the bathroom door. 'Are you okay in there?'

'Yes, yes. Feeling a bit shaky. I think I need to eat something.' Emma opened the door, gave Faith a weak smile. 'I think the baby's getting ready to be born. He's moved. I feel like I'm walking with a bowling ball between my legs.'

Faith's eyes widened, her heart skipping with delight. This might be over sooner than she'd hoped. 'Really? Oh, wow, you better run me through what to look out for. So I know when to get you to hospital.' Not that Emma was going anywhere near a hospital, but she didn't need to know that.

'It's just over two weeks to my due date now, so I suppose he could decide to come at any time.' She still looked pale, Faith thought, and she watched her sway before grabbing the door frame for support.

'Hey, you're not okay, are you?' Faith put an arm round her shoulder, supporting her elbow. 'Come on, let's get you back to bed and I'll sort out some food. We need to keep your strength up and it must be ages since you last ate. You've been asleep for hours.' She pulled a face. 'There's not much in the fridge, but I think there are some ready meals in the freezer.'

Emma lay back against her pillows, hands rubbing her baby bump. 'I would eat anything. Honestly, I don't care.'

'Okay.' Faith beamed, patting her shoulder. 'Shouldn't take long then.'

She hurried back downstairs and set about doctoring a ready meal. Chilli con carne with extra chilli, a dollop of castor oil and a sprinkling of evening primrose oil, washed down with a triple-strength raspberry tea. That should kick start things nicely.

The tray was ready and she was about to take it upstairs

when the sound of the theme tune from the evening news made her heart stutter. Emma had put the TV on in the bedroom. She hurried upstairs just in time to hear the headlines. Something about immigration. But what made her gasp were the words tracking along the bottom of the screen. *Breaking news. Death of Marcey Dubois, ex-model. Initial investigations conclude the house fire was arson.*

She caught Emma's horrified expression and put the tray down, grabbing the remote from her hand and switching the TV off. 'You don't want to be watching the news, love. All that doom and gloom. You need to be watching happy things. Or how about a book?' She spotted the pile on Emma's bedside table and pulled one out. 'Here we are. This sounds lovely. Heart-warming and uplifting, it says on the cover. Exactly what you need.'

Emma was giving her a strange look, like something had clicked in her mind. Her eyes narrowed, and Faith bustled round trying to pretend she hadn't seen the flash of suspicion in them. *Bloody news!* Why hadn't she thought to take the remote away earlier? So many things to think about, it was like spinning plates keeping on top of everything.

She put the tray on Emma's lap and sat on the bed, watching as she ate.

'Aren't you having something?' Emma asked, after a few mouthfuls.

'I ate while you were asleep. I'm sorry, I couldn't wait.'

She seemed satisfied with that and started eating again, stopping after a couple of mouthfuls to gulp down some water. 'Wow, I don't remember this chilli being so hot. And there's a sort of... soapy aftertaste as well.' She grimaced. 'I don't want to be rude, but I'm not sure I can eat it.'

Faith laughed and clapped her hands together. 'Oh, I was just reading about this. What happens to your senses in the latter stages of pregnancy. Apparently, it's an indicator that birth is imminent when your taste buds go a bit haywire.'

Emma looked at her, and Faith could tell she wasn't sure whether to believe her.

'I had the exact same meal earlier and it was absolutely fine.'

Emma hesitated, then started eating again. Faith watched, mentally chewing and swallowing every mouthful with her until it was all gone. She handed her the tea. 'I thought this would be nice and refreshing.'

Emma took a sip and nodded. 'Fruity. Oh yes, delicious.'

They chatted for a bit, Faith making a real effort to establish a bit of normality, discussing preparations for the birth, then Emma's eyes finally closed and once again she drifted into a deep, drugged sleep.

Faith trudged back downstairs with the tray, thinking she could nip over to Penrith and pick up Emma's things from the refuge while she slept. A loose end she needed to tie up. It had been one hell of a long day, though, and her eyes locked on the wine rack next to the fridge. A bit of fortification before she had to face Laura again would be a good idea, she decided. That woman had a suspicious mind, she could tell by the looks she'd been giving her, but then she supposed it went with the job. She pulled a bottle out of the rack and poured herself a generous measure, screwed the top back on. Only one glass if she was driving.

She was savouring her drink, sip by delicious sip, as she wrote a mental list of everything she had to do and tried to sort it into priority order. The sound of a car door slamming made her jump, spilling wine over her hand and onto the floor. *What now? Was Laura back again?*

There was no way she could pretend she wasn't in, with the lights on and her car in the drive. She put her glass down, wiped her hands on a tea towel and peeped through the kitchen window. There was a car parked in front of hers, blocking her in. It had one of those aerials, a dead giveaway that it was a police car.

Her brain froze, all the hairs standing up on the back of her neck. *Oh, for crying out loud. Was nothing ever simple?*

CHAPTER THIRTY-SEVEN

Faith dashed to the door, opening it before they could knock and risk waking Emma. A stocky man and a lanky woman stood on the driveway, studying the broken glass in the boot of her car. *Oh God, so much explaining to do.* She gulped, her mind scrambling for a logical cover story. 'Good evening,' she said with a smile, walking out to meet them. 'How can I help you?'

They turned and looked at her, neither of them returning her smile. 'Looks like you had a bit of an accident,' the woman said, holding up an ID card, the print too small for Faith to read. 'I'm Detective Sergeant Pamela Lamb and this is Detective Constable Ian Brown.' Faith hardly heard the introductions, her mind working full speed on creating a cover story. Anyway, she didn't need to know their names because she'd be making sure she never saw them again.

She looked up at the huge ash tree next to the house. 'It was the other night, you know, when it was stormy. I was getting the shopping out of the boot and a branch fell off the tree, broke the glass and smacked me in the face.' She shook her head. 'I'm going to have to ask the landlady to take it down.'

DS Lamb studied her face, for longer than was comfortable, but didn't comment. 'So you rent this place?'

Keep as close to the truth as possible, Faith advised herself. She had her story sorted out now, felt confident it would be okay. 'No, my brother does. I'm keeping an eye on the place while he's away.'

'And who's your brother?' the constable asked.

Faith frowned, her eyes flicking between the two of them. 'What's this about?'

'Your brother's name?' the constable insisted.

'Sam Barclay. He's an architect, working in Dumfries on a project at the moment.'

'Right. And when did you last hear from him?' The woman was still staring at her. It was unnerving, and Faith could feel sweat pooling under her arms, a nervous tic twitching the corner of her mouth.

She screwed up her face, as though she was trying to remember. 'Um... I'm not sure.' She tapped her chin with her fingers, stringing it out. 'Let me see, I think... It seems longer, but it's probably a couple of days. He called to say the job had hit a glitch and he was staying a bit longer to sort it out.'

The constable was taking notes now. He glanced up. 'Any idea what time it was when he called?'

'Um... early evening, I think.' She gave a tentative smile. 'Can I ask what this is about, please? You're worrying me. He is okay, isn't he?'

The sergeant's steady gaze and lack of words was getting to be unbearable. Ask your questions, then go away, she pleaded in her head, desperate to get back inside.

'And how did he seem when you spoke to him?'

'Oh, his usual stressed-out self. Honestly, he lives on adren-aline and energy drinks. I've told him he's heading for a heart attack or a stomach ulcer, but he won't listen.'

'Can you confirm the number plate of his car for us, please?'

The constable was firing off questions, writing down Faith's answers, while the sergeant watched.

Why would they want to know his number plate? Her heart leapt. *Had they found his car?* Her palms were slick with sweat, her jumper sticking to her back. She hoped she still looked unconcerned, while her mind travelled back to the previous night, putting Sam's body in the boot of his car, driving to the site, parking it in the derelict barn where it couldn't be seen from anywhere. No, they couldn't have found it. *Keep calm, keep calm.*

She pulled a face, glad that she didn't have to lie to answer their question. 'You've got me there. I find it hard enough to remember my own number plate, let alone his. He drives a little sports car. Black. I'm not even sure what model he has now. It used to be a BMW, but I can't be sure he hasn't changed it.' She gave them a bright smile. 'Shall I tell him you're looking for him?'

The constable tapped his pen on his notebook. 'If you could give us his mobile number, that would be helpful.'

She reeled it off, watched the officer write it down. 'I'm sorry I can't be more use.'

DS Lamb looked sorry too, her mouth pressed into the thinnest of lines. 'Do you have the name and address of the clients in Dumfries, by any chance?'

Faith grimaced, apologetic. 'Oh, dear. I'm afraid not. We didn't talk about details like that.'

'Does your brother have any connections in Northumberland?' The sergeant landed the killer blow, and now she knew. This was about Marcey.

She couldn't stop her face from twitching, the question catching her unawares, but there was no harm in telling them now, she decided. What did it matter now he was dead? Especially if her answer helped to protect the living. 'Well, yes. He built a prize-winning house for a client. Marcey

Dubois. Ex-model turned fashion entrepreneur. Lives near Alnwick.'

'You know she's just died in a house fire?' The sergeant didn't blink.

Faith feigned shock, her mouth dropping open, her hands flying to her face. 'No! How terrible. That's awful.'

'The fire service believe it was arson.'

'Not suicide, then?' As soon as she'd said it, she knew she'd made a mistake. It was the look on the sergeant's face, the flash of a raised eyebrow.

'Why would you think it was suicide?' Both of them were staring at her now, and she could feel herself getting hot, her cheeks burning.

'I, um... I believe she had mental health problems.' Shut up, she told herself. Shut up, shut up, shut up. She was digging a hole for herself and she had to find a way to stop. 'Just something Sam said.' She shrugged. 'I didn't know the woman.' She made a show of checking her watch. 'I'm so sorry, but I need to dash off. I help out at the women's refuge in Penrith and I'm going to be late.'

She thought she'd sounded pretty genuine, but the officers gazed at her and she couldn't read what they were thinking.

'Thank you for your time,' the sergeant said eventually, handing her a card. 'If your brother gets in touch at all, these are my contact details.'

'I'll message him. Tell him to call you.'

'Thank you. That would be helpful.'

She had to stop herself from saying anything else, clamping her mouth shut, eager for them to be gone.

DS Lamb turned, gave her a smile that caught her off guard. 'I'm so sorry, I forgot to ask your name.'

'Faith Barclay,' she said, instinctively.

The woman's smile broadened. 'We'd better have your contact details as well, so we can keep you updated if we can't get hold of your brother.' Faith stifled her groan of annoyance and gave them a fictitious number. It would take them a while to realise it wasn't genuine. Hopefully enough time for her to go to Plan B.

Plan B, though, would take a bit of preparation if she was going to get it right.

She could feel something stirring inside her, an excitement at what was to come, the anticipation already making her tingle. She knew it was wrong, but she also knew she couldn't help herself. It had always been this way.

CHAPTER THIRTY-EIGHT

Faith dashed inside, downed her glass of wine and grabbed her bag. Her mind raced through all the things she needed to do. The first thing was to go and get Emma's stuff from the women's refuge. Then she needed to pick up a few bits and pieces from her apartment, ready for Plan B.

Adrenaline coursed through her veins as she clambered into her car and shot out of the drive, her mind so busy she hardly noticed the journey to Penrith. It was just after eight o'clock in the evening when she pulled up outside the refuge. She tried to remember the manager's name, panicking when it wouldn't come to mind. Never mind, she'd wing it, bluff her way through. She only needed to pick up a bag, after all, shouldn't take long.

A small woman with a greying bob opened the door, a worried look on her face. The door was on a chain and she peered through the gap, ready to slam it shut at any moment.

'Yes?' she said, abruptly.

'Oh, hello,' Faith said in her warmest voice, making sure she smiled. 'I was wondering if your manager is in. I met her earlier and she has a bag belonging to my sister-in-law. She was here this morning, but left her things. I don't know if you met her. Emma?'

The door closed and Faith stood on the doorstep for what seemed like an unreasonable length of time. She was about to ring the bell again when the door opened and Laura appeared.

'I'm sorry, I was sure you said you were coming tomorrow.' She showed no signs of wanting to let Faith in, and Faith wrapped her arms round her chest, feeling the cold now.

'Yes, that was my plan, but we think the baby might be on the way and Emma needs her bag.'

Laura peered over Faith's shoulder. 'Oh, you're on the way to hospital. Is she in the car?'

'No, no, she isn't. She wants a home birth.'

Laura looked puzzled. 'Really? That's not what she told me when she was here. She said she wasn't good with pain and she'd organised to go into the maternity unit in Penrith.'

Faith's heart sank and she looked down at her feet while she scrubbed the annoyance off her face. 'Yes, well, it seems she's had a change of heart and I have to go along with her wishes. But don't worry, I've rung the midwife and we're keeping her up to speed with contractions and everything.'

'You've left her on her own?' Laura sounded appalled, and Faith realised she'd messed up.

Oh, for the love of God. Her temper was starting to fray. She laughed, like it was the daftest thing she'd ever heard. 'No, no, she's not on her own...' She paused, her thoughts at a dead end; then, a merciful breakthrough. 'Hilda, the landlady, is with her. She has eight grandchildren, half of them home births where she's been present, and think of all the lambs and calves she's helped to be born.' She was gabbling and told herself to stop talking gibberish. She sounded unhinged. *Just ask for the bag.*

'Anyway, could I please have Emma's things, then I can get back to her.'

Laura hesitated, then opened the door and let her in,

leading her to a messy office at the front of the house. She pulled Emma's bag from behind her desk and handed it over. 'There you go. Please give Emma our best wishes, and I hope you don't mind if I call in and see how she is?'

Persistent was this woman's middle name, Faith thought, as she sighed inwardly.

'Thank you. I'm sure she'd be delighted to see you. But maybe give her a few days to rest and get used to being a mother.'

'Of course.' Laura gave a tight smile. 'Good luck.'

Faith headed out of the building, desperate to get away from the place.

It was only when she'd been driving for a few minutes that she noticed the headlights behind her. *Am I being followed?* The police! She'd completely forgotten about the police.

With her nerves on edge, she drove at random round Penrith until she was sure there were no cars following her, then headed to her apartment. She burst through the door and locked it behind her, groaning when she saw the heap of Sam's possessions filling her living room. All this to get rid of, but it wasn't top of her list. Her priority was Emma and the baby.

Her eyes scanned the room. She had hoped to sort through everything, pick out the most important paperwork. In fact... She nodded to herself as a new plan popped into her head. A quick dousing with petrol, a match, and the evidence would disappear. She and Sam would cease to exist, and wouldn't that be the ideal solution?

Oh, she did like a fire. It got rid of so much evidence, you didn't have to be quite so careful.

She'd been fascinated by fire for as long as she could remember, and there had been 'accidents' at home when she'd been young, before her parents had hidden the matches. Followed by periodic searches of her room to make sure she wasn't concealing anything. As if that was going to stop her.

She'd contented herself with random acts of arson: bins set on fire, initially, progressing to garden sheds. Not all the time, just when she was feeling particularly stressed. The sight of a fire seemed to calm her somehow, and she'd basked in the memory of it for quite some time afterwards.

She'd dreamed throughout her adolescence about burning a house down, but had been happy to keep it as a fantasy until she'd learnt of her parents' duplicity. She had wondered, as an adult, how two well-paid professional people – her father a teacher, her mother a pharmacist – had been so poor, but had never felt able to question them about it in case they threw her out. They had been miserly and miserable, never taking Faith and Sam on outings, no family holidays, always penny-pinching, dressing them in second-hand clothes, budget presents for Christmas and birthdays. Faith had accepted that, believing they were short of money, struggling to get by. Then, when Sam was about to go away to university, they suddenly had cash to splash out on booking cruises and organising home improvements.

Faith was livid, and when she discovered exactly how much they had in the bank, their fate was sealed. She decided her fantasy would become a reality. She'd burn the family home to the ground with her parents in it. But she had to be careful, make sure she knew what she was doing.

There were practice runs. The first being the chicken house in next door's garden. Then the chemistry lab at Sam's school, followed by a derelict cottage used by local addicts. Having made sure she knew how to set the thing up without the suspicion of arson landing at her feet, or the risk of setting herself on fire, she just had to wait for the right opportunity. A time when she and Sam could be legitimately out of the house while her parents were asleep in it.

She organised a camping trip, not far away, sneaking out of the tent while Sam was asleep to do the deed, because he could never know what she'd done. Once the house was in flames, glass shattering, timbers crackling, the thick, acrid pall of smoke hanging in the air, she could honestly say the thrill of it was like nothing she'd ever experienced.

They'd taken out life insurance with their mortgage, which provided a sizeable nest egg, along with the house insurance and their savings.

Unfortunately, she hadn't been able to stay long, needing to get back to Sam before she was missed. But there'd been other opportunities over the years to savour her handiwork. The fire that got Alice being her favourite, because the location meant she could hide behind a wall and not be seen while she watched the whole thing unfold.

Marcey had needed a slightly different approach. She was very susceptible to suggestion, and all Faith had needed to do was embed the idea in her mind that Sam had never loved her, that he despised her and was using her in order to build a statement property to further his career. They had regular hypnotherapy sessions over Zoom, and instead of bolstering Marcey's confidence, she'd used them to chip away at her resolve, take her back to the dark place where she'd had suicidal thoughts, reinforcing all those terrible, negative emotions.

She'd planted the idea of burning the house down. That would show Sam, she'd told Marcey, that would punish him for marrying someone else when he should have married her. She hadn't been sure it would work and was delighted when it had.

Not once had she been questioned about the fires, and she was confident that she could work her magic once again.

Quickly, she went to her desk and found the folder with all the bank details, birth certificates and her passport. Put it in a carrier bag together with a couple of framed photos of her and Sam. Nothing else was important. None of her professional certificates, nothing like that, because she couldn't be that person any more. She would have to reinvent. Quite how she wasn't sure, but necessity was the mother of invention and she was certain she'd come up with something.

She went to close the curtains, feeling exposed with the black night reflecting her image on the glass. There was a car parked in the shadows on the road outside the building. Her breath hitched in her throat, her pulse quickening, recognising something wasn't quite right. How odd for someone to park there when there were several free spaces in the car park. She pulled the curtains, turned off the light and peered through a tiny gap she'd left, which allowed her to see outside without being seen. After a few moments, her eyes became accustomed to the dark. She spotted the aerial on the roof.

It was the police.

CHAPTER THIRTY-NINE

She was ninety per cent sure it was the same officers who had spoken to her at the cottage. They must have followed her here, and she cursed herself for not being more careful.

The ring of the doorbell made her jump out of her skin, and she pressed herself against a wall, still as a statue. If she was quiet, she hoped they'd go away. Unless they had a search warrant, of course. Her heart fluttered, panic lodging itself in the middle of her chest. *Not now, please.* She was so close. So very close to having this situation all wrapped up.

The doorbell rang again, followed by a loud knocking. 'Open up. Police.'

Fat chance of her obeying that order, she thought. She couldn't move, couldn't give any clue she was still inside. Of course they would have seen the light on, but now she'd turned it off, she hoped they might think she'd left. That's if they'd realised there was a back door on the ground floor. Or gone to bed.

Finally, her brain started to work. If he was ringing the bell again, it meant he didn't have a warrant, otherwise he would have forced the door. Her breathing started to calm. She was safe, for now.

After a while, when the quiet had settled around her, she crept back to the curtains. The car was still there. *Dammit.* For the moment, she was trapped. She'd have to bide her time.

She went to grab a small suitcase to pack a few clothes. That done, she glanced out of the window again. No change. She slumped onto the sofa, her hand tugging at her hair, wondering how to get herself out of the apartment without the police noticing. It didn't seem possible when she needed her car, which was parked out the front.

She closed her eyes, her mind taking her back through the sticky times in her life when, out of nowhere, she'd not only got herself out of a mess, but accrued significant wealth in the process.

At the start, after her parents had died, she'd been foolish, spending on luxuries she didn't need, just because she could. It was shocking how fast the money had disappeared, but she and Sam travelled the world and had so many wonderful experiences, she didn't regret any of it. Once she'd got a taste for luxury, though, she couldn't let it go. They'd spent all their legacy by the time Sam was in the middle of qualifying as an architect, and then she'd had to get back to work and get creative.

Sam started the first scam on a small scale, people wanting applications for planning permission. He charged a fee, secured the job, then scarpered without actually doing the work. That was online, and pretty low-risk, and it was easy enough to disappear and pop up as a new company on a regular basis. He had carried on with that over the years when big projects dried up.

Then Alice had come into his life, and he was totally in love, swept along by her ethical approach to life, her eco-vision. Suddenly he hadn't wanted to do the scams any more. They'd earned enough by then to provide a nice nest egg for each of them, but it wasn't enough for Faith. And sharing her son with another woman wasn't going to work either.

The stress of being pushed out of his life had reignited her pyromania. Blowing up Alice's parents' boat had been a new trick she'd learnt, one she thought she might repeat in the future because it was so... dramatic. But it was over in a flash, so to speak, so the satisfaction wasn't quite as strong as a house fire. Still, it was a means to an end. All part of the plan, the longer game she was playing with Alice, letting the money accrue from her inheritance first before she got rid of her, knowing that it would all come to Sam.

My goodness, it had worked a treat. Afterwards, although she'd hated to see Sam so distraught and broken, it had cemented their relationship. Made it stronger. She was there to comfort him, to piece him back together, support him through all those interminable police interviews, the accusations.

It drove him back to her and he vowed he'd never get over Alice, happy for their life to be just the two of them.

It was at that point that Faith branched out into bereavement counselling. She could see what a malleable clientele these distressed people presented. There were opportunities if she could get Sam to work with her. She had an idea for a new scam. A much bigger opportunity that would accelerate progress towards their goal.

These wealthy people she was seeing had more money than sense, and she felt they were at such a low ebb she could probably talk them into anything. The trick was to pick the right personalities, with no family to question and interfere.

The first project, Sam overcharged for services and materials, inventing problems that had to be overcome and that bumped the price up. The woman hadn't noticed because she was clueless at managing finances. Her dead husband had looked after all of that. She bought into the idea of downsizing to a new-build bungalow with gusto, and she totally loved the finished product, so she was left happy while Faith and Sam had boosted their savings considerably. *No real harm done, was there?*

Marcey had been their second project, coming to Faith after her marriage had broken down and her father had died. She'd been a mess and a perfect target, so susceptible to suggestion it was a dream come true. Faith decided to ramp up the scam. It was a much bigger house, after all, and Marcey was away with the fairies half the time. She could be persuaded that she'd agreed to all sorts of things, when she actually hadn't.

For some reason, Sam appeared to be attracted to the silly women she earmarked for their scams. Still, that had worked to their advantage with the first woman, so she didn't take any action when it happened with Marcey too. It all seemed to be part of the process for him. It was like the client and the build became one entity. He was besotted with his design for Marcey's house, dreaming of winning prizes and getting industry accolades for his work. He was rather vain like that, and she'd played on it to achieve her aim of getting closer to a couple of million in the bank. Then they'd stop. That was her promise to herself, although the process was rather addictive, she'd found.

If Marcey had paid the final invoice, their goal would have been within touching distance. But she had proved to be more of a challenge than Faith had realised, the money not forthcoming, and she had moved them on to the next project.

Emma had appeared to be such a good opportunity. Perfectly ditzy and a self-confessed risk-taker where money was concerned. Ideal. Until she revealed she was pregnant. Then Sam proposed to her. Neither of those things was supposed to happen, and it had thrown Faith for a while until she'd worked out a solution.

Once Sam realised that planning permission wasn't going to be given, Faith had encouraged him to start siphoning off the money. It was all tucked away in an offshore bank account via a series of shell companies. But there should have been more, so much more. Unfortunately, Sam had turned on her. Said he didn't want this to be a scam. He wanted a life with Emma, wanted to build this house for her, bring up a family together. He was done.

That was when she knew she had to take control. Force the issue.

She puffed out her cheeks, weary beyond words, but she couldn't allow herself to sleep, not with the police outside. She crept to the window again, her heart giving a flip of relief when she saw that they'd gone.

It was time to exit, right now, before they decided to come back.

First, though, she needed to give them something to keep them busy. She pulled the can of petrol from under the sink, sprinkled it round the apartment, being careful not to splash it on herself, fashioned a fuse from a bed sheet, then set it alight, closing the door behind her.

She hurried down the stairs, her jaw set as she focused on Emma and the baby and how she was going to deal with that little dilemma. Thank goodness she wasn't squeamish.

CHAPTER FORTY

When Emma woke, the house was quiet and still, the light of the moon seeping round the edges of the curtains. Her stomach was griping, and she dashed to the loo, sank gratefully onto the seat. Whatever Faith had given her to eat, it was definitely cleansing her digestive system. After an uncomfortable ten minutes, wondering if she dared get off the toilet, she decided to risk it and waddled over to the bed, flopping onto the covers feeling completely exhausted.

Her stomach tightened, the weirdest sensation, making her gasp, her hands clutching the skin as she held her breath. Then the muscles relaxed again.

Was that a contraction? She lay back against the pillows, sweat beading on her brow. Christ, she was hot all of a sudden. The baby's leg kicked out, catching her under the ribs. He was definitely in a different position now, and it was the first movement she'd felt for a little while. Her breathing was ragged, panicky, and she tried to calm herself down.

Her mind went back to the last antenatal class she'd attended, a Q&A session discussing labour and what to expect. People telling stories of friends who had taken days, others whose labour had been so quick, their babies had been born in the back of taxis, by the side of the road, in supermarket toilets. 'There is no such thing as an average labour,' the midwife who was leading the class had said. 'Everyone is different, every baby is different.' She gave a knowing smile. 'You have to expect the unexpected.'

That was what was so hard about your first baby: you hadn't got a clue, not even an inkling of the reality. Being told things was a world away from actually feeling them for yourself. And her body had already taken a beating. How was she going to cope? How much pain was she going to be in? Her heart raced, her mind sabotaging all attempts to be calm.

'Faith!' she called. She listened, could hear no reply, no movement in the house at all. 'Faith!' she shouted, as loudly as she could. 'Faith!' The last call was a strangled cry, cut off when she felt another contraction starting, this one a bit stronger than the last.

She panted her way through until it subsided. How long had that one lasted? She was supposed to monitor the length of the contractions and the time between them, wasn't she? Slowly, her breathing went back to something approaching normal. Perhaps Faith was sound asleep. After all, she'd had a busy day – she had to assume it was Faith who had moved Sam and all his belongings and that was no mean feat on her own.

As she thought about that now, she acknowledged for the first time that it had been a strange thing to do. Sam was Faith's *son*. If it was true, would she really just dump his body? Surely the normal response would be to call the police. Have every-thing officially sorted out so you could organise a respectful burial.

Unless you had something big to hide. Something more important than burying your own child.

Emma hadn't been thinking straight yesterday, knocked off kilter by her own guilt. But it would seem that Faith had guilty secrets of her own, and it confirmed Emma's conclusion that she and Sam were scamming her. That's why Faith didn't want the police involved, didn't want them finding evidence.

Then it hit her. *Am I evidence too?*

It was odd that Faith hadn't answered her calls, and she clambered off the bed, peered outside. Faith's car wasn't in the drive. She'd left Emma alone.

She stumbled to the bedroom door, pulled at the handle, but it wouldn't open. She tried again, rattling it in its frame, but it soon became clear the door was staying shut. There was no lock, so she couldn't work out what was going on. Unless... She peered through the crack between the door and the frame, and could see a bar going across. How odd. Then she realised what it was.

A bolt.

Her heart skipped a beat. There didn't used to be a bolt on the outside of the door. This must be Faith's doing. *She's locked me in.*

She hammered on the door, shouted Faith's name again, but there was still no response, and after a few minutes she had to give up because another contraction started. Only when it had finally subsided did a question explode into her mind.

Was Faith planning to wipe out her existence? Was that why she'd shut her in the bedroom? Thoughts of Marcey and Alice filled her head. She could almost hear the crackling of fire, checked the door to make sure there was no smoke creeping underneath.

No, she wouldn't. Faith wouldn't do that to her, would she?

Her mind sorted through everything she'd found out about Alice and Marcey, remembering Faith's adamant denial that Sam had had anything to do with their deaths. So... if Sam hadn't killed them, maybe they were accidents. Maybe her imagination was running away with her again.

Or maybe Faith had done it.

Had she been jealous of the women close to Sam? Emma gave an involuntary shiver, felt another contraction building inside her. She wished she'd gone to more of the antenatal classes, wished she was more confident about what to do.

Breathing. It's all about the breathing.

She puffed her way through the pain, not sure if she was doing it right, but at least it gave her something to focus on. As the contraction subsided, she knew that one had been stronger and longer than the one before.

Feeling restless, she paced up and down, a dull ache at the base of her spine, wondering if Faith was coming back or if she'd gone for good.

No, surely not. She wouldn't lock Emma in and then leave her. What would be the point of that? *To make me suffer. Revenge for killing her son.*

A sob erupted from her throat, then a surge of nausea, as another contraction started to build inside her. Her baby was on his way, and it looked like she would be giving birth on her own, with no pain relief and very little idea of what to do.

Women died in childbirth. Babies died too. Giving birth was not a risk-free process, and it was only now that she understood the stark reality of her situation. The danger she was in. *The danger we're both in.*

Fear gripped her scalp, squeezing and squeezing until she couldn't bear it any longer.

She screamed and screamed, hoping that somehow, somebody would hear.

At that point, her waters broke. The baby was definitely on his way.

CHAPTER FORTY-ONE

The following day, Laura was in Appleby, helping a client who was moving out of the shelter into a new property. She decided she'd ignore what Faith had said and pop over to see Emma. It didn't have to be a long visit, just enough to put her mind at rest, because she had a bad feeling about the whole situation. Faith had been cagey and elusive in her answers to questions the previous evening, and Laura had learnt, over the years, to trust her gut.

She popped into the florist to pick up some flowers for Emma, and was paying when she overheard a conversation between two women who had come in behind her.

'It was on the local news this morning. What a shock. Hilda Gregson's place. You know, that holiday cottage she rents out at the top of Battlebarrow. Went up in flames and nobody knew a thing until this morning. Of course, by then it was too late. Roof had caved in and everything. Only the walls left.'

Laura spun on her heel, shock clawing at her chest. 'I'm sorry, I don't mean to butt in, but I couldn't help overhearing... about the fire.' She swallowed; she could hardly bear to think of what might have happened. 'I think I know the tenant who was living there. Emma. Did they say anything about survivors?'

The women glanced at each other, shrugged. 'Don't know anything about that,' said the one who'd broken the news. 'They just said the place had burned down.'

Laura rushed out of the shop and jumped in her car, hoping the woman was wrong and they were talking about a different cottage altogether. But as she got closer, she could see a road-block manned by a police officer. Her heart felt heavy. It was true, then.

She stopped and wound down the window as the officer walked over, introduced herself. 'The lady who lived here, Emma, came to the refuge a couple of nights ago. I wanted to make sure she's okay.'

The officer frowned. 'You sure she was here? The landlady reckoned the tenants must have been away, because neither of their cars was in the drive. She said the tenant was heavily preg-nant. We're just checking which hospital she might have gone to.'

Laura considered that for a moment, knowing something wasn't right. Faith had said Emma had started in labour, so it was possible she'd changed her mind about a home birth and headed for the hospital. But... Faith had also said Hilda was with Emma, keeping an eye on things while Faith came to collect her bag. If that had been true, Hilda would have known for definite where Emma had gone.

Faith had been lying.

'I don't think everything was as it seemed in that house,' she said. She told the officer the whole story, and he got out his note-book and wrote down the main points. 'I got a feeling about Faith, the sister-in-law. She seemed jumpy and she wasn't being honest with me.' She could see clouds of smoke billowing into the air, the wind pushing it in her direction, the acrid smell catching the back of her throat.

'Thank you,' the officer said, tucking his notebook into his pocket. 'I'll pass on your information. Make sure they check for a body.' He grimaced. 'The fire had really taken hold before it was noticed, though. I mean, it's just a pile of rubble. It's going to take a while to sift through it, so...'

He didn't finish the sentence, but his meaning was clear. There wasn't going to be much in terms of physical evidence.

CHAPTER FORTY-TWO

The baby wouldn't stop crying. She'd longed for a child to mother for so long but never expected it would be so hard to cope on her own. It was a nightmare trying to get anywhere with him screaming at the top of his lungs. Was he hungry, or windy, or was it a nappy change? It was impossible to know, but the crying was relentless.

She tried singing, driving faster, driving slower. Stopping to pick him up, rocking him, but still the screaming wouldn't stop, his wails set at a frequency that blinded her senses to everything but him. She couldn't concentrate on driving or even think straight. Of course, that's what nature intended, but it was far from ideal on the motorway and to say she was stressed would be an understatement.

There was an urgency to their trip, though. The police would be on her tail, so she'd tried to push on, but there was a greater need to get the baby to settle so she could actually drive. After stocking up on supplies in Penrith, she'd headed north, deciding that the emptiness of Scotland would provide her with the best opportunity to disappear.

It felt like hours since she'd left Penrith, although in reality it was less than thirty minutes, when signs for a service station had her gasping with relief. She veered off the motorway and into the car park. For a moment, she scanned her surroundings, looking for CCTV cameras, working out the lie of the land. She'd parked in a far corner, the damaged window out of sight as she reversed up against a hedge. At least she wasn't so noticeable now and she'd had the presence of mind to muddy the number plates before she left so she wouldn't get picked up so easily by the ANPR cameras.

She'd bought a scarf in Penrith to cover her head and face so the worst of the bruising wasn't visible, but she was nervous about mixing with people. Unfortunately, she was going to have to stay away from the main building, however much she yearned for a coffee to keep her going.

The baby's wails amplified, and she unclipped him from his car seat and held him to her chest, jiggling him up and down and shushing him. Thank goodness Sam had taken the initiative and bought some baby equipment a few weeks ago, including a sling. Poor Sam, he didn't deserve what had happened to him. But at least she had the baby, a living, breathing part of Sam to call her own.

She put the sling on, slipped the baby in and set off at a brisk walk round the perimeter of the car park. After a few minutes, his screams turned into whimpers and finally she was able to revel in the blissful quiet.

Without the distraction of the incessant crying, she noticed how every bit of her body was aching, how exhausted she felt after all those hours of effort and no sleep. She'd never worked so hard for anything in her life. But it had been worth it. She'd got away with the baby and Emma was dead. It had all worked out in the end.

Amazing what adrenaline could do to keep you going, but now she felt like she was running on fumes. The idea that she had to drive further brought tears to her eyes and a heaviness to her heart. In truth, she couldn't face it, didn't feel she was safe to be driving and if there was an alternative, she would grab it with both hands.

Making sure she couldn't be traced was proving to be more complicated than she'd imagined. She'd ditched the bank card once she'd taken out as much as she dared from the cashpoint. That was one less way to trace her and she couldn't use that account now. She chewed at a fingernail as she carried on walking, mentally totting up the price of fuel, the miles she could travel, overnight stays, meals, possible ferry costs.

Going over and over the figures, she realised she'd made a terrible mistake. At the time, she'd thought that taking out a modest amount wouldn't alert the banking authorities to unusual behaviour, but now she could see she hadn't been thinking straight. Tiredness had got the better of her. The bank getting twitchy was the least of her problems after she'd set fire to the cottage. She should have withdrawn the absolute maximum she could. Now she only had enough for a couple of weeks at the most.

Disheartened, she trudged back to the car, unnerved to see a minibus parked not far away. A number of people stood around next to it, chatting and laughing, their dark robes flapping in the stiff breeze. It was unusual to see a group of nuns these days. As a child, she'd been educated at a Catholic school and nuns had been part of everyday life. Now, though, they seemed to be an endangered species, hidden away.

As she got closer, she could read the writing on the side of the vehicle: *Dysart Carmelite Monastery, Kirkcaldy, Fife.* They must be heading back to the east coast of Scotland.

Hidden away.

An idea sparked in her brain, and before she had time to talk herself out of it, she skirted round her car, like it was nothing to do with her, and found herself hurrying over to the group.

'Excuse me, I'm so sorry to interrupt, but I wonder if...' She took a deep breath, pushing herself past the point of no return. 'Could you help me, please?' She glanced over to the main building, loosened her scarf from her face so the bruises were visible. 'My husband...' She gulped. 'It's taken me so long to find the opportunity to do this. I've got to get away from him.'

Seven faces turned towards her, ranging from the plump flesh of a late-twenties adult to the wizened skin of old age. All of them wore the same shocked expression, but instinctively, they huddled round her, effectively hiding her from view, while their eyes studied her intensely. 'He did this to me.'

'Oh, dear child,' said a middle-aged nun, who appeared to be the only one willing to speak. Or maybe she was the one in charge and the others were waiting to follow her direction. 'How can we help you?'

'Take me with you.' She put her hands together in prayer. 'Please, please take me with you,' she begged. 'It's not just me in danger, it's my baby too.'

They glanced at each other, clearly unsure.

'Only for a couple of weeks. Until I can find a longer-term solution.' She tripped over her words in her rush to try and convince them. 'He keeps finding me at the women's refuges I've tried. I don't know how he does it, but he's never far behind me. He'd never think of looking for me at a convent.'

The nun gave a heavy sigh. 'Our monastery is a place of peace and contemplation. We're all getting older and I'm afraid we can't offer the help we used to when we were younger and there were more of us.'

She knew this was the best chance she would ever have to properly escape. To hide where nobody would think to look for her until things had quietened down. She had to try harder. 'I went to a convent school. I would welcome some time to reflect and reconnect with my God.' She was close to tears now, a sob in her voice. 'I want to ask for forgiveness. Guidance. I want my child to have a better life. To know God for himself.'

She broke down then, covering her face as she sobbed. A hand touched her back, then another, and another. A whispered conversation was going on behind her but she couldn't hear what was being said.

Finally, she heard the nun clear her throat. 'We can offer you temporary refuge, my dear, if you don't mind our humble furnishings and basic accommodation.'

'I'll help,' she said, giddy with relief. 'I'll help in any way I can. I'm so grateful, I can't tell you.' And in truth, she couldn't put into words how she felt. It was like divine intervention, the perfect hiding place presenting itself like this. Confirming to her that she'd done the right thing, getting the baby away from that dreadful woman, who didn't deserve him.

'I'm Sister Ruth,' the nun said. 'I'm the abbess at Dysart.' She angled her head, a kindly smile on her face, concern in her eyes. 'And what's your name, dear?'

There was a moment of silence as her brain tried to work out the best thing to say, her mouth automatically wanting to form an 'F'. She swallowed, telling herself this was a new chapter. 'Hope,' she said, with a quick smile. 'My name is Hope. And this is baby Sam.'

That was close enough to the truth, she thought as she climbed into the minibus, her grateful smile reflecting her feelings. These old dears would never need to know much in the way of details. All that mattered was that they were safe, Emma had gone from their lives, and she could enjoy being a mother at last.

PART FIVE

CHAPTER FORTY-THREE

TWO DAYS AGO

Zach checked his messages. Absolutely nothing from Emma. He threw his iPad back on the bed with a dissatisfied grunt.

Nina, the nurse who was organising his morning medication, gave him a sympathetic look. 'No news?'

She'd yet to meet Emma, but he'd told her all about his wife, what a great artist she was, how she'd struggled after his accident to come to terms with everything. It helped him to talk about her, look at her pictures. Then she felt a little less absent.

He liked Nina. In fact, she was his favourite. She always made time for him and, more than the other staff, she was in tune with his mental well-being, how he was feeling, knowing when he needed a lift, a joke, or a companion to sit and chat for a little while.

He sighed, feeling frustrated and disheartened and more alone than he had for a while. It was the fact she'd said she was on her way back that had caused the problem, raising his hopes and expectations, only to have them dashed by her last message. The silence ever since. 'Nope. Not a thing. I mean, she could send a few words, couldn't she?'

Nina nodded. 'I know you're worried about her.' She gave

him a little container of pills and a glass of water, watched while he swallowed them down one by one.

He slumped back on his pillows. 'Of course I'm worried. She said she'd been in a car accident. What if she's badly injured? What if she's alone somewhere and can't get help? I mean, I don't even know where in the world she is at this moment.' He could feel his blood pressure rising, the thud of a headache behind his eyes.

Nina put a hand on his shoulder, the warmth of her touch so comforting he closed his eyes so he could savour it for a moment. This was what he missed so much. The human touch. It was different to when the nurses were helping him wash and dress and get in and out of bed. Nina's touch was gentle and sympathetic and brought an emotional response he wasn't expecting. A tear rolled down his cheek, quickly followed by another. His jaw tightened. Her hand stayed where it was and he clasped it in his for a moment before he let go and she stepped away.

'I was thinking,' she said, as she put the medicine away in the little cabinet on the wall before locking it. 'If you want to know exactly where she is, there are apps we could use. I know you like Apple products, so I was thinking, if she has an iPhone or iPad, we could try to find it that way.'

He stared at her, amazed he hadn't thought of doing it himself. A bolt of excitement sent a shock through his body and he picked up his iPad again, opened it up. 'I've tried ringing, but it says the phone is not in use, so she must have got a new one. We did share a laptop, though. A MacBook. I bought it for my work, but she used it as well. I wonder if she took it with her?'

'It'll only work if you've set it up already,' Nina cautioned.

He laughed. 'Oh, yeah, I had to do that. I get so distracted when I'm working on a project, I kept leaving it places. Thankfully I always got it back.'

Nina perched on the bed, watching him open the app.

He frowned. 'Well, that's odd.'

'What is?'

He glanced up, met her gaze. 'It's showing my laptop as being in Penrith, Cumbria. That can't be right, can it?'

He handed her the screen and she pulled a face, clearly as puzzled as he was. 'You're right. Let's zoom in, see exactly where it is.' She handed it back. 'Eden House.'

He stared at the screen, unable to understand what he was seeing, his brain trying to work out what it meant.

'She's in the UK. I can't believe it. Why didn't she say?'

The pressure was building behind his eyes, the ache intensifying. She'd said she was travelling back from India, he was sure of it. He went back into his messages and scrolled through them, skimming the content. It was funny, but he could see now that her responses were all quite vague. Going north, she'd said. No specific mention of places or people, just generalities about yoga practice and meditations. How she was missing him and hoped he was feeling better. Sometimes he'd had to wait a few days for her to respond to a message and sometimes she sent just a couple of lines, even when he'd written what amounted to an essay.

He couldn't pretend it didn't hurt, but he'd always given her the benefit of the doubt, always knew it was a tough call expecting her to love him now he was so badly injured. But she'd promised to be there for him. That was what marriage vows were all about, wasn't it? In sickness and in health. She'd promised she'd be back. Now he didn't know what to believe.

Nina's hand squeezed his shoulder again. 'Don't get yourself worked up about it. I mean... you don't know if it's her. The MacBook could have been stolen. She could have left it with a friend. Sold it. All sorts of things. It's no good jumping to conclusions based on one piece of information.'

Of course, she was right, and he took a deep breath, relieved there could be a simple explanation. One that didn't mean his wife had been lying to him.

'Why don't you find out more about Eden House?' she suggested. 'It might be a guest house or something. You could give them a ring. Then you'd know for sure instead of guessing.'

His brain jumped into action, glad to have something to keep him busy, stop him making up scenarios with no basis in reality. 'Good idea. I'll send her another message as well, ask her where she is now.'

'I hope you've told her that the consultant thought you'd be ready to go home soon?'

Zach pulled a face, wondering if he should have done. 'No, I didn't. I want her to be surprised. Delighted, hopefully. I mean... I was such a wreck when she left.'

Nina looked unsure. 'Maybe you need to tell her what you can do now. Don't you think the fact that you're almost ready to move out of here might help to entice her back?'

He thought about that for a moment. 'Or frighten her away? She might not want me at home. It might be too much for her.' That was his real concern, although he'd never spoken about it before now.

She gave his arm a gentle squeeze. 'I've told you before not to worry about things that might never happen.' She stood. 'Anyway, I'm sorry, but I've things to do. I'll be back in a bit, though, see how you're getting on.'

He smiled at her. 'Thank you. I was about to have a meltdown then and you stopped me.' Their eyes met. 'I do appreciate the way you keep doing that.'

She laughed. 'All part of the job.' And with that, she was gone.

He settled back against his pillows and wrote Emma a message:

Hi, babe, missing you like crazy, as always. How are you feeling today? I hope things are a bit better and you can continue your journey home. Where are you now and how long do you think it will be until you get here? The anticipation is killing me. I can't wait to hold you in my arms again. Love you so much, Zach xxx

He heard the whoosh as it went zooming off into the ether. He'd given her a clue that he was better than she was expecting, that he would actually be able to hold her in his arms, something that had seemed impossible when Emma had left.

Feeling happier, he tapped Eden House into the Google search bar and settled down to find out what he could about the place.

CHAPTER FORTY-FOUR

Zach was woken a couple of hours later by a nudge from Nina, his iPad on his lap.

'Sleeping on the job,' she teased. 'How did you get on? Find anything helpful?'

He yawned. 'My poor brain is so out of practice.'

'It's good for you to have projects, gets you thinking for yourself again. Did you send Emma a message?'

'I did.' He brought his iPad to life, excited to see that she had sent a reply:

I'm okay, a bit sore. Can't be precise about arrival, though.

That was it. Short and blunt, no endearments, no kisses or even a sign-off. Odd. She always signed off as *Em x*.

Nina frowned. 'Hey, what is it? You look so sad all of a sudden.' She leant over, scanned the message and pulled a face. 'Short and sweet.'

'It's not sweet, though, is it?' He puffed out a breath. 'That's like a holding message, not wanting to give me any details. Or hope.'

'Hmm, I wonder if you might have been a bit too vague. Spell it out for the girl. Tell her how much better you are.'

He read through his message again and decided Nina was right, started to compose a new one.

Are you okay, babe? You don't sound like yourself. I was keeping this as a surprise, but if it encourages you to come back sooner, I think it's best I tell you now. I'm so much better than when you last saw me. I mean mega improvements. I'm in a wheelchair now, can use my arms, can speak properly and I'm painting again. I've also become a gym fanatic! More than anything, I want us to build a life together. I know it will be different to the life we had planned but I love you so much and I hope you can learn to love a different me. A better me. Please say you'll be home soon. The waiting is killing me. All my love, Zach xxx

He read it through, happy that there was no ambiguity. If that didn't elicit a proper response, then he'd know for sure what he already suspected.

Later that evening, he was sitting by the window in his chair, with his head in his hands, when Nina came in to give him his medication.

He felt her hand on his back. 'Hey, fella. Are you okay?'

'I have a feeling she's not going to come back,' he mumbled. If he was being honest with himself, he'd had this thought at the back of his mind for a while now. Especially with delay after delay and her messages getting shorter and further apart. Those were not the messages of a loving wife. 'She's been lying to me.'

Nina frowned. 'What makes you say that?'

'Because I've confirmed that she's in the UK.'

There was a moment of silence before Nina spoke again. 'Perhaps she only just got back?'

He dropped his hands and looked up at her. 'I don't think so. You can stop trying to put a positive spin on things.' He gave a derisive huff. 'I found out that Eden House is a women's refuge.' Nina's eyes went round, her jaw dropping, mirroring Zach's reaction when he'd found out. 'Anyway, I rang them and I had a strange conversation with a woman called Laura, who runs the place.'

He plucked at the blanket on his knees, not wanting to see the pity in Nina's eyes. 'I mean, she was cagey, because she's there to protect the women in her care, so she wouldn't confirm or deny. I did most of the talking, explaining what had happened and how I came to be ringing.' He sighed as he recalled their stilted conversation. 'She seemed a bit taken aback. You know, lots of awkward silences. And she asked me a few weird questions.' He pinched the bridge of his nose, telling himself to stay strong. 'Long story short... I got the impression Emma had been there. But Laura was talking in the past tense, so I don't think she's there now.'

'So, she left her laptop there?'

Zach nodded. 'That's what I'm thinking. I took your advice earlier and wrote her a second message, putting my heart on the line, telling her everything, and she read it but didn't reply.'

Nina sat on the chair next to him, reached for his hand. He couldn't look at her as he blinked hard, not wanting her to see how upset he was. 'I'm so sorry, Zach.'

He squeezed his eyes shut, willing himself not to cry, but when he spoke, his voice was thick with emotion. 'I sort of knew I was losing her. I mean, that lack of communication was a big clue, wasn't it? But I've chosen to wear blinkers, keeping my hopes up. Making all sorts of excuses for her. The thing is, Emma writes massive messages. Great long stories. That's how it's always been between us. Then after she went away, the messages got shorter and shorter, with sometimes no response for days.' He gave a hollow laugh. 'I've been kidding myself. If she's been at the women's refuge, that implies she's been in a relationship with someone else. Someone who hasn't been treating her well.' His voice sounded the way he felt. Defeated.

He looked down at Nina's hand, held in his, and had a moment of clarity.

'It was the thought of being with Emma again, being able to hold her and love her, trying to get some of our old life back, that gave me the motivation to do the physio, to put my all into improving and getting as well as I can. It worked, it really did. But it seems I was chasing a dream that wasn't real.' He gave a harsh laugh. 'You know, I always used to joke with her that she only wanted my sperm, not me, because she was obsessed with having a baby. Then she had a miscarriage and she was devastated. Not long after that, I had the accident.' He turned to Nina, the look of sympathy in her eyes bringing fresh tears to his own. His chin quivered. 'I think I always knew I would never be enough for her if I couldn't give her a child.'

He swiped the tears from his cheeks. 'I think she's left me and not told me. I think she moved on months ago.' He frowned. 'In fact, did she even go to India? I mean, that sounds like a cover story, doesn't it?' His fist banged the arm of his wheelchair. 'I feel so stupid for believing her. Encouraging her to go. And all those ridiculous messages I sent, which she obviously wasn't interested in.' Anger hardened his voice. 'How could she? How could she do that and not have the decency to be straight with me? Haven't I lost enough already?'

Nina held his hand a little tighter. 'I think... well, you're making some pretty big assumptions there, mister. You might not be right. But...' She caught his eye, must have seen that he had no patience for pacifying words, because her demeanour changed. 'Okay... you've got a point. I'd have to say her message is in no way loving and is not a meaningful response to yours.

So, you could be right. But you don't know for certain.' His eyes dropped from hers, his hand wriggling free from her grasp. She stood. 'Do you want me to leave you in peace? Let you process things for a little while?'

He gave a snort, thoroughly riled up now. 'No, no, I've had plenty of time to process. I've had all year to consider the what ifs, but I've always hoped for the best.' He stroked his beard, his thoughts crystal clear. 'I think I know what the score is now. She obviously considers me a burden since the accident. Something she wants to forget about.' He gave an emphatic nod, sure in his mind what he was going to do. 'I'm going to ask her for a divorce. Then she'll be free to live the life she wants and I won't feel guilty for not being able to give her the child she's desperate to have. It would always be a barrier between us and I don't want to live my life consumed by guilt. I've felt enough of that since the accident as it is.'

Was that relief he was feeling? It would be wonderful not to have to carry the weight of knowing he wasn't quite enough, and he'd felt torn for quite some time. Yearning for his wife, while acknowledging how hard his accident had been for her as well. Both of them had suffered. Perhaps he'd be happier on his own. He'd certainly discovered a contentment over recent months, accepting his limitations, but hopeful for the future. He couldn't pretend he wasn't bitterly disappointed in the way Emma had behaved, though. Perhaps he hadn't known her as well as he thought he had?

He forced a smile. 'I've decided what I'm going to do. I'm going to use my compensation money to buy a house, get it adapted and move on with my life.'

Nina beamed at him. 'Attaboy. I always thought she'd done a number, deserting you when you needed support. That's what we all thought. You deserve so much better.' Her eyes shone and she reached over to ruffle his hair. 'Somebody much better than her is going to fall in love with you, because you are one hell of a fella.'

'Come on, now, don't get carried away.' He laughed, feeling lighter by the minute. All that uncertainty, that fear of rejection had been such a waste of energy. He had friends, he knew a lot of lovely people. He was painting again and enjoying his life. 'I don't suppose you can help me talk to an actual human being at the bank, can you? I need to know where I'm at with finances, then I can start looking at properties.'

The situation with Emma had been a shock, a rude awakening, but it did mean he'd had to face reality. It was clear his wife didn't want him any more. But now, he found to his surprise that he didn't want her either. Not if it meant he had to live with the guilt of not giving her what she longed for. He'd let her be free, if that's what she wanted. That's what they said, wasn't it? *If you love someone, set them free.* And if they leave, they were never yours in the first place.

CHAPTER FORTY-FIVE

Zach realised that waiting for Emma, pining for her, yearning for her love when she obviously wasn't willing to give it had been making him feel unworthy and less of a man.

As his psychologist pointed out, he'd been letting her dictate his feelings of self-worth, and he didn't have to do that. He was taking control of his own life instead of waiting for her to come and look after him, and it was such a positive step forward. It was scary, but he could feel a thrum of excitement he'd thought was long lost.

'Good on you, mate,' the physio said with a huge grin, shaking his hand when Zach told him he'd decided to move out to a place of his own. 'The fact you're in a wheelchair shouldn't stop you from doing things. Where there's a will there's a way and all that.' He tapped his head. 'This is where the power lies, not in your body.'

Zach found himself buoyed by everyone's positivity and tried even harder with his rehab activities. Later that day, the chief medic came to talk to him with the independent living co-ordinator, Kerry, and they started to plan for him leaving, discussing the sort of care package he might need at home and the costs. 'It's going to be months yet,' Kerry said, trying to temper his expectations.

Zach nodded. 'I know. And I'll have to get a place adapted. That's if I can find something suitable.'

'Yes, but it's good to know what you're aiming for so you can make sure your budget allows what you want.'

'Talking about budgets, I still haven't spoken to anyone at the bank yet.'

'Ah, yes,' Kerry said. 'I believe we have someone coming to see you. We insisted they come here, so you can have an advocate in the meeting with you.'

Zach frowned. 'I don't think I need an advocate, do I?'

'Well, it sounds a little... complex. And it can't do any harm. Two minds are better than one, as my mum always tells me.' She gave him a reassuring smile. 'It's a way of making sure there are no misunderstandings, that's all.' She looked away and jotted something in her notes. 'I can start looking for properties if you like. You are staying in Manchester, aren't you?'

He shrugged. 'You know, I haven't thought about any of that. But I think I'd like to be close to here to start with. Then it won't feel like too big a step.'

Excitement fizzed in his chest, and he took himself outside for a whizz round the gardens while he considered the question of where he wanted to live. What he wanted the next chapter of his life to be like. He was lucky to have so much help and the money to pay for what he needed. Thank goodness for the compensation payout.

That afternoon, once the client manager from the bank had explained the situation, it was clear that his dreams would have to be severely scaled back. He was so glad Kerry was in the meeting with him, because the information was indeed hard to grasp. And shocking.

'So, his wife has spent a third of the money?' Kerry said, aghast.

'Invested, I'd say,' the client manager said, defensively. 'She's building a bespoke property to accommodate Zach's care needs.'

Zach snorted. 'No, she's not. She's left me. I haven't seen her for months.'

The client manager looked at her notes, clearly flustered. 'Well, she's been actively working on the build. We let a tranche of the money go for purchase of the site, then another to cover initial build costs. It should be progressing nicely now.'

'And where exactly is this property?' Zach asked, disgusted that Emma should have been allowed to use so much of the funds without consulting him. Furious at her betrayal. He understood when the account was first set up, they weren't sure if he had brain damage or even if he was going to live, so she had been given legal powers over his affairs. It looked like she'd taken full advantage of that status.

'It's just outside Appleby,' the client manager said, flicking through her folder of notes. 'In Cumbria, not far from Penrith, I believe.'

The meeting ended on a subdued note, all of Zach's hopes dashed.

As much as he'd like to believe that Emma was building a house for him, he couldn't. She'd been too elusive, too distant. If she was doing something wonderful like that for him, she would have been excited to get him involved. No, whatever she was building, it wasn't for Zach. It was for someone else. He gritted his teeth. She had lied to him and stolen his money.

CHAPTER FORTY-SIX

Five days after Zach had made his complaint to the police, and started a case against Emma to retrieve his money, Sergeant Mark Meadows came to see him with his sidekick, Constable Sharon Wright, who looked fresh out of training, all bright-eyed and eager.

Zach was in the gym, having just finished a physio session, wiping the sweat off his face with a towel. He'd worked hard and his muscles were so tired his arms were shaking.

'I have some difficult news, I'm afraid,' Mark said, pulling up two chairs so they could sit next to him. He was as thin as a stick and looked like he might be reaching retirement age, his face crumpled in a permanent frown.

Both officers were looking sombre, and Zach dropped the towel onto his lap, preparing himself to hear he wasn't getting his money back.

'I'm sorry to have to tell you...' The sergeant paused, blinked a couple of times. 'We have reason to believe your wife has died in a house fire.'

Zach gasped, his heart stuttering, the stark delivery of the news landing like a physical thump to his chest. 'What? Dead?' His voice was incredulous. 'She can't be dead.'

'Unfortunately, the situation is more complex than we'd originally thought. Our colleagues in both Northumberland and Appleby got in touch when we issued an alert for your wife. They've been working on a different case and it appears we have an overlap. They had started to piece things together, with the help of a witness from the local women's refuge.'

'Laura?' Zach asked. 'You mean Laura? I spoke to her too.' Now he was beginning to understand the reason for her confusion. *But Em can't actually be dead. She can't be.* He was feeling light-headed, floaty, not quite in the room as he struggled to comprehend what he'd been told.

'It appears your wife had been leading a double life. She'd remarried and was living in Appleby with her husband, Sam Barclay, who was an architect.' The officer shifted in his chair. 'This is where it gets a bit more complicated. His body was found on the site where they were building a new house. I don't need to go into the details, but the pathologist believes he was murdered.'

'What?' Zach could hardly believe what he was hearing. *Murder?* This was getting surreal, more like a TV drama than his life.

'We also believe that your wife's death is suspicious, and that is being treated as a murder inquiry as well. The fire brigade have reported that their initial investigation suggests an accelerant was used to start the fire.'

Zach's head hung between his shoulders, his hands covering his face. The news was getting worse by the minute, too terrible to absorb. *Emma murdered.* And she'd been messaging him just days ago. It didn't seem possible that she was gone.

'Northumberland police are looking for Faith Barclay, Sam's sister, as their prime suspect, but the trail has gone cold. She used her bank cards in Penrith on the morning after the fire, and they found her car at a service station on the M6 close to Carlisle, but there's been no sign of her since.'

Zach felt numb. Of course, he hadn't been happy with Emma's decisions and apparent deceit, but he'd never in a million years anticipated this. It was too much, and although Mark carried on speaking, the words didn't register for a while.

Emma's dead.

He felt as though a little part of himself had died with her. His unpredictable, talented soulmate. Bouncy and bubbly and so full of life. Addictive, that was what she'd been. A star that burned brightly, dazzling him on the day they first met and keeping him entranced ever since. However much he'd tried to hide his hurt at her desertion, his love for her was still there in his heart.

She left you, deceived you, took your money and married somebody else, for God's sake. But still, the sadness wouldn't leave.

'I'm sorry to be the bearer of such bad news,' Sergeant Meadows said. 'There is one more thing I think you should know. A witness who saw Emma in the days before she died told us she was very close to giving birth. We believe the baby perished with her.'

It was too much to take in. Zach stared at the officer and through his disbelief he felt a pang of sympathy for Emma; she never got the baby she so wanted.

'But I can assure you the investigation is very much ongoing, and as soon as I have any further news, I promise I'll let you know.'

'So... what about a funeral?'

The constable cringed and Zach understood there was more they weren't telling him. 'I'll let you know when your wife's... remains can be released,' Sergeant Meadows said, standing. 'And if you have any questions, or information you think might be useful, then please don't hesitate to call.' He cleared his throat. 'Obviously there are more details if you want to know them, but I think that's probably enough for the time being.'

Zach nodded, not wanting to hear any more. He watched them leave the gym, feeling hollowed out and empty, then took himself back to his room, needing to be alone with his thoughts.

Along with his photographs, all he had left of Emma were her messages. Every word was now precious because they were the last ones she'd ever speak to him. He even looked at the location of her laptop, desperate for a connection with the woman he had loved. But the signal was no longer there. It must have died in the fire along with Emma.

CHAPTER FORTY-SEVEN

FIVE MONTHS LATER

The staff huddled round the car as Zach was helped into his seat, Nina jumping in beside him. It was a new start, and it felt exciting and overwhelming in equal parts.

'Oh God, I might cry,' he whispered to Nina, who held his hand and leant over to give him a kiss.

'You'll be fine.' She grinned. '*We'll* be fine. You'll have your very own live-in nurse now.' She squeezed his hand. 'Nothing to worry about.'

'Have you got the keys?'

She delved into her pocket, held them up. 'I have indeed.'

A shiver of anticipation ran through him. It was finally happening. 'It's going to be great, isn't it? The developers were brilliant with the adaptations. I can't believe how lucky we were to get the last bungalow.'

'Ah, it was meant to be.' She kissed him again and he looked at her, love filling his heart. Nina was special. She saw who he was, not the brokenness of his body. She was the sort of woman who could tackle any problem, and he loved her more than he'd loved anyone else in his life. Funny how things had worked out.

Twenty minutes later, they drew up outside the new property. There were balloons and banners saying *Welcome Home* and a little gang of friends who'd come to welcome them. That was the strange thing. He had the best group of friends now. Not the ones he'd been to uni with or knew through Emma. These people had been with him all the way on his journey to recovery.

There were a couple of lads from work, and his old boss, who'd made a point of coming to visit regularly ever since the accident. The physio, who'd become a friend for life, and the doctor who'd looked after him for the last year and was as proud of his recovery as if Zach was his own child. Zach felt he'd been adopted on the sly, but was happy to go along with it. He would never forget his wonderful mum, who he was sure would have loved the doctor too. Finally, there were the nurses who had shared a house with Nina.

He blinked back tears as he looked at his new home, thankful he'd had enough money left in the pot to buy it. He was hopeful he would get the rest of his payout back, although he'd been told it would take some time to get everything sorted. At least his care costs were going to be drastically reduced now he'd left the unit. He'd become more or less independent over the last few months, and Nina would be able to help him with the few things he couldn't manage for himself. She glanced at him and his heart leapt. A new start, a new future, and he knew they'd make it work.

A month later, they had settled into their new life. Zach was starting an art project based around spirituality, an interest that had developed since his accident. He was researching images online when an article caught his eye. It was a collection of modern artworks reimagining old Christian classics, and at the top of the first page was a striking painting, a replica of Botticelli's *Madonna and Child*. There was something about it that made him enlarge the picture, studying it closely, his heart speeding up, his breath caught in his throat. *It couldn't be, could it?* He recognised the face of the Madonna, the nose, the hair, the secret smile. It seemed so unlikely, but he was certain. *It's Emma.*

He enlarged the picture even more, wondering if his eyes were deceiving him. He pulled out his phone, found the most recent photo he had of his wife, compared it to the painting, his eyes flicking from one image to the other. If it wasn't her, it was freakishly similar. He looked even closer, studying the composition, the brush strokes, the colour palette used.

Now he was convinced Emma was not only the subject of the picture, along with a plump baby boy with a shock of dark hair, but the artist too. Every artist had unique elements to their painting style, and he'd know her work anywhere. It was like a physical shock, seeing her work in print, sending a flood of memories washing through his mind. It must have been a portrait she'd done years ago, he decided, before they met. That was when he noticed the name of the artist at the bottom of the picture. *Hope McKenzie.* He felt deflated for some reason. Not Emma after all.

Puzzled, he studied the painting again, trying to work out how he'd got it wrong. Curious to know more, he read through the article, found out where the painting was housed and a few minutes later, he had a phone number to call.

A careful voice answered, with a crisp Scottish accent. 'Hello, Dysart Carmelite Monastery. Sister Ruth speaking. How may I help you?'

He introduced himself and explained why he was ringing, his curiosity about the painting.

'It's rather wonderful, isn't it? You won't believe how much interest we've had since that article. It's not for sale, though. It was a gift, you see.'

'Oh, I don't want to buy it. I just wondered how you came to have it. I thought I might know the artist, you see.'

'Hope? To be honest, I don't know much about her background. In fact, we didn't know what a fantastic artist she was until she presented us with the picture as a leaving present. It's a self-portrait, you know, of her and her baby.' There was genuine affection in his voice and he could tell the artist had made quite an impact. 'She painted it as a thank you for letting her stay for a few months while she sorted herself out. To be honest, we were all sad to see her go.'

'Oh, I see, so it was her baby?'

'That's right. Little Sam.'

Sam. The name lodged in his brain, and after a moment, he realised why. It was the name of Emma's dead husband. What a strange coincidence. In fact, the whole explanation left him feeling uneasy and unsettled.

He thanked Sister Ruth and disconnected, tapping his chin with the edge of his phone as he thought. He studied the painting again. Perhaps Hope looked remarkably like Emma. With the veil over her head, hiding her hair apart from a few escaped curls, he supposed it was hard to tell. Although... not many people had the same springy hair as Emma. It was one of the things that had attracted him to her in the first place. Was it too much of a coincidence that the artist looked like her *and* painted like her?

He sighed, closed the article. Perhaps he was seeing things he wanted to see, making things add up that didn't. Emma and her baby were dead. He wanted to forget the whole thing, but his mind kept asking the questions. Could she still be out there? Or was he still struggling to let go?

CHAPTER FORTY-EIGHT

Hope shivered in the cool night air, leaning to kiss the baby's nose as he gazed up at her from his buggy. It got her every time, that likeness to his father, stirring the guilt.

It was the middle of June, and it was still light, even though it was getting late now. Darkness would have been her friend, but she couldn't wait once she'd found his address. From her position, hidden behind the trunk of a tree, she watched Zach wheel himself into the living room. The shock of seeing him again took her breath away, his red hair gleaming in the glow of the dipping sun. Her eyes scanned his body. Muscular torso, broad shoulders, strong arms. She closed her eyes and remembered the feel of his embrace, the smell of him, the taste of him on her lips.

If only I could turn back time. The ache intensified in her heart and she knew she had never wanted a person more in her life.

She opened her eyes, needing to feast on her view of him, absorb every little detail and commit it to memory, to be enjoyed at her leisure when she went back to the hostel. He started spinning himself around in his chair, the faint boom of a bass beat humming through the air, and she realised he was dancing. He'd always loved to dance, and it made her smile, remembering the fun they'd had when they first got together. He looked happy on his own.

He'll be happier with me.

Could she go back to her old life now she had Sam's baby, though?

She'd been over this so many times and had come up with a couple of plausible explanations for her son's existence. A holiday romance. Or a drunken one-night stand when she was feeling miserable. He knew how much she'd yearned for a child, but would he be willing to accept Sam's baby as his own?

It would give their relationship a positive focus, she reasoned, but could their love survive her betrayal? Only if she didn't tell the truth. The baby had Sam's colouring, his dark hair. A story about a mad fling while overseas would work, she thought, if she was vague about the baby's age and he didn't think too hard about timing. Would he punish her for one mistake? Or would he welcome a baby into their lives, knowing the child wasn't a product of any sort of lasting relationship?

It was going to be harder to explain the fact that she hadn't died in a fire, when she'd left all the clues to suggest that she had. Hmm, she had no idea how she was going to get round that one yet.

She'd lived off her wits for the last six months, but it was exhausting, and hard to find decent places to stay. She'd reached the end of that road and was desperate for a permanent place to live where she could settle with her son. That's why she'd come back. A life with Zach was by far her best option.

As she watched, another figure appeared. A woman in a nurse's uniform. She must have come to help with his evening routine or something. But then she leant towards Zach and kissed him on the lips, his hand reaching up, caressing her neck as the kiss deepened.

Emma reeled back, appalled. *No, no, no!* This wasn't supposed to be happening. *He's mine.* How unprofessional of the nurse. She pulled her phone from her pocket and took a couple of pictures. Once she'd sent them to whichever agency the woman worked at, she'd soon get her sacked and out of the way.

The nurse pulled away and disappeared, leaving Zach as the centre of Emma's attention once again. But ten minutes later, she came back, wrapped only in a towel, her wet hair hanging down her back. *Oh my God!* Emma's mouth dropped open. This wasn't what she'd thought. This woman was actually *living* with Zach. They were in a *relationship*. The realisation hit her hard, as though she'd walked into a wall, leaving her dazed and incredulous.

Never for one minute had she considered that Zach might have moved on from her. Never, ever, ever had that thought crossed her mind.

Her teeth clenched, along with her fists. Her chin jutted forward. If she had to fight for him, she would. She knew exactly what a fight for survival felt like after her tussle with Faith. It was amazing how much strength you could muster when it was a genuine case of life or death. Even when you'd just given birth. She'd turned into an animal, a feral being, snarling and biting and scratching and gouging. Grabbing the bedside lamp and hitting with all the strength her body could muster until Faith lay motionless on the floor.

Of course, the element of surprise had helped, hiding behind the door when Faith unlocked it, baby Sam lying on the bed, wrapped in a towel, as bait to draw her in. She'd hated using her son like that, but she had to get them both to safety.

Her initial instinct had been to grab her things and leave as fast as she could, locking Faith in the bedroom. But when she saw the can of petrol Faith had left by the door, along with a knotted sheet to act as a fuse, she realised she could completely reinvent herself if it appeared they had died. She shook the rest of the images from her head. No need to go back there. She wasn't proud of her actions but it had been a case of survival, making sure her child had a chance at life.

Finding the nuns had been an amazing stroke of luck and they'd doted on her and Sam, thrilled to have a baby in their midst. One had trained as a nurse and she checked Emma over when they arrived, keeping an eye on her for a few days to make sure there was nothing amiss. She'd been lucky, she knew, not to have any medical complications. Of course, there were complications of other kinds. Like the lack of identification, which meant she couldn't register Sam's birth. And the lack of money, now that she'd had to leave her own and Faith's bank cards behind. But as the saying goes, necessity is the mother of invention and she was sure, given time, she'd work it all out. In the meantime, she'd begged, stolen and borrowed her way down from Scotland to Manchester when the nuns had started asking too many questions and she had to leave.

The draw to Zach had been too strong to resist.

Her eyes rested on her husband, on the smile lighting up his face as he gazed at the half-naked woman. She wanted that smile to be for her and her alone, like it had been not that long ago. She took a deep breath. Oh yes, she was definitely up for the fight.

Where there's a will there's a way, she reminded herself. Once Zach knew she was alive, there would be no contest. She was all he'd ever wanted, she was sure of that. Just look at his last messages, full of love for her, even though she'd been away for months. He was hers, they were still married, and she'd have to make this woman understand there was no place for her in Zach's life.

Once Emma had moved in, Zach would be besotted with her and the baby and nobody would need to know the details.

She nodded to herself, noting the woman's slight build. Her

mind got to work. Life was dangerous. Accidents happened all the time and in the strangest of places.

She smiled, looked at her child and then at Zach.

At least she had the element of surprise on her side. It wouldn't take long.

A LETTER FROM RONA

Dear Reader,

I want to say a huge thank you for choosing to read *The Bigamist*. If you enjoyed it, and want to keep up to date with all my latest releases, just sign up at the following link. Your email address will never be shared and you can unsubscribe at any time.

www.bookouture.com/rona-halsall

The idea for this book came from a conversation with my previous editor, Isobel Akenhead. We were throwing ideas around and generally gossiping (as if!) and it was a snippet of a conversation that really made my ears prick up. An idea took root. As usual, the original idea evolved and transformed and finished up as a roller-coaster ride of a story, because that's the way my brain works. I believe the theme is compelling. Who doesn't want to know how and why someone becomes a bigamist? Apparently, having done the research, it's a situation that is more common than you'd imagine, even though few people are charged. Bigamists are out there – you might even know one...

My aim is to entertain my readers and I hope I've hit the mark with this one – it was fun to write, but it took a while to work out how best to tell the story!

I hope you loved *The Bigamist*; if you did, I would be very grateful if you could write a review. I'd love to hear what you think, and it makes such a difference helping new readers to discover one of my books for the first time.

I love hearing from my readers – you can get in touch on my Facebook page, through Twitter, Instagram or my website.

Thanks,

Rona Halsall

ronahalsall.com

 facebook.com/RonaHalsallAuthor

 twitter.com/RonaHalsallAuth

 instagram.com/ronahalsall

ACKNOWLEDGEMENTS

First of all, my books would be nothing without my readers, whose feedback and enthusiasm for my stories makes me get on with the next one. Thanks to all of you for egging me on!

As usual, there are a lot of people to thank in the creation of this book. Even though it's my tenth book, and you'd think I would have got the hang of writing by now, this one has been a tricky little customer.

Firstly, I would like to thank my editor, Isobel Akenhead, who has been with me for all ten books, for her initial edits and for giving me the idea in the first place. Then I must thank my new editor, Maisie Lawrence, who has picked up the baton halfway through. She has been fabulous, and her insightful second round of edits made sure this book has become the story it deserved to be.

Big thanks also to my wonderful agent, Hayley Steed of Madeleine Milburn Film, TV and Literary Agency, who always has my back. This book was written in difficult personal times and Hayley is always there to help when I need it.

Thank you to my team of beta readers (Carla, Mark, Wendy, Chloe, Sandra, Alice, Kerry-Ann and Gill), who were presented with a less than perfect first draft and gave some fantastic feedback that has made the story so much better.

I would like to thank the whole team at Bookouture – marketing, publicity, audio production and everyone else who has worked on my book behind the scenes: you guys are amazing! Huge thanks to the brilliant designer, Lisa Horton, for creating a wonderful cover for *The Bigamist*. It might be my favourite of all the covers she's done for me over the last five years, although they are all pretty special!

I have some very lovely friends to thank who have kept me going when times have been tough – special mention to Susan O'Hanlon, Audrey Corrin, Beryl Baker, Kerry-Ann Mitchell, Sandra Henderson and Alan Pye for your loving kindness, which is so appreciated.

Finally, thanks to my children, John, Amy, Oscar and step-daughter Kate, who I love with all my heart and are always supportive. And then there's my husband, David, chief cheer-leader and my one and only love.

I forgot the dog! My crazy collie pup, Maid, who is my writing buddy and in charge of my fitness regime, making sure I'm out in all weathers and up with the lark. Every. Single. Day.